Well, Well, Well

Titles By Randall Miller

The Ability to Reason
Random Samples
Several Possible Conclusions

Well, Well, Well

Randall Miller

Well, Well, Well

First Edition

ISBN-13: 979-8-9917163-1-4

Dedication

To Alex, who was the inspiration for this um---
American classic?

To Collin, my son and my friend

Thanks to Doyle Geddes, my brother from another mother
who contributed the drawings in this book.
To see more of his work, please go to:

www.doylegeddesart.com

Thanks to Brett Grimes for the cover design.
To see more of his work, please go to:

www.brettgrimes.com

Table of Contents

Part One

Take Me To Tahoe

THE FOUR FRIENDS, and BENNY

They were four friends who met in high school, well five if you count Benny. When it came time for college each of them moved to a different part of the country, except for Benny who still lived at home with his parents. Somehow though, through all of life's adventures with marriages, kids, graduations and divorces, the four of them (make that five) managed to stay in contact.

Once a year, good old Benny would send out invitations and help with travel arrangements to bring them back to their hometown, the place where they went to high school, to spend a few crazy days together. Benny would be there too as he still resided in the old hometown, actually only a block away from their high school.

The four friends, Jimmy, Mike, Trevor and Adam were human success stories.

Jimmy was a self-made millionaire. He was the kid that turned a lemonade stand into a food truck and then built a fast-food empire with a string of mini drive-thru burger kiosks in Utah.

Mike had always had a summer landscaping job. Now he owns a thriving landscaping business in South Carolina.

Trevor turned an obsession for golf into a golf instruction school at a luxury resort in Tampa, Florida.

Adam was the bookish one. He never missed a good time *or* a homework assignment. He parlayed this focus and discipline into becoming a practicing attorney in Mystic, Connecticut. He was excited about this year's get together so that he could announce to the group that he was making partner at his firm.

And then there was Benny, who was *still* in high school. The same high school he and his four buddies had attended in Ohio. Not as a student of course but in a janitorial position. He could walk to work from his parents' house and most days he did exactly that, which was just fine by him. Benny was happy with his life. For better or worse, who is to judge really, Benny never got caught up in the pursuit of wealth or a "better life." He was comfortable in his old room at his parents' house and they loved having him there.

Benny sometimes wondered if the guys were ever jealous of him. They had big-time jobs with big time pressures, large homes with large mortgages and the demands of keeping a marriage going or surviving a divorce. He didn't have any of that to deal with and felt that he was a happier man for it. Back when he was actually attending high school he was written off as a nobody and walked the halls in anonymity. Now though, he was something of a celebrity. The kids liked him and respected him. True, he was not rich or a business owner or an attorney. He was nothing "fancy," just "Mr. Benny" to the kids in the high school but that was all the "title" that he needed in this world.

THE GATHERING

And so it was that every year the four of them (make that five, don't forget Benny!) would gather for their annual get together to reminisce and tell stories of the past. One of the highlights of this gathering was the telling of 'tall tales' with each one being more outlandish than the last. This telling of 'tall tales' had become quite a tradition. The same level of tradition held true for the all too anticipated (and expected) reply from Benny each year when called upon, as he would simply say "Pass."

Try as he might, Benny just never had a tall tale to tell.

The guys would of course take this in stride and go about telling their tales. Woven into the conversation at some point would be the proverbial "hey, just kidding, you know we love you!" jab at Benny.

Never failed, someone had to bring it up. Benny was always voted least likely to go to a party, or any social outing really, so there was the inevitable comment, "go to the party, drag Benny." Ha-ha, hilarious but Benny didn't really mind. Or at least he didn't think that he did.

Benny knew that he wasn't flashy or good looking, super-smart or popular. He was *just* Benny and that was okay by him. It was okay by the group as well. He may have been seen as a misfit from the outside looking in but Benny was their most trusted friend. He had been there for each of them when it counted the most.

Back in their high school days he had driven each of these guys home at *least* once when they were too drunk and stupid to drive. As the years passed, he had been the one to take their calls when life had dealt them a bad card. He was the one that always remembered their birthday and reached out to them when a parent had died. He was the one thing that they all aspired to be, just a truly good guy.

It was those feelings and emotions that gave them pause when he surprised them all with his tall tale about "Tahoe Tom." As they listened there was something just not right, something off just enough that they simply could not get it out of their heads. Although none of them said it aloud they were all thinking the same thing.

Could it be that this 'tall tale' was actually a *true story*?

Was "Tahoe Tom" just a character in a tall tale?

Or was Benny leading a double life and this was Benny's alias?

THIS TIME BENNY DOESN'T "PASS"

Fast forward to Memorial Day weekend. It is the twelfth year of their annual gathering. This year's get together, like every other year before it, had up to now been a great time. They were natural friends meaning that they had the ability to pick up exactly where they left off. Time and distance placed no challenges on their friendship.

So now the five of them are sitting at a table in a bar at their neighborhood Applebee's. They have arrived at what has become their favorite part of the gathering, the telling of 'tall tales.' It is tradition to start the round with Benny because Benny *always* says, "Pass." Tradition dictated that they would have a good laugh at this, order another round of beers, and then continue.

This year was different. This year Benny said solemnly, "I have a tale to tell."

Jaws dropped, eyes got big and each member of the group looked from one to the other. This had *never* happened. Benny *always* says, "Pass." But, this time, *this time,* Benny *doesn't* pass. So, more beers were ordered and Benny began to tell *his* 'tall tale'...

THE TALL TALE of TAHOE TOM

I work with a guy by the name of Tom. Actually I call him "Tahoe Tom." You will understand why very soon. Tahoe Tom had visited Lake Tahoe a few years back. Upon his return he shared the details of his trip with his coworkers. Each of them had normal *questions such as, 'What was the weather like?,' 'Did you have good food?,' 'Did you go skiing?,' that kind of thing. No big deal. One of the coworkers however,* "Al" *we'll call him, asked a somewhat unusual question, 'Why didn't you take* me*?'*

Everyone laughed, except of course Al. Because his question was genuine. He really had wanted to go to Tahoe. With Tom. Somehow he got it in his head that this trip might yet happen and so began the daily ritual of Al stopping by Tahoe Tom's cubicle and saying simply, "Take me to Tahoe."

The four guys at the table shared a glance of 'where do you think this might be going' but kept their comments to themselves and toasted the occasion of Benny's first "tall tale."

At first this was all in good fun. Tahoe Tom did his best to wave it off as a joke that had gone beyond its shelf life. Every joke has a "best by date" but this one had gone rotten and was starting to smell. The thing was that this wasn't *a joke to Al. He* really *wanted to go to Tahoe! Still! First thing every Monday morning, amidst everyone asking one another about their weekend, there is Al leaning over the side of Tahoe Tom's cubicle saying, "Take me to Tahoe."*

As it turns out, Tahoe Tom actually did *have a return trip to Tahoe already planned. What* wasn't *part of the plan was taking Al with him. Tahoe Tom was excited about his trip and couldn't help but tell a few of his coworkers. He was careful who he shared this with as he certainly didn't want Al to know. He was fairly certain that no one had let on because each day the same words were spoken by Al, "Take me to Tahoe."*

"Excuse me, Benny. Can I stop you there for a minute?"

"Sure," said Benny. "What's up?"

"Well, just making sure here, you know we tell 'tall tales,' kinda wild and crazy stuff, right? This just seems like a, I don't know, like a regular old work story. No offense but do you know what I mean?"

The others nodded their heads in agreement. They all wanted Benny to participate but he was killing the moment with this boring story about a friend's coworker.

Benny nodded at this and said, "I think if you will just bear with me for a few more minutes you will see where this is going."

Benny said this with a confidence they rarely saw in him. They quickly agreed to give him the floor and let him spin his yarn. They all owed him this much whether his story fit the bill as a 'tall tale' or not.

As it turns out, it did.

Actually, it topped them all.

The day came when Tahoe Tom was to leave for his trip to Lake Tahoe. One thing was certain, he was not *going to miss the daily "Take me to Tahoe" comment from Al. He felt a little guilty about not telling him of his trip, it was almost like he was sneaking away in the middle of the night but he knew those feelings would soon pass. He had been looking forward to this trip for some time now.*

The previous visit had been in the wintertime, which was great. He had visited the ski resort, seen the lake from a distance and enjoyed the season. This time however, he wanted to actually get out on *the lake and do some fishing. He needed a respite from the everyday routine and this was going to be his dream trip. He boarded his flight and made his way through the cabin to his seat.*

The moment he arrived at his row is when everything, everything, *one right after another like a line of dominoes, began to go terribly wrong.*

Everyone's ears at the table perked up when they heard the part about how everything began to go wrong. It sounded like maybe this story was just starting to get good.

Tahoe Tom checked his ticket twice before he said anything. 'Excuse me, I think that little girl is in my seat.'

He said this to the person whom he believed to be the mother of *the child who was occupying his seat on the plane. The mother was quick to explain that her daughter was fearful of flying and they felt that the window seat might help in that regard.*

Tahoe Tom was, he felt, an understanding person however that was his *seat.*

And he had a ticket to prove it.

Much of the excitement of the journey (for Tom anyway) was to look out the window during the flight and see all that there was to see. While he was pleading his case, the flight attendant, the pregnant *flight attendant, encouraged him to please take his seat. Somehow he reasoned that his desire for the window seat that he purchased would be completely lost on her so he didn't even try.*

The mother of the little girl said 'why not just take the window seat in the other row? No one is sitting there.' And that was certainly true until just then *when a large man plopped himself down into that seat. Before he could even think of challenging the man for the window seat Tahoe Tom let out an involuntary groan followed by, "Oh no!"*

"Is there a problem?" asked the flight attendant.

Rather than cause a scene Tahoe Tom said no and looked for an open seat. There was only one vacant seat and that was next to none other than the person who had claimed the window seat, his coworker, Al.

'Well, well, well,' says Al, 'it looks like we are on the same flight.'

So what, his coworker Al is on this flight. It was of course a rather unwelcome surprise, and an odd coincidence to be sure, but rather than gain any more unwelcome attention from the flight attendant Tahoe Tom decides to just accept the proffered seat.

'Well, well, well,' *Al had said.*

To Tom those three words would soon be like aluminum foil on his teeth.

Tom looks back over at Al. No additional words need to be exchanged but in Al's world, that is simply not the case.

Al smiles at Tom and says, "Glad you could finally make it."

What the hell does that even mean?

Coincidence? *I think not.*

For the remainder of the flight Tahoe Tom is just miserable. He watches with building irritation as the little girl who has taken his *window seat, (and* only *to spite her mother mind you), absolutely* refuses *to look out the window and then even pulls the window shade shut.*

Next to Tom is Al who, after managing to power through eight bags of stale airline pretzels, has now fallen asleep for the duration of the flight. He has rested his head on a pillow, and has situated the pillow against *the window, essentially blocking the view and shutting out the beautiful blue sky.*

Tahoe Tom considers himself a good *guy but right now he is definitely* not *a* happy *guy.*

"Damn, it sounds like this Al character really knows how to get under Tom's skin," said Adam.

"You could say that" replied Benny, "but as you will hear, there is much more to Tom's story."

"Alright then, I guess we need more beer!" Everyone agreed. Their server brought another round and Benny resumed the telling of his 'tall tale.'

Tahoe Tom makes it through the flight and although he is not happy, they have arrived in Reno and the two are certain now to go their separate ways. First things first, Tom heads over to the rental car counter to claim his all-important transportation for the week. There is a twenty-minute wait for a spot at the counter but Tom prides himself on being a fairly patient man so he has nothing but smiles for the woman at the counter when she waves him over. The smile is gone instantly when he hears that they have run out of vehicles.

What?! No cars?! But this is what you do, he argues. This is ALL that you do, rent cars. How can you be OUT of cars? How about a truck then? I will take a truck. You did not listen sir, she explains, I said we are out of VEHICLES. No cars. No trucks. No vehicles.

Tom walks away from the counter aghast. How is this even possible? How was he going to get to Lake Tahoe from Reno? And how would he get around once he arrived? Uber everywhere? He didn't care for that idea. He didn't care for that idea at all.

'Well, well, well,' *he hears from behind him.*

Tom turns around and there is Al with keys in hand from a different rental car agency. 'It looks like you *need a ride.'*

Tahoe Tom has his pride and he decides no way *he is getting in a car with Al after that three-hour flight from hell he has just endured. However, what he* actually *hears himself saying is, 'What a kind offer, let me grab my bag.'*

Al gets in the car first, on the driver's side. As Tom slides into the passenger's seat Al makes the unnecessary comment, "Glad you could finally make it."

Tom cringes and scrunches up his face unable to hide his inner torment.

You have* GOT *to be kidding me!

It is about a 45-minute drive from Reno to Lake Tahoe, the resort area where the hotels and casinos can be found, that is if you go directly *there. This is something that Al has elected NOT to do. Why not drive AROUND the lake? It's beautiful this time of year he says. This, however, will add an hour to the trip.*

Tahoe Tom is once again less *than happy.*

It appears however that fortune has finally smiled on Tahoe Tom when he learns that they are booked into different hotel properties. Tom has reserved a room at Harvey's and Al is booked at Harrah's. While the two hotels are linked by an underground walkway these are two entirely different properties.

As Tahoe Tom is attempting to check-in he is mortified at the fact that he cannot seem to locate the American Express card which he used to book the room. There is an expectation to show the card and run it for additional expenses but he cannot present what he does not have and now he is beside himself with disbelief.

'I know I had it when I booked the room' he is saying to himself, realizing that the card is probably still right there on the kitchen counter where he called the hotel and jotted down his confirmation number. A quick check of his wallet confirmed that his policy of traveling safe and light meant that he had no other credit cards on him and only about $100 in cash. The room was surely more than $200 a night. He wondered for a brief second why he didn't notice the card was missing at the rental car counter until he remembered they never got that far. No vehicles. No need for a credit card.

Tahoe Tom steps away from the counter wondering what he can do with no room and no money.

'Well, well, well,' *he hears behind him.* Not again! *he thinks to himself. 'It looks like* you *need a hotel room.'*

Tahoe Tom is not of the belief that lightning strikes twice but now he is of the opinion that perhaps tornadoes do.

'What a kind offer,' he hears himself say once again and soon Al and Tahoe Tom are bunkmates. Fortunately, it is a room with two

queen beds. Tom promises to pay for his half of the room when they return to work. He hopes it isn't much; he doesn't want to overpay as he is comparing in his head the room he had booked to where he is now.

The hotel room they are sharing has a second-floor view of the main street below. There is a patch of blue visible if you angled your neck just right. He was fairly certain that that might *be Lake Tahoe. The room that Tom had booked was on one of the upper floors. It was a corner room with floor to ceiling windows offering an amazing vista of Lake Tahoe only a tenth of a mile away. While he was missing out on the amazing view he would have had from his room at least he was saving money.*

It was now Jimmy's turn to comment.

"Please don't tell us that Tom went to the casino and played table games. That guy has zero luck. Plus it sounds like this guy Al might have the natural ability to be a cooler."

"Well, you're getting ahead of the story just a bit but you guessed it. Tom just couldn't help himself. What little cash he had on him disappeared at a Blackjack table with Al standing directly behind him to show his support."

There was laughter and a round of high fiving at the table as Jimmy exclaimed, "Nailed it!"

"So what happened next?" asked Mike.

Tahoe Tom has found himself in the very uncomfortable position of spending the remainder of the week living off of the kindness of Al. On a positive note, he ate at great restaurants and did much of what he came to do. On the other side of that coin is the fact that he and Al ended up spending most *of their time* together. *Tahoe Tom is a guy who prefers to be alone so this was like a prison sentence for him. Now consider this, sharing a plane* and *a car were both a huge challenge for Tom but now he finds himself sharing a hotel room for* five nights!

The point of telling you this is to prepare you for the fact that Tahoe Tom was obviously nearing the end of his rope. The last straw was well within his view.

Trevor spoke up this time.

"Something tells me we are nearing the end of the story and something really bad is about to happen."

Benny looked at each of his friends in turn, nodded his head and related to his friends the remainder of his first ever 'tall tale.'

The one thing that Tahoe Tom had really come to Lake Tahoe for was fishing. It should have been obvious that Al was only joking when he told Tom that there was no way he was paying for a boat, that he had done enough already. Tom was absolutely beside himself with frustration. Al was enjoying (probably too much) the temper tantrum that Tom was throwing. Tom was always such an in-control guy that this moment just screamed *to be captured on video, which Al did. It went viral. At their office.*

Is it fair to say that Tom was less than pleased?

Al doesn't want to push Tom too far so he announces that he has already secured a boat for the next morning. As it is already late afternoon, the owner of the boat has offered them early access so they are free to load their things onto the boat this evening. This will guarantee an early start in the morning. Suddenly Tahoe Tom has this crazy look in his eyes as he tells Al that he will be back in a short while, that he has a surprise *for him tomorrow when they are out on the boat.*

Upon his return he says, 'Don't peek!' or you will spoil the surprise. Al likes a good surprise as much as anyone so he follows Tom's command and is now eager for the boat excursion in the morning.

All four of Benny's friends are leaning in now knowing the payoff to this story is coming soon. They can almost feel the tension between Al and Tahoe Tom.

What will come next they can only imagine...

The next morning finds a chipper Tahoe Tom eager to start the day. He seems to have a spring in his step. Whatever his surprise for Al might be he is certainly anxious for that moment to be at hand. Al however seems to be moving in slow motion this morning. He had a good day yesterday and capped it off with more than a few cocktails in the casino while playing at the Blackjack tables. He is sluggish and a bit under the weather. He would rather just stay in bed.

But Tom is pestering him to get ready.

Al is wondering to himself, as the boat was already reserved and Tahoe Tom had intimated on several occasions that he prefers to fish alone, why then did he appear to be so worried *that Al might not be able to join him?*

Who knew, Tahoe Tom was a strange bird.

There was just then a few minutes when everyone seemed to want to take a break from the telling of stories. A couple of them scanned the various TV screens to see what sporting event they might catch. The others were busily working their phones, catching up on texts and emails they may have missed.

The man who was "Benny" used these few moments to engage in some deep introspective thought. There was *much more* to share than what he was sharing, like for instance the true reason why Tom was at odds with Al in the first place. There was some *critical* paperwork which has been left *undone.*

By Al.

Until that paperwork was complete Al had Tom over a barrel so to speak which made him uneasy, uncomfortable and unsettled.

Should Benny share Tom's concerns about the paperwork owed to him by Al?

Before he could make that call, Mike spoke up to say, "Benny! C'mon brother, don't leave us hangin' like this!"

The others laughed, turned their attention away from the TV's and their phones and shook their heads that 'yes!' they were ready for more. Benny looked at each of their eager faces and allowed himself the random thought of *'hope this doesn't sound too much like a confession...'*

An hour past *the time when Tom had planned to head out onto the beautiful blue waters of Lake Tahoe Al finally feels better and is now up for the boat ride. Tom has shown a patience that Al would not have guessed possible. This "surprise" must be pretty special to him. That was the only reason that Al has finally decided to go along on this crazy fishing expedition. After months of saying that Tom should take him to Tahoe, they are now here and why not enjoy every bit of the adventure.*

The two board the boat and take their seats. Tahoe Tom will be the Captain and Al will quite possibly play the unseaworthy passenger. The lake has more of a chop to it than Al had expected. His worry over getting sick out on the water was beginning to increase with each wave, however, Tom seemed to have an exact point in mind for where he would be fishing and was wasting no time in getting there.

The boat was rising and falling as it cut through the waves. While Tom guided the boat Al had time to look about and noticed that there was something concealed under a red tarp.

Ah! That *must be the surprise!*

Benny stopped for a moment to gauge the level of interest from the group. All eyes were upon him and eager to hear how about the surprise so he ventured forward with his tall tale.

The Big Finish

They were making good time, easily making up for Al's tardiness. Al assumed that Tahoe Tom must be quite anxious to either go fishing or share the surprise (or both!) as he had the engine at full throttle. The bow was bobbing up and down.

'Let's get there alive!' yelled Al.

Tahoe Tom looked at him strangely at first and then said, 'Yes. Yes of course. That would certainly ruin the surprise if we did not!' And then he smiled a rather evil smile which Al chose to ignore.

Tahoe Tom began looking about, his eyes focused on the shoreline, turning his head slowly to take it all in with a panoramic view. Al was looking at the shore as well but his gaze was centered more on the hotels and casinos and the ski resort that climbed the mountain in the distance.

Speaking of distance, what Tahoe Tom was actually not *doing was taking in the view. What he actually* was *doing was calculating the distance from their spot in the lake to the shore. He purposefully had not taken them to the center of the lake as he had told Al earlier. They were actually in a bit more remote area that was further away from the town proper. There were small motels and cabins and luxury homes dotting the landscape surrounding the lake but the place where they had arrived could easily be considered the* furthest *from civilization and casual view from the shore.*

Al readily accepted the fact that Tom would prefer a quiet spot for fishing. There were other boats and fishermen out on the lake but none of them had chosen to travel as far from the harbor area as Tom.

Suddenly Tom cut the engine to the boat which slowed immediately and then came to something of a rested stop allowing the waves to tug them back and forth with the moving current. Tom left his post and then navigated the area inside of the small boat to be able to sit down across from Al, now facing him.

Al had his eyes on the red tarp wondering if this might be the moment for his big surprise. That is when he noticed something odd.

Where was all the fishing equipment?

The lures and reels might be found under the red tarp but unless the fishing rods were collapsible, there were none to be seen.

'Well, well, well,' *said Al. 'It looks like you have forgotten to bring your fishing equipment.'*

Those three words were like nails on a chalkboard for Tom but somehow he checked himself and showed no outward anger.

Tom simply said, 'Oops!'

Al smiled at this and commented, 'Well, you told me that you throw the small ones back in anyway. That can't be that much fun.'

'Did I say that?' asked Tom.

Al was shaking his head yes.

'What I actually meant to say,' began Tom, 'is that it is the big ones *I throw back in. Here, stretch your leg out towards me.'*

Al complied and Tom reached under the red tarp and pulled out some heavy chain which he wrapped around Al's ankle. Tom looked up at Al, gave him a wink, and then threaded the shackle of a lock through a couple links of the chain, tested it and then fastened it. Al was curious but sat patiently watching as Tom went about his business of preparing the big surprise.

Once he had completed his task Tom sat back looking bemused but satisfied. Whatever it was that he had planned for this surprise Al could see that Tom had a nervous energy about him in the way in which he was preparing for the big reveal. Perhaps he was just now second guessing this big surprise?

That is when Tom lifted the red tarp and Al discovered what lay beneath.

'Well, well, well,' *said Al. 'You brought me all the way out here to give me a cinder block. How disappointing.'*

Tahoe Tom looked long and hard at Al and said, 'Al, you are making this quite easy for me. I thought I might have some reservations about this as the burden has been on my shoulders for some time but-- not now. I have no qualms about shifting that weight *over to you.'*

'The weight of the cinder block you mean? Is this a riddle?' asks Al.

'Oh, it is much *more than just that!' exclaims an oddly animated Tom.*

Al is looking at Tom now with a piqued curiosity yet urging him to continue.

'Al, I want you to look around and take it all in. Breathe in that cool clean air, that comfortable breeze coming off the water, the warmth of the sun, the breathtaking beauty of the mountain vistas and the clear blue sky. It's all so peaceful, right?'

Al nodded his head in agreement.

'Al, this is perfect for fishing but we're not *fishing, are we?'*

Al shook his head no.

'No Al, we're not *fishing. But I* do *still plan on going fishing.* Alone.'

Al put his finger up, presumably to make the point that Tom could have gone fishing alone today but rather encouraged Al to accompany him. Tom waved him off and said, 'You see, I can't go fishing alone, and enjoy myself, *until I meet my obligation. I know that now. I would feel terribly guilty if I didn't own up to this obligation* first.'

With that Tom turned the cinder block over and asked Al to stand up. He held the cinder block up for Al to see it better. Al could now see that Tom had painted something in black letters on the cinder block.

The letters read, "Ticket to Tahoe."

'Well, well, well,' *Al said with a smile, 'so* you *are finally taking* me *to Tahoe.'*

Unable to believe the moment they were sharing Tahoe Tom is grinning and shaking his head. He looked to Al and said, 'Do you remember that I told you that I actually throw the big ones *back in?'*

Al nodded his head yes.

'Well my friend, you're a big one! *Welcome to Tahoe!'*

And with that Tahoe Tom tossed the cinder block overboard. Al had a huge smile on his face, even as he noticed that the chain wrapped about his leg was securely attached as well to the cinder block. He felt a slight tug, lost his balance and then went overboard!

Al's descent must have been rapid because there were precious few bubbles rising to the surface as Tahoe Tom studied the water. In a celebratory act of brushing his hands off after a dirty chore was completed, Tom slapped his hands together a few times and then sat down to drink in the moment. He had expected to feel guilty, on edge like someone had seen *him doing something wrong. Instead he felt calm. And invigorated. The remainder of his time spent there at Tahoe would be his to enjoy.*

Alone.

Tom fired the engine back up and headed for shore. That evening he happily drank more than his share of a local craft beer and later when to the hotel room alone and slept like a baby.

"Wow! That was some story you told there!"

"Yeah, that was a tall tale for sure. Welcome to the Club!"

"Wait guys, the story isn't finished."

"What?!" they all said in unison.

"Yeah, there is a little bit more to tell." Benny surveyed the group, taking in their reaction. None of them seemed eager to continue. "Guys, don't you want to know how it ends?"

"Look," said Adam. "If the guy's body washes ashore and the police show up to arrest Tahoe Tom we get it, that is a fitting ending but it is also a bit anti-climactic for our 'tall tales' segment, don't you think?"

Benny thought for a moment and said, "Well yeah, I get it. That wouldn't be much of an ending but that's *not* what happened."

"It isn't?"

"No. *Not at all.*"

The guys looked back and forth at one another and then said, "More beers then and on with the tale!"

Tahoe Tom woke up the next morning feeling refreshed and invigorated. He felt like he had run a marathon and finished with energy to spare. If guilt was supposed to be his constant companion he hadn't shown up yet for his shift.

Tom was hungry and he was eager to find a spot for breakfast at a restaurant which was situated almost right on the lake. There was a "beach" of sorts that led from the lake up to the weathered tables and chairs.

Tom found a spot closest to the water. It was peaceful hearing the water lapping on the shore. It would have been more peaceful though if there wasn't so much conversation going on about him. There was a buzz in the air. Everyone wasn't talking about something. *He had noticed it in the lobby as well. What was going on?*

The server arrived at his table with a glass of ice water and poured him a cup of coffee from the decanter she carried. As he took a sip of the strong, hot coffee he managed to ask, 'What's the buzz about?'

'Oh you haven't heard? Some man swam ashore *with a cinder block* chained to his leg! *They think he might be a mob boss from Chicago!' The server had barely said this when a burst of hot coffee spewed out from Tom's mouth onto her face and blouse.*

The server was in shock at what Tom had just done.

Tahoe Tom was in shock from what he just heard.

And that's when a man's voice was heard from behind him.

'Well, well, well.' *Those damn three words again!*

'Glad you could finally make it.'

Al followed this up with, 'I see that you decided to have breakfast without me.'

Tom is flabbergasted at the sight of Al. His appearance speaks volumes of what he had gone through to make it back to shore alive. At this time he had made no effort to clean himself up. A crowd of onlookers had gathered to see what would happen next.

'I-I-I,' stammered Tom, trying to come up with something to say. The sight of Al standing there was too much to take in and process.

Al standing at his table, somehow still dripping wet with the cinder block still in hand.

What?! Are you serious??? Why, why, WHY?! *was that cinder block* STILL *chained to his leg?*

Al approached Tom and set the cinder block on his table with a loud 'THUNK!'

Tom looked at Al with fear in his eyes, unsure of what might happen next.

Al looked him dead in the eye and said, 'That was quite an adventure I just had. And I only have one thing *to say to you.'*

'Yeah?' said Tom in almost a whisper. 'What is that?'

Al suddenly flashed a huge smile at Toma and said, 'Tahoe was fun. Now--- TAKE ME TO VEGAS!!!'

Part Two

Take Me To Vegas

"Wait! You mean there's more??!!"

Jimmy, Mike, Trevor and Adam exclaimed in unison, loud enough to garner the attention of everyone in the bar area of the restaurant. This caught Benny off guard. He nearly fell off his chair!

"Well, yes," answered Benny after he regained his composure. "There is the '*Vegas*' story."

"Are you telling me that after all of that you just shared, this Al and what did you call him, *'Tahoe Tom,'* went to Vegas *also? Together?!"*

"Well, they did have some help," answered Benny.

"What do you mean by that?" prompted Jimmy.

"They went there on an all-expense paid trip courtesy of a local radio station."

"*What?!* Come on, you've got to be making this stuff up. This story keeps getting *crazier!*"

Benny posed the question. "This *is* our *'Tall Tales'* night, right?"

All four guys nodded their heads yes.

"And you have to admit that this *is* a 'tall tale,' yes?"

Benny looked for affirmation from the group. Another round of bobbing heads.

Mike added, "A 'tall tale' and then some!" This was followed by a bout of laughter from all.

"Yeah, Benny," Trevor said. "You hit this one out of the park!"

"Nothing like saving it all up for years and putting the rest of us to shame, right?" Adam said, elbowing Trevor who was sitting beside him.

"Aw guys, I didn't mean to—"

"Benny, it's all good." This came from Jimmy in a conciliatory fashion. "He's just kidding around with you and he's saying the same thing we're all thinking. You have one hell of a story that you're telling here. And this is *way more* than a 'tall tale.' This sucker is as tall as a *'Sequoia tree'*! Right fellas?"

The other guys nodded their heads in agreement and clapped each other on the back. There was nothing but love and support for Benny who seemed to have suddenly come of age and risen to the head of the pack all in one evening. The boys were proud of him and eager to hear more of the story.

"Thanks, but I don't feel right. I went first and none of you have had a chance to tell your story yet." Benny said.

"Gentlemen, as your general counsel," began their attorney friend Adam as though he were addressing the court, "I am of the opinion that it is our duty as colleagues, and friends," he made purposeful eye contact with each member of the group before continuing on, "that we put this matter to a vote. All in favor say, 'Aye'."

"Aye!!" said all four at once.

"Well then, it appears as though the 'ayes' have it and you sir," continued Adam, pointing at Benny, "are hereby overruled and remanded to sharing the continuation of the aforementioned story, *"Take Me to Tahoe"* with the amended version to be identified as *"Take Me to Vegas."* Do we have a quorum?"

"A *what*?" asked Benny.

Mike jumped in. "All he is saying in that 'lawyer speak' of his, which is just a bunch of B.S. mind you, is let's get on with telling the story! We ALL want to hear it!"

"Oh okay," Benny said meekly. "I hope you like this second part."

"Hey, if it's as *crazy* as the first part, I think we're gonna *love it!*" exclaimed Trevor.

"Oh, it's *crazy* alright." Benny stated. "Crazi-*ER!*"

"Wow!" said Jimmy. "I can't wait! But hey, how about we ditch Applebee's and head somewhere with a bit more atmosphere? And a bit more of a beer selection. Whaddaya say?"

"I'm all for that," said Mike. "You got something in mind?"

"I sure do. That new brewery on the east side of town. It is perched up on a hill overlooking the airport with an incredible view of the city skyline in the distance."

"Sold!" shouted Trevor. "That sounds amazing! Do they have outside seating?"

"Of course!" said Jimmy. "Come on guys, let's pay our tabs and head on out. And Benny, you keep that story warm until we get there, okay?" He said this last part with a wink of an eye and a pointing finger.

"Sure. Will do, Jimmy." He said his name as though he were reminding himself of the name and to which one of them it belonged.

The brewery is exactly as advertised. It is set on what was arguably the highest peak of land in the city with a grand view of the airport and the downtown area to the west with buildings reaching up to the sky. This had come as quite a surprise to Benny as he had always thought of the city as being rather flat and boring. This new vantage point was exciting and might lend some additional perspective to his 'Tahoe/Vegas' story.

After they parked their cars, the group of five headed inside the brewery. The interior of the brewery was impressive. The interior of the building was crafted like a defunct brick factory. Using the bourbon barrels that they aged their beer in as props gave the brewery the look and feel of a prohibition-era speakeasy. This 1920's mob ambiance put them all in a Vegas type of mood. After all, Vegas had once been the jewel of the mob's gambling crown. A man by the name of Bugsy Siegel had recognized a diamond in the rough of what was once just parched desert land. Over time that tiny desert oasis would blossom into an entertainment paradise.

The five of them are now gathered inside the brewery gawking at the beer offerings handwritten on a chalkboard. Each one in turn made their selection. Since Jimmy had made his first million selling lemonade out of a food truck he naturally chose a lemonade shandy. Mike was in the landscaping business so he gravitated towards something crisp and refreshing. His pick was a pale lager. Trevor spent a good amount of his time at or near a golf course. He owned a golf instruction academy so he preferred to keep his drinking light. He opted for a nice wheat beer. Adam, always the bookish one of the group had developed a taste for the sour beers. He drank alone when it came to this type of beverage. His buddies would always wave off any offers when he was buying which was just fine with him. He considered his manner with money 'frugal.' His friends would just say that he was 'cheap.'

It is Benny's turn to order. As he started to open his mouth Jimmy cut in and said, "Now don't embarrass yourself here, Benny. This is a *craft* brewery where they make their own beer. They don't have Bud Light!" This comment elicited a round of giggles from the group which Benny ignored and then placed his order.

"I'll have the Imperial Milk Stout. That looks creamy and delicious."

"Hey Benny! You're not ordering ice cream here!" joked Jimmy.

"No, I am definitely *not* ordering ice cream," said Benny as a large glass filled with a very dark liquid was handed to him. All four of his friends were quiet as Benny took a sip. As he savored the brew he noticed that he had the rapt attention of his friends.

"What the hell *is* that?" asked Trevor. "It looks *dangerous!*"

"It looks--," Adam piped in, "like motor oil. *Old* motor oil."

Another round of laughter followed that comment. Benny headed for the door to the yard area outside where Adirondack chairs were situated, each of them with a view facing west. His friends followed. Once they were all seated in a haphazard semi-circle Adam spoke.

"Hey, you still haven't answered Trevor's question. What the hell is that stuff?"

Benny smiled after taking another sip. "This 'stuff' as you call it, is a chocolate coffee Imperial milk stout." This piece of information he had provided them was not helpful.

"What!?" they asked in unison.

"It is a dark beer with chocolate and coffee notes all brewed into a frothy goodness. How does that sound?"

"I would say that it sounds better than it looks!" chimed in Mike. "And certainly not a beer I would expect *you* to be drinking." The others nodded their heads in agreement.

"Well boys, maybe you just don't know me very well. Cheers!"

Benny lifted his glass and the others followed suit. It was now time for Benny to share the next part of his story about Al and Tahoe Tom. He was in the middle of the group and they offered him their full attention as planes came and went with a pleasant drone overhead to the airport nearby.

Benny looked from Jimmy to Mike, then to Trevor and Adam. Their eyes said it all. Go ahead and tell your story. Benny cleared his throat and began.

"It all started, this part of the story anyway, *before* Tahoe Tom and Al met up in the Reno Airport at the rental car agency..."

The five of them, all with beer in hand, had settled in for the Vegas portion of the story. Benny looked at each of his friends to be sure that they were still interested. Each nodded in the affirmative so Benny began to tell the story.

Day One: **The Vegas Story, starring *Al*-vis!**

On his way from the plane to the baggage area Al had passed by a kiosk with a life-size standup poster of Elvis holding a sign that read, "ENTER TO WIN!" *Not one to pass by an opportunity to win something, (Al was a gambler at heart), he just had to stop to see what this was all about. The man standing inside the kiosk explained that this was an Elvis impersonator contest. The winner from each of these kiosks (there were similar kiosks in other Nevada airports) would win an all-expense paid trip to Las Vegas for a grand finale Elvis impersonator contest to be staged and televised live at the Stratosphere Hotel & Casino.*

This was simply too good to pass up but unfortunately Al was in a hurry to get to the rental agency to pick up a rental car. Not to worry, said the man at the kiosk. Just pick an Elvis song, none of them are more than three minutes long, suit up in the provided Elvis costume, step inside the recording booth there and wail away. Your performance will be recorded in the booth. After that you will fill out an entry form and be on your way. We will notify you if you win. Easy as that! Who could resist?!

Well, Al of course could not resist. He chose 'Burning Love' as his song of choice. The man behind the kiosk stepped out of the kiosk area and walked around to meet Al who did a doubletake. Something weird had just happened. This man who had only moments ago been eye level with Al was now at full height just up to Al's belt buckle. Al was at first caught by surprise. The man looked up at him and asked, "Hey buddy, do we have a problem?"

Al looked him squarely in the eyes and said, "Not your problem that I am freakishly tall. I have learned to live with it. So, do you think you have an Elvis suit that will fit me?"

The man winked at Al and said, "Okay my large friend, we will get along just fine. As for the suit, since we figure that most people are not tall enough for their weight, we'll go with the 'later years' Elvis for you, if you know what I mean." This was followed by another wink and a nod. Al snickered at this not sure that the comment was all that clever.

The man disappeared for a moment in the back of the photo booth then reemerged with a sequined and bedazzled Elvis cloak. "Here, try this on."

Al tried it on and it fit like a glove, the kind of glove that OJ might have worn.

Al grabbed the microphone that the kiosk man handed to him and then went into the photo booth to gyrate and belt out the very best Elvis impression of 'Burning Love' that he could muster. The kiosk man standing outside the booth could not contain himself. This was too viral-ready to pass up so he took a short video of the recording booth rocking and rolling back and forth. He then posted it to social media with the caption, 'If the booth is a-rockin'...'

Three minutes later Al was filling out the entry form and after that was on his way to the rental car area.

"Wait." Jimmy cut in. "So what happened with the Elvis thing?"

"Oh, the contest you mean?" Benny asked.

"Yeah that, did he *win?*"

"Do you want me to tell you that *now?* Or wait for later in the story when it starts to make sense?" He looked to each of them and they all seemed to be in agreement that they were curious to know that part now. "Well alrighty then, it looks like we have a consensus.

So Al *won* the contest! *And* the 'all-expense paid trip to Las Vegas'." He said this last part using air quotes.

"*Really!?* Wow!" exclaimed Mike. "What *luck!*"

Benny scrunched up his face and said, "Not so fast. There are two things here at play that I must share with you."

"Okay, what?" asked Trevor.

"Well, first of all, I don't think it was a *legit* contest if you know what I mean."

"Pray tell as I for one do *not* know what you mean." This from Adam who most certainly had been the captain of the debate team in high school.

Benny continued. "I am of the opinion that this was not a contest to find the *best* Elvis impersonators."

"No?" queried Mike.

"No. I think this was a *sham.* I think it was a ruse to be able to find the *worst* Elvis impersonators. A way to discover the hidden talents of the *truly bad* singers with little to no rhythm but definitely *not* lacking in confidence. The grand finale Elvis show was destined to be a hodgepodge of the *best* of the *worst*, with every one of the impersonators placed on stage clearly to make an absolute fool of themselves."

"The prize *was* awarded though?" questioned the ever-vigilant attorney Adam.

"Oh sure, sure. Al *definitely* received *his* 'all-expense paid trip' to Vegas." This comment also made with air quotes.

"Wait, quick question. I thought this was an all-expense paid trip for "*two*" which is why Tahoe Tom signed off on going with Al."

"Good catch, counselor. Tahoe Tom *assumed* that it was for two which *is* why he went. Tom was cheap, cheap, cheap (primarily because he was poor mind you) so a *free trip* was a no-brainer. Plus he needed to work on how he might smooth over that whole '*tying*

Al to a cinder block and pushing him off a boat into the deepest part of Lake Tahoe thing.' Somehow, some way, Al saw that as a friendly prank. Tom needed to keep him on track with believing just that, if for no other reason than to keep *himself* from going to jail."

"So who paid for *Tom's* trip?" Mike was curious as were they all.

"*Al* paid for it. *100%.* He didn't want to go alone and he knew that Tom would not accept his um, shall we say, generosity. Tom hated to be indebted to anyone. For *anything.*" This last part Benny shared with an odd bit of defiance.

Mike has a couple of follow up questions to pose.

"So, did Tom ever find out? That Al had paid for his trip? And if so, how did he handle it?"

"To answer your questions, yes, yes, and not well. But we'll get to that."

"Yeah, right. Let's get back to the story while our beer is still cold!"

This proposal from Jimmy met with cheers from all. Benny nodded his head and continued. "So now you know why and how Al and Tom got to Vegas. Here is what happened next..."

The Vegas Story, with a gambling problem

Things went south for Tahoe Tom and Al before they had even checked into the room at the fabulous Luxor Hotel and Casino. *While strolling through the casino (which is the only way to get anywhere while in Vegas) Al encourages Tom to gamble with him. "Let's play craps!" he says. Tom is quite reluctant to do so knowing that the only luck that comes his way is bad.*

Al reminds Tom that their hotel stay is being provided for them courtesy of 'W.H.O.A.' radio, the station promoting the Elvis impersonator contest.

The good news for Tom is that that bit of information was 100% half-true. The hotel stay is *being covered by the radio station* but-- *it's not* this *hotel and it's not* this *evening. Tom will find all that out soon enough. For now he has a gambling problem. He* wants *to gamble but he has* no *money.*

As it turns out the radio station folks have brought with them a small camera crew and are eager to capture whatever exploits these two juxtaposed friends might have to offer. Right out of the gate there is a DJ from the station on hand to egg on Al and Tom at the craps table. Each of them is generously handed $100 of free "radio money" with which to gamble. This sudden change of fortune sways Tom's opinion on gambling so he steps up to the table eagerly. What he should *have done is to listen to that little voice inside his head reminding him that he has* zero luck *at gambling* but-- *with free cash in hand, he ignores it completely.*

In just under fifteen minutes (!), Tom is down by $500, which is $400 more than he had to begin with if you're counting in the free radio money. The DJ is actively calling a play by play of Tom's losing streak, jokingly comparing it to the National Debt in terms of the rate of debt accumulation. This is all being caught LIVE! by the camera crew. The disparaging looks on Tom's face are priceless!

Al on the other hand, has amassed a whopping $3,500 in winnings, making him once again the shoulder that Tom will need to lean on when it comes to covering his debts. Al is winning big but oddly he is standing alone in his moment of victory. He hears the excited shouting of an assembled crowd but sadly it is not for him. It is for Tom, the biggest loser.

Well, Well, Well

Tom is standing at one end of a craps table where an enthralled throng of onlookers has gathered. He is baffled by the fact that he has somehow become the center of attention with a crowd of *spectators who are eagerly cheering him on (or is it* jeering *him on) with his amazing display of rapid misfortune. Tahoe Tom is fuming, barely able to keep control of his temper, yet he continues to play to the crowd (and the camera) by gambling with money he does not have---.*

Just then a comforting hand is placed on his shoulder and a friendly voice that grates like sandpaper in his ears.

'Well, well, well. *It looks like you are in quite a pickle.'*

"Oh man! Without bad luck this Tom dude would have no luck at all!" exclaimed Jimmy around a mouthful of food truck chicken wings. He clapped Benny on the back and said, "Isn't that hilarious?!"

"Yeah, I guess so," said a rather sober Benny. "Maybe it's just a matter of perspective. Don't you have any concern for *Tom's* feelings?"

"Well, this *is* just a story, right? It's just a made-up 'tall tale,' right?"

Benny sported a completely blank stare for a minute before responding with, "Of course! I mean, yeah, it's just a story! All made up. None of it is real. I mean, how could it be, right?"

The guys all looked at one another, each thinking that this seemed like a *weird* thing to say. Benny sensed their discomfort and hurriedly jumped back into his story. There was so much more to tell...

The Vegas Story, the conundrum of how to cleverly share misfortune

Tahoe Tom is embarrassed and humiliated once again with this episode at the craps table. Sure Al has bailed him out financially once again, (even tipped the croupier which Tom would not have done), so now the crowd has dispersed. Even the camera crew left for a much-needed coffee break.

Tom wants to leave as well but knows that he has made a commitment. Moreover he is quite cognizant of the fact that he needs to keep up the ruse that his attempted "murder" of Al at Lake Tahoe was just an incredible prank.

Tom found himself leaving the casino area with Al to check into their hotel room. Some of what just happened had become something of a messy blur for him. The jerky ride up the "inclinator" (not elevator) at the Luxor *got Tom's blood pumping and stirred his imagination for perhaps another creative mishap for Al.*

The Luxor *is a 30-story casino hotel built in the shape of the great pyramids of Egypt. The* Luxor *name itself is derived from a city in Egypt. The property is situated on the southern end of the Las Vegas strip. The facade is black mirrored glass and although the* Luxor *does not rise to the height of the Great Pyramid in Giza, the massive Great Pyramid of Cholula in Mexico could rest comfortably inside what was once recognized as the world's largest atrium.*

To crown the pyramid is the Luxor *Sky Beam which is considered to be the strongest manmade beam of light in the world. Such a feat is achieved by using curved mirrors to collect light from 39 Xenon lamps and focus them into one narrow beam which is visible from space. On a clear night it can be seen from over 200 miles away by aircraft cruising at altitude.*

Outside there is a scale replica of The Sphinx with a tunnel at its base to welcome guests arriving on the casino-to-casino tram. Several of these intrepid folks had climbed quite a few steps to get to this point. They were coming from... the famous (or infamous, your choice) Las Vegas Strip.

If all of that was not enough to pack into one venue the use of "inclinators" rather than elevators to access each floor of the hotel was a fascinating addition. At the four corners of the pyramid shaped building hotel guests ride these inclinators to their assigned floor. The inclinators are positioned at a 39-degree angle and move at a rate of 700 feet per minute. Al and Tom are riding in one now. While Tom felt that not having glass in the car to show off the awe-inspiring view of the atrium below was a big miss, Al who is possessed of a fear of heights felt that the architects made the right call.

After having taken a few minutes to freshen up in their room, Al and Tom head back down to The Strip to board a waiting trolley style bus. This vehicle will afford them a street level view of the iconic casinos that line the strip on their way to their destination which is the towering Stratosphere Hotel and Casino.

Now that he is comfortable, sitting next to a window and across the aisle from Al, Tom can take in the sights and sounds of the strip while he allows his mind to wander. After that horrendous loss at the Luxor *casino, Tom begins to consider the many possibilities that Vegas might have to offer when planning his annoying friend's demise.*

And there are *many...*

The first of course would be a fall from one of the highest floors in the Luxor *to the incredible atrium below. Al has already quashed that idea by requesting a lower floor citing that whole fear of heights thing. When boarding the bus Tom had looked behind him to see* Mandalay Bay. *He had heard that they had a gigantic wave pool. A spectacular drowning incident sounded quite interesting at first until he remembered that Al was* obviously *a powerful swimmer to have made his way back from the deepest waters of Lake Tahoe to the shore with a cinder block chained to his leg. Scratch that idea!*

Excalibur *came up on his left. Tom had read that there was live jousting in that place. Perhaps he could get Al to participate. Impalement sounded like a medieval way to meet your maker. There were probably safeguards to prevent that though, bummer.*

New York New York *was next on his left. Tom looked up at the superstructure and his eye caught something moving. Weaving around the skyscrapers of the New York skyline replica was a rollercoaster. Tom chuckled at the thought of Al's seat restraint malfunctioning and the momentum of the coaster ejecting him into one of the hotel rooms.*

What a surprise that would be!

Room Service!

The MGM Grand *passed by on the right but nothing came to mind. The giant figurehead of the* MGM *lion that might have gobbled Al up was long gone. The trolley guide mentioned that entering a lion's mouth was considered for some international travelers to be bad juju.*

ARIA Resort & Casino *and* The Cosmopolitan *both escaped his attention on the left while* Planet Hollywood *passed by unnoticed on his right. The* Bellagio Hotel & Casino *is on his left. Hmm, a tumble into the lake! Oh wait, never mind, been there done that with the water and swimming thing, that didn't work. Besides, the fountains always had their share of gawkers who might catch his untoward actions and post on Tik Tok.*

To his right Tom sees the fabulous Paris Las Vegas*. He chuckles to himself thinking that there are not enough beignets in the world to break a fall from the replication of the iconic Eiffel Tower! But-- there we go with that fear of heights thing again. Good luck with that. Next!*

Caesars Palace *now on the left, the* Flamingo *(where it all started!) and* The LINQ *to the right. So much to take in. Vegas is incredible!*

Ooh, look at that! Lava spewing from a live volcano at The Mirage*! A tumble into red hot lava would be terrifically horrible, right?! Of course it's not* real *lava. Move on.*

And then Tom sees Treasure Island. *Is that a* real *cannon? And a* real *pirate ship? A walk on the plank might make for a nasty death. That sounds so appealing! Lots to consider.*

The Venetian Resort *appears on his right but the thought of a boating accident involving slow-moving gondolas was simply too silly to consider. The last possibility before arriving at the* Stratosphere *is* Circus Circus. *How amusing it would be to see Al swinging on a trapeze above the casino crowd.*

Look Ma! No net!

And then to crash into the slots and table games below. Sounded amazing but absolutely no way to make that work. Al was definitely not *a circus performer.*

Just then an advertisement in the trolley catches Tom's eye. They have a zipline hanging above Fremont Street?!? Keep that one in mind, Tom thinks to himself. They do have plans to go to Fremont Street during their visit. How safe is that zipline anyway? That cable could snap at any time, right?! Tom's daydream smile faded as once again he was faced with that stupid fear of heights thing again. Dang it! There would be no way to get Al to ride the damn thing. Foiled again!

Jimmy said, "Hey! Is it just me or does this Tom dude seem to have some twisted obsession with killing Al? What's the deal? Al seems like a nice enough guy."

"Yeah?! Well you don't know him now, do you?!" Benny fires back.

This sudden outburst caught all of them off guard.

"Hey man, are you alright? This *is* just a story, right?" Adam inquired with real concern.

Benny looked around at the worried looks on the faces of his friends. The mood had changed. Did they think these were *actual* events? Did they think that *he* was *Tom?!*

Benny burst out laughing. "Guys! I was just playing you! It's just a *story!* Give me a break!"

The intended reaction of laughter from the group did not happen. Benny took a huge gulp of beer, draining his glass. "I'm going for another! Who's with me?"

Something wasn't right. The group looked around nervously at one another unsure of who should be first to speak. Adam spoke up. "I could use another. Let's do it. I *really* want to hear the remainder of this story *now.*"

Once the five of them had regrouped with fresh beers in hand and a sincere concern for how it might end Benny continued on with his tale.

The Vegas Story, the thing with the backpack

"Al, tell me again why we're going to the Strat.*"*

"Because that's where the Elvis contest is going to be held."

"So we have to come all *the way down here* again?*!"*

"Yep, but it's not that big of a deal since we'll be staying here."

"Wait. What? You lost me. I thought we were staying at the Luxor*."*

"We are. Tonight. When they hold the Elvis contest we'll be here at the Strat *courtesy of* WHOA *radio."*

Al gave Tom a huge smile certain that he would receive one in return. He did not. He got an angry scowl instead.

"Wait, if we're staying at the Stratosphere, *then who is paying for the* Luxor?! *What the hell?!"*

"Don't you worry about a thing. I *am covering our expenses at the* Luxor. *Your welcome. You can owe me." Al said this magnanimously.*

"I don't want to owe *you anything!" exclaimed Tom with a quick-fire reply.*

"I'm just teasing. As long as I keep winning all this money I am willing to share!"

Tom stomped off, fuming once again. Al just didn't get it. Tom doesn't take charity*. He doesn't* give it *either to be fair. Before he can continue with his tirade, Al shares a new problem. Somewhere along the way he has forgotten his precious new backpack.*

"We have to go back to the Luxor. *Sorryyy." Al drug out the last word to show how badly he felt about the inconvenience this would cause for Tom.*

"What do you mean "we" *have to go back? That's all on* you*. It's* your *backpack.* I'm *staying right* here*."*

"You're making me go back alone?*"*

"I'm not making *you do* anything*. You want your backpack? Go get it."*

Al made a pouty face but then agreed that he would run the errand alone.

"You will wait for me here?"

"I promise that I will not leave this very spot!"

"I don't believe that for a minute."

"Would you look at that! You're finally getting to know me."

"You're silly," said Al and headed back towards the Luxor. *Tom breathed a sigh of relief as he watched him leave, eager for some time on his own.*

Some things just irritate Tom, he can't explain why, they just do. Like this backpack that Al feels a compulsion to wear. Everywhere. *The fact that he has to go all the way back to the* Luxor *to retrieve it was super annoying to Tom. The backpack, in Tom's estimation anyway, looked like something that was designed for military use. In other words, it was all function and lacked any fashion sense. Brother Al wore that thing like there was a baby inside. He was overly cautious, so much so that he was careful to lean forward at all times when seated to be certain not to put any undue pressure on the pack.* Crazy. *Given the chance Tom would like to throw that damn thing from the top of the* Stratosphere*...*

...which just gave Tom the kernel of an idea.

The "alone time" Tom suddenly found himself with would afford him an opportunity to put some more thought to this kernel of an idea rattling around in his head like so much un-popped popcorn.

The camera crew was still present but not particularly interested in the exploits of only one of the daring duo so no filming was taking place.

As Tom wandered away from the crew he saw a sign which was exactly what he was looking for, the elevator to the top of the Strat, *which intrigued him.*

When Tom entered the elevator it occurred to him that he had forgotten all about the fact that this casino hotel featured a revolving restaurant at the top of the tower, not to mention the fact that it was the tallest point in Las Vegas.

The Stratosphere Hotel & Casino*, or just* "The Strat" *as the locals called it, was an iconic landmark in the heart of Vegas. Visible throughout the city, the structure seemed to dominate the skyline which was saying something with a skyline as diverse and whimsical as Las Vegas. A revolving restaurant, the "Top of the World," was the crown jewel of the tower offering diners a 360-degree view* of *the city with a full revolution every 80 minutes.*

And there was more!

Tom busied himself reading the posted literature inside the elevator car. He read that this elevator would whisk him to the top of "SkyPod," a 1,149-foot-tall observation tower, the tallest freestanding observation tower in the United States. This was all great stuff but what really grabbed Tom's attention were the thrill rides perched on the rooftop.

There is the "Big Shot." The marketing piece read, 'Strap in and be catapulted 160 feet into the air at 45 miles per hour in mere seconds!' Not to be outdone there was also "X-Scream," which was described as 'a roller coaster ride like no other!' As he read on he learned that the car in which one is seated actually teeter totters 27 feet over the edge of the tower!

It was truly a special moment for Tom when his eyes landed on something listed as the "SKYJUMP." The elevator car had reached the top but he was eager to learn more so he held the door open with one foot and read on.

He read that the "SKYJUMP" was an open-air leap of 829 feet to the strip below. The attraction holds the record as the highest commercial 'decelerator' descent facility. The rate of descent for those choosing to take the leap was 40 mph. That kernel of an idea in Tom's brain was now starting to pop. He would soon add a pinch of salt and a drizzle of butter to make the idea really tasty.

Tom finally allowed the elevator car to continue its service as he made his way to where the thrill rides are located. The view was spectacular from this vantage point. Getting Al to even come up here was going to be a challenge but Tom put that concern on the back burner for now. This SKYJUMP thing just seemed too good to be true.

Tom walked over to the staging area of the jump to watch for several minutes. He wanted to see if he could learn anything about how it is operated. What he saw were two men, young men perhaps in their mid-twenties, working the thrill ride. One was suiting up the riders and going over the safety regulations. The other was operating the mechanism itself. In the short time that Tom was watching, one of the two young men walked over to say something to the other. Tom moved in closer to see if he could make out what they were saying.

"No worries dude, I got this. Besides, it's kinda slow right now. You'll be back way before the evening rush hits, right? Enjoy your break and tell Melinda I said hi! Later dude."

The young man who had been suiting up riders headed for the exit. The other young man was on his own now, performing both tasks. A good-sized gentleman has just been suited, hooked up and ready to go. The young man operating the ride gave the man a thumbs up which was returned by the rider. He then yelled "Bombs away!" and the rider disappeared from view.

Tom walked up to the young man with the thought in mind that he would ask some basic questions about what it's like to work up here at the top of the world. He lost his train of thought when he saw what was embroidered on the young man's blue denim shirt.

It was not something that he recognized--- as a name.

"Excuse me," said Tom.

"Yeah Mr. Dude, how can I help you?"

Tom scrunched up his face with the "Mr. Dude" *comment.* WTF? *Whatever.*

"Yes, I couldn't help but notice the words that are embroidered on your shirt there."

"Oh here, you mean?" the young man pointed to the words on his shirt. "Yeah, that's where the name goes on these work shirts."

Tom scrunched his face up again but decided not to be rude. "Yes, I can see that but correct me if I'm wrong but it appears that it reads, 'Part-Time.' *May I ask what that is about?"*

The young man laughed and said, "Yeah, isn't that funny as shit?! The fellas did that for me. They actually PAID for it. Too cool. I like it. Do you like it?"

"I guess I like it but I don't really GET it. Is it like an inside joke or something?"

"Yeah for sure," he explained. "My name is really Marc but the guys call me 'Part-Time.'

"And why is that? If you don't mind me asking."

"Not at all. You see, I have this A-D-D thing and sometimes I—Whoa! Check out that plane! It is HUGE."

"What?!" Tom looked around for a plane and found one far off in the distance. THAT distracted him? He looked back to Marc. "You were saying...?"

"I was? What was I saying?" Marc asked as though being caught totally off guard.

Tom was getting weary of this already. "You were saying how this 'Part-Time' *nickname made it on to your shirt."*

"Yeah, the guys pitched in and got it for me. Pretty cool. I like it, do you like it?"

"We have already been through this once," Tom said, now starting to show his frustration.

"Really? *Have you been here before? Sorry man, you don't look familiar."*

"What?!" Tom was beginning to realize that no explanation was necessary but he asked again anyway. "WHY do they call you 'Part-Time?'

"Oh that! Yeah, they call me 'Part-Time' *so they put it on my shirt."*

"Um, I think you're forgetting something." Tom said, referring to the fact that Marc had neglected to answer his question.

"Oh yeah! Thanks man! You're right! Damn, you're good. I just remembered that I forgot to check to make sure that big dude made it to the ground safe-like. Not a blob of blood and guts, you feel me?" Part-Time (Marc) winked. He then held a walkie talkie up to his mouth and said, "Hey Ground Control! We good down there? Did our passenger land safely? Over."

"Yep, about five minutes ago. Thanks for staying on top of the situation like always 'Part-Time.' Out."

Marc winked at Tom. "Did you hear that? They call me 'Part-Time' like what's on my shirt. Do you wanna know why?"

"I would LOVE to!" Tom exclaimed. "Wait! Where are you going?"

"Who? Me?*"*

"Yes. You.*"*

"Oh, my bad. I thought I was on break. I kill *me." Marc laughed out loud.*

"Oh yeah? Well if you don't, I will,*" whispered Tom to himself.*

"What's that?"

"Nothing. For the last time, why do they call you 'Part-Time?'

"Yeah, the guys call me 'Part-Time.' I don't know why. Maybe it's because I have A-D-D. Or maybe it's because I don't always finish what I start. It might be because I don't always show up for work. Or maybe—it's because I don't always do all that safety stuff *we're supposed to do. Let me tell you man, there is a LOT to remember. I don't know man. I'm drawing a blank on this one. Wish I could help. What is that you wanted?"*

"Never mind, you answered my question. Thank you, 'Part-Time.' Tom said this with a snicker.

"Hey man, that's what the guys call me. How did you know that?" Part-Time (Marc) then looked down at his shirt to see the words embroidered there, laughed and said, "Oh man, you must think I'm an idiot!*"*

Tom, with a plan taking shape in his brain, shook his head and said, "Nope! Actually, you're my new best friend."

"Whoa, that's so cool. I'd say let's go check out the strip but I think I have to work right now."

"You know what? I think you're right. By the way, how often do you work up here?"

"Oh that's an easy one. Five days a week but I couldn't tell you which ones, you know what I'm saying?"

"Sure. Thanks for your help. I will be seeing you around. Take care."

"You too. Hey man, you're going the wrong way. This is how you get down." Part-Time pointed to the edge of the rooftop.

Tom winked at him and said, "Maybe next time. This go round I'm taking the elevator. See ya."

Whatever Part-Time said in return was missed by Tom as he hurried onto the elevator. Once he had returned to the lobby he headed directly for the desk of the Concierge.

Tom spotted an incredibly well-groomed man in a suit and said, "Can I ask you a question?"

"Certainly sir, how may I be of service?"

"I have what may seem like a pretty random question. A friend of mine would absolutely LOVE to do the SKYJUMP but he is deathly afraid of heights. Do you have any ideas for how I might help him to overcome his fear and cross something off his bucket list?"

"This question comes up more often than you might expect. I have a possible solution for you."

"You do?!"

"Yes. Has your friend ever tried indoor skydiving?"

"Um no, what is that?"

"It is exactly what it sound like. You are inside a building; you get a parachute strapped to you just like the real thing and then you step out onto a net. There are walls all about you and if you look up you will see there is a ceiling as well."

"Okaaaay—" *Tom drew this out prompting the gentleman behind the desk to continue.*

"If you were to look below you, you would see a giant fan with a 1,000-horsepower motor which blows wind speeds of up to 120 mph. That's enough to give you lift and get you flying! Or free-falling, however you want to look at it."

"Wow, that sounds amazing. Is it expensive?"

"Sir, you don't want to look at it that way."

"No?"

"No. Don't ask if it is expensive. *Ask instead if it is* worth *it. If this gets your friend to overcome his fear and actually* do *the SKYJUMP is it not* priceless*?"*

Tom pondered this for less than ten seconds and then exclaimed, "Yes! Thank you! What is this place called anyway?"

The Concierge smiled and said, "They have a very clever name. It is simply 'Indoor Skydiving Vegas'."

"Well that sounds easy enough to remember. Thank you for your assistance."

"Thank you sir and enjoy your stay in Las Vegas."

Tom gave him a thumbs up as he walked away. All the myriad pieces of his plan were now coming together nicely. It was an evil plan to be sure. He looks around guiltily to see if Al has returned. He has not. Tom quickly walks in the direction of where they were standing when Al left.

As Tom is strolling through the casino at the Stratosphere, he sees a slot machine that captures his attention. It is a James Bond 007 machine replete with the sounds of gunfire and car chases. Tom watches for a moment as a woman sits down to play. She pulls the lever and the wheels spin. As each wheel stops spinning an image is visible in the window.

Villain. Villain. Villian.

She loses.

'Story of my life' whispers Tom to himself.

Just as he is beginning to walk away a young boy of about eleven or twelve approaches him and says, "Hey Mister, I'm not old enough to play but I have some money. Will you play that James Bond game for me?"

Tom chuckles at this and says, "Get lost kid. Gambling is for suckers."

"Please," the boy whines. "Just this one time. Pleeeeease."

"Where the hell are your parents?" Tom demands. "Are children even allowed in this place?"

"My parents are busy and I am not a child." This statement was made with conviction as he stared Tom down. "I thought you were a nice man but maybe you're just a jerk."

"What?! Where did you learn to talk like that anyway? Someone needs to wash your mouth out with soap or spank you or whatever the hell parents do these days to punish their kids." Tom looked around searching for the parents of this errant boy.

"They put me in 'time out,' that's what."

"What?" Tom asked, unsure of what the boy had just said.

"My parents put me in 'time out' but I don't care. I just play video games on my phone."

"You have a phone!? At your age!?" Tom asked in obvious surprise.

"You have a phone at your age?" parroted the boy and mocking Tom.

Tom sneered at the kid, actually wanting to take a paddle to his backside for his insolence. That is when it occurred to him that he could kill two birds with one stone. "Hey kid, I'll be honest with you. I have the worst luck of anyone alive which is why I don't gamble. Listen, if I put your money in this machine it's a pretty safe bet that you will never see it again."

"Oh yeah? Well I will take that bet."

"Hey, I'm serious. When I gamble or play slots, one thing is absolutely certain."

"What's that?" asked the kid.

"That I will lose."

"Okay, well the way I see it is that since it is my money," the boy said smugly while pointing at Tom, "YOU got nothing to lose."

Tom considered this for a moment, finding the angle the kid was posing quite amusing. And totally accurate. "Okay kid, you got yourself a deal. Give me your money and I will play for you but—"

Tom narrowed his eyes and pointed his index finger at the boy and said, "no crying or bellyaching when I lose. Sorry, make that when YOU *lose. You can't say I didn't warn you. Got it?"*

"Got it," said the boy excitedly.

Tom reached out his hand and the boy eagerly deposited the sum of his net worth into the palm of Tom's hand. Tom looked down at the coin and said, "A quarter? Really? This is what you want me to "gamble" with?" He said the word "gamble" using air quotes.

"Hey, what do you expect? I'm just a kid!"

"Ha! Finally you admit it you little rug rat!"

The kid had a retort but choked it back because he didn't want to lose the opportunity for this man to play his quarter in the machine. Tom eyed him for a moment, hoping for another snide comment from the kid that would give him a reason to hand back the quarter. It didn't come. He was committed now to playing the game and losing this kid's quarter. Tom stepped up to the machine. Just before he deposited the quarter he made the declaration, "Well here goes nothin'! And I do *mean "nuthin'"!"*

As the wheels spin, the slot machine plays the James Bond theme and sound effects of both hand-to-hand combat and explosions emanate from the speakers. The young boy giggles with delight. Tom tries to tone down the kid's enthusiasm by saying, "Remember, it's your dime kid."

"Hey! I gave you a quarter! *" the boy asserted, not allowing for this man to pull a fast one.*

"Give me a break kid," said Tom. "It's just an expression! Geez!" Tom then gave the one-armed bandit a mighty pull. The three wheels spun for a few seconds and were coming to a stop from left to right. The first wheel offered up a "0". Big fat zero thought Tom. I tried to warn the kid!

The second wheel stopped on "0" as well.

Tom started to chuckle to himself, this will shut that kid's mouth.

The final wheel stopped. It was another number but hey, what's this? Not *a zero? That's* crazy, *it's a "7". That's a lucky number in Vegas, right?*

Just then a siren went off and the machine Tom was playing was making a whole lot more noise. There was suddenly a crowd of people surrounding this slot machine. Security officers appeared out of nowhere as the machine was steadily ringing up the amount of the player's winnings. Whistles and cheers from the onlookers added to the excitement. A few were patting Tom on the back and shouting, "You won! You won!"

"Oh my gosh! I WON!!" exclaimed Tom. The camera crew had materialized before him and was capturing every exciting moment of his amazing good fortune.

"I WON! I WON!" shouted Tom into the lens of the camera.

Tom could not believe it! He never won anything! *and now with the help of some young kid* this *was his moment.* Oh no! The kid! *Tom looked around quickly hoping that somehow the kid had been lost in the crowd. That was not to be. He was front and center. And what's* this*? Standing just behind him was a big burly man who said aloud, "I saw the whole thing. This kid gave that man a quarter to play the machine. It's the* kid's *money. It's the* kid *who won."*

Tom's eyes were huge as he looked at the man with rage.

"Listen buddy, that kid should not even be *here in this casino. He's underage and unattended. I don't see his parents around anywhere so that makes this money* mine. *ALL MINE!" With that Tom looked back at the machine to see that the total winning amount had finally been tallied.*

$1,500.00!!!

Tom is beside himself with excitement. This was his big payday. Finally *his ship has come in!*

'Not so fast,' said the hand of fate laid upon his shoulder. The large intimidating man who was standing behind the kid speaks up again and says, "Hey 'buddy,' *care to know this kid's name?" This comment garnered the crowd's attention. The security guards looked his way as well.*

"It's Spencer. He's in the fourth grade. You wanna know how I *know that?"*

Tom shook his head nervously, not liking where this might be headed.

*"*I *know that because Spencer is* my *son. So let's get something straight. This is the part where you shake his hand and congratulate him on the first deposit he will make into his college fund." As the man stared him down Tom could feel the sentiment of the crowd shifting to the man's side. "I'm waaaaiting," said the man impatiently.*

Just as Tom was preparing to speak up and stand his ground, a grating voice he recognized all too well came from behind his shoulder spouting those three words that made his skin crawl.

"Well, well, well. *Abetting the gambling addiction of a minor and stealing from the kid's college fund as well. This must be a new low for you, am I right?"*

Tom saw red as he turned and stared into the eyes of a man who should rightfully be fish food right now at the bottom of Lake Tahoe.

"YOU!" *Tom screamed as he felt his hands reaching for Al's throat.*

A security guard stepped in front of him quickly and immediately brought civility to the matter by taking Tom by the arm and saying in a hushed tone, "It would appear that this kid has a prior claim to those winnings and by the looks and size of his father, I would offer this bit of sage counsel. Give the kid his money and go soak your troubles in a stiff drink. Cocktails are complimentary as long as you are engaged in play. Whaddaya say?"

The guard did not wait for an answer but instead turned to the boy and said, "Hey kid, what do you want to be when you grow up?"

The kid responded quickly and said, "I want to be an attorney*! Like my* Dad*!"*

The security guard turned back to Tom and said, "Well, how do you like that? His dad's an attorney. Kinda gives you some additional incentive to see things from the kid's perspective, don't it?"

The next thing that Tom knew he was signing over his winnings to the boy's father and just like that, he was penniless once again.

Al put his arm around him and said, "Take heart in the fact that you're doing the right thing. Besides, either way you look at it, you wouldn't have that $1,500 hundred dollars in your pocket right now anyway."

"Oh yeah?! And why is that?" demanded Tom.

"Well because the way I see it you still owe me about $3,000 for this trip when all is said and done."

"Oh yeah?" Tom shouted into Al's face.

"Yeah," stated Al nonchalantly.

"How do you figure?"

"You owe me not only for the hotel stay but also for all the fun things we will be doing. All this stuff ain't FREE you know."

"What are you talking about?! I thought you said we won an all-expense paid trip to Las Vegas. 'All-expenses paid.' *That means it's* FREE!*"*

"Correction. I *won an all-expense paid trip to Las Vegas.* You *have come along as a friend. And I want you to know that I appreciate having you around." Al flashed a toothy smile at Tom.*

"You sneaky sonuvabitch!" Tom's hands were grasping for Al's throat once again.

Out of thin air the security guard materialized once again. "Are you planning on making trouble for me this evening?"

Tom's hands fell to his side and in a sobering moment he lost the will to do anything but cry in his beer. "No sir."

"Well then, I suggest you go have that drink now."

"Yes sir," said a resigned Tom. His world had just EXPLODED with good fortune and then just as quickly deflated *like a popped balloon. For the moment he was willing to fall in line and head to the bar with his "friend" Al. It escaped him that* Al *was buying the drinks thereby adding to the total of Tom's tab.*

Since Al was in effect paying for Tom's trip he felt that he was owed a certain amount of—allegiance, shall we say from Tom. Unknown at this time to Tom, Al had laid out quite an itinerary for the two of them. Even though it was under false pretenses, Al would be claiming that each of these escapades was at the behest of the radio station sponsoring the Elvis competition. Al bolstered this nonsense by stating that a full report of their exploits would be shared in an interview later in the week. And of course Tom went for this, hook, line and cinder block.

"Is that it?" asked Trevor. For some reason Benny had just stopped talking. "What happened next?"

"Yeah dude, don't leave us hanging like this!" added Jimmy. "Does this guy Tom make lemonade out of lemons or what?!" This of course comes from the man who made a fortune selling lemonade out of food trucks before moving on to become a drive-thru burger kiosk mogul.

"Please," said Benny. "Don't say *"dude."* That reminds me of *'Part-Time'* and I have had more than my fair share of *him!*"

"Hey! This *is* just a story, right? I mean, you seem to be taking this story rather personal. Is there something that we all should know?"

The table got quiet as all eyes were now on Benny. These were his friends or so he thought. Why did this evening suddenly feel like an intervention? Benny looked at each of his friends, making strong eye contact with each one.

"I think that you all need to hear the rest of the story before you start jumping to any conclusions. Is that fair?"

Benny receives nods of approval from each of them. They seem a bit put off by Benny's statement almost as if they had been rebuked. Benny took some small amount of comfort in knowing that he had once more taken control of the situation.

On with the story.

The Vegas Story, Tom's 'Trouble with Tribbles'

The itinerary which Al had put together for them included a multitude of events unique to the world of Las Vegas. The first of these 'escapades,' as Al was wont to call them, is a visit to the 'Star Trek' Convention being held at, you guessed it, the Stratosphere Hotel & Casino. *Tom is completely unaware that Al is cleverly maneuvering him from the casino to the ballroom where the event is currently underway. Tom is a willing partner at the moment as he is wishing to escape the craziness of the James Bond slot machine fiasco. Little does he know that, like the old expression, he is being plucked 'from the frying pan and being tossed into the fire.'*

Tom being the smartass that he is nudges Al and says, "Hey! You got your backpack? 'You can't leave home without it!'"

"That's a good one!" says Al and smiles. Have all the fun you want; thinks Al. Things are about to go deep South for you my friend. An evil smirk plays over his face.

The two arrive at the level where the ballrooms have been transformed into sections of the infamous 'Star Trek Enterprise.' The attention to detail is amazing. As they pass the "bridge" of the Enterprise, one would swear that they were actually on board the ship. There is a large turnout of fans done up in full character costume. As Tom is a 'Star Wars' fan, not 'Star Trek,' while impressive, most of this is lost on him. He is of the opinion that they are simply passing through this exhibit. He could not be more wrong.

"Where the hell *are we going?!" demands Tom as Al leads them deeper into the world of the 'Trekkies.'*

Tom is an introvert so the last *thing that he wants to do is participate in some 'Star Trek' episode reenactment in front of a large group of people. Of course this is* exactly *what Al says is expected of them by the radio station in return for* his *"all-expense paid" trip. All 'BS' of course from Al but hey, all in good fun, right?*

Tom finds himself on what he thinks is something of a makeshift stage but is actually an elaborate construction of one of the many crew spaces of the Enterprise featured on the television show. A small group of willing actors (with the exception of Tom) will be reenacting a fan favorite, "The Trouble with Tribbles."

Alex will be the circumspect "Scotty" which makes perfect sense. Tom, however, cannot fathom how (or why) he has been chosen to play the lead character, Captain Kirk. Besides knowing absolutely nothing *about the show, Tom suffers from stage fright!!!*

An audience has assembled for this showing while a visually nervous, shaking and wide-eyed "Tahoe" Tom, donned the uniform of none other than Captain James T. Kirk. Throughout the reenactment Tom was mortified and clearly in shock.

And the crowd loved it!

At the end of the skit Tom is directed to open what looks like the overhead bin of an airplane. Immediately he is pummeled by soft balls of fur which are the "tribbles." Tom is having 'trouble with tribbles' for sure. Once Tom is completely buried in "tribbles" you could not have paid *Al to have enjoyed himself more in that moment.*

Al got a bit teary-eyed at seeing his pal Tom giving his all to adequately portray the infamous 'Star Trek' Captain Kirk. Tom of course saw things quite differently. He was absolutely humiliated and mortified by his appearance in front of such a large crowd of onlookers. They may have been cheering but he was certain that it was at *him, surely not* for *him. Now in his lowest moment, when he, as Captain Kirk, is fully immersed in a haystack of tribbles, Tom hears the* one thing *that always sets his nerves on edge and makes his eyes burn.*

"Well, well, well. *It looks like you got yourself some trouble with tribbles."*

Al laughs heartily and overly loud which elicits a chorus of shared laughter from the crowd that assaults Tom's ears.

"Help me out of this mess!" Tom yells angrily.

Al steps over to him but before he helps him up, he takes a quick pic of the beleaguered Tom and summarily posts it to social media with the caption, 'Captain James Kirk is in "Terrible Tribble!'

"I don't get it," said Adam.

"It's just a stupid play on words. You know, like terrible '*trouble*'? To be honest with you, I don't get it either. Not funny. That Al can be a real *dick*."

Mike said, "Hey Benny, you alright? That last comment sounded downright *personal*."

"Sure Mike, I'm fine. I laugh at things that are funny all the time. *That* wasn't funny, so what?"

"Alright, alright. I didn't mean anything by it. Just go on with the rest of the story."

Mike shot a look at Jimmy who gave the same look back of *'what the hell was* that *about?!'*

"Should I continue?" asks Benny.

"Sure, why not?" says Mike. "Keep on rolling."

"Okay. It's just that you guys got quiet all of a sudden."

"We're good. Keep going." said Adam.

"Okay." Benny continued on but now something felt a little different. The guys were looking at him strangely. Maybe they were just getting a little drunk. Who knew? Benny continued on with the story.

So the 'Star Trek' thing is over and Al wants to make another trip back to their hotel room to drop off his stash. His backpack is filled with phasers, communicators and the like; cool souvenirs he has purchased at the convention. Tom of course balks at this because they are staying at the Luxor *which is on the other end of the strip.*

Tom proclaims, 'We're not coming back here to the Strat *if we're going all the way back to the* Luxor, *I can tell you that!'*

Tom ignores Al's sad face and stands his ground. But Al has one more trick up his sleeve by suggesting that they take the monorail this time. 'It will be much quicker!' No dice. Tom is done for the day. He has had enough. So they head back to the hotel to stay for the remainder of the evening.

Tom barely speaks with Al after returning to the hotel room. Al doesn't want Tom going to bed all sour so he throws out an unexpected surprise. How about Al "treat" the two of them to a round of golf tomorrow at the Wynn resort and *an incredible dinner afterwards at the restaurant* Sinatra*? This gets Tom's* full *attention. "Treat" does not sound like "charity" plus he absolutely* loves *to golf. Suddenly the events of the day are forgiven (well set aside at least) and Tom is able to settle in for a good night's rest.*

Tom is soon sleeping soundly and snoring loudly. Like a foghorn. Al listens to the raucous noise while he contemplates how to break the news tomorrow to Tom that he has been less than honest about not only their trip itinerary but also the extent of time they would be spending in Vegas. Although Tom was sure to be upset, like he has been about everything else that has happened, it would all soon be water under the bridge.

Or so Al hoped.

Day Two: **The Vegas Story, Golfing in paradise**

Day two of the Vegas trip starts out wonderfully for Tom. He wakes up in a fantastic mood. Today is a golf day and he loves *to golf. What makes this day even better is that today's round will be* free! *"Free" just makes everything better as far as Tom is concerned. And the course itself?* Wow.

Tom had seen the course from the monorail yesterday on their way back to the Luxor *from the* Stratosphere *as they passed the* Wynn Hotel & Casino. *One of the many fabulous features to be found at the Wynn resort is an exclusive golf course which, although hidden from the street, is amazingly situated right on the strip. Thousands of unsuspecting visitors walk right by the cleverly concealed course not knowing that there is actually a cascading waterfall on the other side of the nondescript wall that skirts the sidewalk.*

Tom is beside himself with excitement as he gets out of bed and readies himself for the day. The Wynn Golf Course has been on his bucket list for some time now. He never really expected to find himself in this moment. Tom is giddy with excitement and has already told himself that today, is a "be nice to Al day." It won't be easy but he needs to remind himself that dear annoying Al is picking up the tab for everything. Being here in Vegas and playing golf at Wynn are both things that Tom knows he would not have been able to do on his own. Thank goodness that Al passed the test of making it back to shore after "falling" out of that boat in Lake Tahoe with a cinder block chained to his leg. That is how Tom was choosing to remember it now anyway.

So now Tom is raring to go and of course, of all days, today is the day that Al is wanting to sleep late, claiming that yesterday had been exhausting for him. While there was no real concern of *missing their tee time, Tom is still quite anxious to get things moving. He is eager to get to Wynn and be in the moment, hoping to turn this trip around and have some fun! There was also that little Post-it Note reminder in the back of his head telling him to find time to get Al talked into trying the indoor parachute thing. Tom has convinced himself that today will be a good day for that conversation and that Al will be a willing participant. Just then Al tumbles out of bed mumbling that he would be ready in fifteen minutes. Tom smiles. Everything is starting to come together nicely.*

Wynn Las Vegas *is a product of the imagination of one Steve Wynn, truly a legend and an icon of the Las Vegas scene. In a city where "winning" is the goal, the name "Wynn" was pure gold. It only makes sense then that Steve Wynn would be the man that brought the Golden Nugget back to its former glory. He was also the man behind such marvels as* The Mirage, Treasure Island *and* The Bellagio. *This is the man who then chose to put his own name on what is considered to be his crowning achievement, one of the most unique properties in all of Vegas, the* Wynn Resort. *Now comprising two curved juxtaposed towers sporting wraparound bronze reflective glass, the eponymously named* "Wynn" *and the addition of its newer sibling,* "Encore" *are proof that there can truly never be enough of a good thing.*

Unique to the Wynn *resort is an absence of "theme." Pick any casino resort in Vegas and you will clearly see the inspiration behind the design and architecture. Not so with* Wynn. *According to* Wynn Resorts, *"the property, rather than a theme, will be the attraction..."*

Al and Tom arrive at the Wynn *and start to wander around the resort in awe. It is a sprawling property encompassing some 5 million square feet but somehow the interior designers have found a way to make it feel intimate and immediately comfortable. Al points out to Tom that the color "red," a lucky color for Asian gamblers, is prominent throughout the resort. Tom mentions to Al that he thinks there are more five-star restaurants in this resort than in most cities.*

As the two walk through the casino area Al can't seem to just pass by the gaming tables. He must *stop to play. Tom glances at his phone to check the time. This is a necessary function as there are no clocks to be found in a casino. He is relieved to see that they still have plenty of time and the good news is that Al is already doing what Al does,* winning!

Thirty minutes later they walk away from the table and Al proclaims, 'Hey! I just won enough money to tip the caddie!' This was followed by that annoying new catch-phrase of his, 'Aren't I the lucky one?!' *This is done of course with the emphasis on the pronoun* "I" *and both thumbs raised and pointed towards himself.*

'Lucky bastard,' *Tom mumbles under his breath as they make their way to the pro shop at the golf course.* 'Let's see how lucky you are when you jump off the Strat with good old "Part-Time" as your safety guide!'

Al smiles broadly as Tom finds himself uncharacteristically putting his arm around Al in a friendly embrace. 'You did great back there,' says Tom through gritted teeth. 'I'm a proud papa!'

'Aw, thanks Tom!' Al hugs Tom, grateful for the comment. Tom cannot fathom how those words made it out of his mouth. Perhaps a mixture of tension and excitement of knowing he would soon be playing an incredible golf course for free!

And then tomorrow he will enjoy watching this annoying man plummet to his death with the comfort of knowing that he would be among the crowd that is crying out, 'Oh my God! How did it happen?!'

The big moment has finally arrived. Tom is standing on the first tee of the Wynn Golf Course. *The view is nothing short of spectacular. This course rivaled any course in the country for layout and visual appeal. Tom ponders the fact that the parcel of land which makes up this course must have cost a fortune. Think of what it must cost to operate this course compared against what it might generate were it a casino. Nope. Not doing the math. That's Wynn's problem. Tom prefers instead to just say thanks to the vision of Steve Wynn that there is this jewel of a course in the most unlikely of places, the Las Vegas Strip.*

Tom takes in the panoramic view. The course is both visually stunning with gently rolling hills and well-placed trees throughout. The course is also immaculate with the scratch-your-head how do they do that trick with making checkerboard fairways and perfectly maintained greens. This could easily be the host venue for a professional tournament. Today however, it is here for the likes of Al and Tom to enjoy as members of an elite club.

Tom says to himself, 'Nothing could possibly spoil this perfect day.'

Famous last words?

Al and Tom are sharing a caddie. The caddie's name is "Joey" and he was described by the man who checked them in at the pro shop as "full-on Italian with an 'interesting' sense of humor, you either love him or you hate him." While that seemed like a rather odd characterization of a person Tom felt like they would get along just fine. It would be Al that might take issue with him, not Tom.

Tom is on the tee and ready to hit his shot but thinks to himself, 'I have a caddie, why not use him?'

'Hey Joey!'

'Yeah, bro, what's up?' Tom cringed at being called 'bro.'

'Do you have any words of advice for me on this hole?'

Joey sidles up to Tom and gives the hole a professional look, taking in the slopes, contours and potential hazards. 'Okay, my friend, the way I see it is that what you got yourself here is a straight-ahead golf shot on a par four with no *hazards and* no *sand. The fairway is plenty wide for just about any wayward shot and both sides are actually angled inward so that your first shot of the day has a better than average chance of ending up smack dab in the middle of the fairway. What do you see?' Joey stepped back to allow Tom to comment.*

Tom's face had colored up a bit from that assessment. As he looked at the golf hole again he could not help but notice that it was truly a gift to a nervous golfer standing on the first tee. The odds were in the golfer's favor. Hitting an errant tee shot seemed to be almost impossible.

'Um, I guess I see it the same way.'

'Fair enough, hit away!'

Tom is put off by the interaction with Joey and decides to step away from the tee box. Rather than admit his capricious behavior he makes a grand gesture of offering the first swing to 'the man that is making this all possible, his good friend, Al.'

'Why, thank you, Tom!'

As Al steps up to the tee Joey asks him if he knows his handicap. Al thinks for a moment and then says, 'I am a very giving person so sometimes people feel as though they can take advantage of me.'

Joey looks at Tom with a 'what the hell answer is that?' look on his face. Tom answers by mouthing the words, 'I don't know that he has ever golfed before.' Joey's predictable reply was a wordless, 'Oh.' Inside he thinks to himself, this is going to be a long *round.*

Al is ready to play. He brings the club back and swivels his hips nicely as he then swings the club through the ball exactly as intended. Both Tom and Joey watch in awe as the ball arcs up into the cloudless blue sky and then lands with authority on the high right side of the fairway due to Al's exaggerated slice. But then, just as Joey had accurately described it, the angle of the fairway gave the ball a friendly kick and urged it back towards the fairway. The ball rolled several more yards before settling almost exactly in the middle of the fairway leaving Al an approach shot of about 150 yards.

'THAT!' Joey said, pointing to Al's ball in the distance, 'was a golf shot!'

Al is beaming with pride. He looks to Tom and says (you guessed it), 'Aren't 'I' the lucky one?!'

Joey puts his hand on Al's shoulder and says, 'You need to take that luck *to the casino!'*

Tom balls his hands into fists and thinks to himself, how freakishly annoying can one man be?! There goes his great day.

'How about you, player?' asks Joey. 'You a first-timer too?' Joey points to Tom, then to the tee to indicate that it is now his turn.

Just then by some twist of misfortune Tom suddenly has to pee. Really bad. He asks the caddie if there will be a place where he can go to the bathroom just up ahead. The caddie laughs and says that he is "shit out of luck," no pun intended. He then points to the restaurant just to the right of the first golf hole and suggest that he run in there to do his business. Tom was gone in a flash.

So now Tom has returned to the tee and he sees that his indiscretion has met with disapproval by the group now waiting to tee off behind them. Before he has the time to apologize Al speaks with that other phrase of his, "Glad you could finally make it." That little gem brings tears to the eyes of the caddie.

Although much of Tom's confidence has been squelched by the perfection of Al's earlier impossible *drive, he is quick to share with the caddie that he has a 12 handicap. Joey nods in acknowledgement and steps back to watch what he is expecting to be a slightly better than average golf swing. What happened next explained how urban legends are born.*

Tom plants his feet, waggles his club, takes a sideways glance towards his target, pulls the club back and then swings through with all his might. The ball takes off from the tee like it was shot out of *a cannon!*

And then the ball veers **hard right**, *(away from the golf course, mind you), in what is called a "banana slice," bending in the air like a failed rocket and then shooting straight for the ground. Thankfully, unlike a rocket, there is no fiery explosion, not counting of course Tom's* explosive *reaction. There* are *screams though which accompany the landing of his ball. This is due to the fact that the ball has found the restaurant perched just above the course. The architects had deemed it safe from play. Tom had just proved them wrong.*

'What the hell just happened?!!' *shouts Tom.*

'Well,' began Joey in full caddie mode to an obviously inexperienced golfer, 'the way I see it is that you shifted your feet during the swing, you cocked your wrist a bit to the left, you fell back a little as you made contact, you didn't keep your head down which in turn made you take your eye off the ball, then you tilted your shoulders to the right on the follow through--,' Joey was losing breath as he finished his run on sentence, 'and then at the end of the swing you totally lost your balance and almost fell down.'

'Thank you for that synopsis and your play by play of the action.' Tom gave Joey a hard stare as he said this, thinking there goes any chance of the two of them getting along the rest of the day. Tom then said, 'Okay smart guy, where the hell *did that ball* go?!'

Joey took the driver from Tom's hands as he walked by and muttered, 'It's in the shit, bro.' As Joey was placing the driver back in Tom's golf bag he said, "Had I known you were going to hit your drive at the restaurant I would have told you to take your pee break after your tee shot."

Joey, Al and the four golfers in the next group and their *caddie thought this might be the funniest thing they had ever heard in their life. Tom hung his head in shame as he walked off the tee,*

As the round progressed things did not improve for Tom. Al continued to hit shots better than he should have been capable of and Tom continued to struggle. He could not get past the first hole in his own mind. After he and Joey had had words Tom clamored on wanting to know why the caddie would not retrieve the lost golf ball. He and Al were both using rental clubs. One sleeve, three golf balls, seemed hardly enough for a big course like this, and losing a ball off the very first tee surely did not bode well for the round.

Tom was absolutely flabbergasted with Joey's response to retrieving the lost ball. He told Tom that for twenty bucks he would gladly visit the restaurant which overlooks the course to see which plated entrée his ball might have landed on.

'How is that even possible?' Tom had implored.

'Exactly,' agreed Joey. 'But hey, look on the bright side,' he had said, 'that shot of yours, if it did *land on somebody's plate, it would be more rare than a double eagle!'*

If that comment was intended to make him feel better, it did not. Tom had trudged on through the day with his head hung low and moping like a child.

Al and Tom have now arrived at the signature par three hole on the back nine. Truth be told, this course could arguably say that it consisted of eighteen *signature holes. So they arrive at the tee and there is a pop-up canopy with a Vegas showgirl in full feathery costume standing beneath.*

'Hello boys,' she says in an ultra-sexy Mae West drawl, 'would you care to place a wager on your golf shot?'

Simultaneously Al and Tom respond.

Al excitedly says, 'Sure!' *while a dour Tom simply says,* 'Nope!'

Hearing Al only, the showgirl says, 'Great! Let's go over the rules of the wager.' She then proceeds to explain that for a twenty dollar buy-in you have the opportunity to:

a) get $10 back if you hit the green,

b) break even and get your $20 back if your ball lands within three feet of the cup or,

c) shoot a hole in one and win an all-expense paid stay at Wynn's all new Asian-themed resort, **Tokyo Vegas** *to compete in a million-dollar hole in one playoff.*

Tom doesn't have twenty dollars to his name but that doesn't stop Al from pressing a twenty-dollar bill into the showgirl's hand on his behalf and saying that Tom was all in. Another twenty pressed into her hand meant that Al was in as well.

Tom was quite nervous but decided that he would go first. He didn't want a crappy shot from Al to get in his head and mess up his shot. Tom placed his ball on the tee and took a good look at the golf hole. He checked the golf app on his phone as well for yardage and slope of the green. Joey looked like he wanted to help but Tom waved him off. That guy had done enough for one day.

Tom fought off the urge to take a picture of this golf hole. He needed to focus on his shot but it was difficult not to appreciate what the course designers had created. A pond of cool blue water offered definition to the front portion of the hole. (It was also there to gobble up any shots short of the green.)

The green was heavily bunkered on the right which to many a golfer's chagrin meant that it was the only bailout area. An incredible (and realistic) rock wall behind the green with a roaring waterfall (in the desert mind you) anxiously awaited any golf ball hit farther than intended.

As if there was not enough challenge already, the green itself sloped purposefully towards the water so that too *was a problem. Simply stated, this was a fantasy golf hole surrounded by a* world *of trouble.*

Tom pulled an 8 iron from his bag. The flag was measuring 138 yards off the tee. This would be the perfect *club for that yardage.* If *he hit it well. And that was the rub wasn't it. Golf was hard. Unlike other sports, you were not reacting to the ball being hit or thrown. Instead, the ball just sat there on the tee,* waiting *for you to swing.* Waiting *for you to screw it up. It was infuriating how difficult that motionless object could be at times. Tom tried his best to clear his head of bad thoughts and just hit the damn ball.*

'Here goes nothing' he said to himself and swung the club.

Tom, Al and Joey watched as the ball soared off the tee and into the air. 'How about that,' murmured Joey as it looked like Tom had just struck "the" *shot that was sure to go in the hole. And then the ball, like a plane with a failing engine, began losing airspeed and just dropped from the sky. Next came an incredibly loud PLOP! as the ball entered the water and completely dashed Tom's hopes of it landing on the green safe and dry.*

'That's wet, bro.' Tom gave Joey another vicious glance. So that was it. Game over. Tom was crushed. He looked as though he was going to cry.

Al said, 'You owe me twenty bucks, Tom.'

Al said this with a straight face, waited for just long enough before he broke out laughing. 'I'm just messing with ya!' Now Joey and the

Vegas showgirl started laughing as well. Tom of course was the odd man out. 'The joke's on me,' thought Tom. 'Again.'

Al gave Tom a friendly punch in the arm and said, 'Hey, this is just for fun! Let it go! You can laugh at my shot when it goes in the water right next to yours!' That comment actually cheered Tom up a bit as he now hoped that Al's shot would make a bigger splash.

Al stepped up to the tee with Joey at his side. The two spent several minutes talking and pointing. Tom was beginning to get irritated with all this needless preparation. Al's ball was going in the water whether it be short into the pond or long into the waterfall. Why prolong the madness?

Finally the two decided on a game plan and Joey walked over to stand with the golf bags. Al put his tee in the ground and placed his ball on the tee. Tom was at first curious what club had been selected before thinking that it really didn't matter. You could use any club in the bag to hit a golf ball into the water.

Al is waggling his club and moving his behind in unison. That was not pretty. When the swing actually happens it looks like it is a surprise to Al even though he is the one swinging the club. What a comedy of errors! The ball is in the air and going left which is not good. Oddly enough it looks as though it might actually be short of the water which would give Al at least a chance to knock it onto the green.

But that is not to be. The ball has just enough carry to go over the corner of the pond where it hits a large rock angled, as luck would have it, towards the green. Tom groans. He can see it now in his mind's eye. The ball will probably land safely on the green.

But that is not what happens.

The ball strikes the rock solidly and jumps high into the air where it sails over the green and hits the rock wall. This is the moment *where physics seems to take the day off. The ball should actually drop straight down into the water but that doesn't happen either.*

Al, Tom, Joey and the showgirl, look like they are watching a ping pong match as their heads swivel rapidly to the left and right following the ball as it goes from place to place. The ball finally lands out of harm's way on the back of the green but it does not land on the grass. The ball actually finds a sprinkler head! Hitting the hard plastic cover of the sprinkler head then amazingly propels the ball back *into the air.*

'What is happening?!' *Tom wants to scream.*

The golf ball has now ended up in the most unlikely of places, on *the green, and rolling* towards *the cup!*

This is all playing out now in slow motion. As it reaches the edge of the cup the ball seems to hesitate for just a second longer than seems physically possible. Had this shot been televised the camera would have had a money shot of the ball, a tight view of the logo and number, 'Titleist' 1. What would have made this image so memorable however was the fact that Al, thinking he was being clever, had crossed out 'Titleist' and wrote in the word 'Lucky' so it now read 'Lucky 1'.

The Vegas showgirl screamed in delight as the ball fell into the cup.

Joey jumped up and down yelling, 'YES!!!'

Tom was doing the exact opposite, squawking, 'NO!!' through gritted teeth.

Al had been silent during all of this, mostly because he was in shock. But now he was back to being Al and he just can't help himself. After all, there would never be a better moment than now *to say it. He spread his arms out wide and bellowed out his new catch phrase.*

'AREN'T I THE LUCKY ONE?!'

Tom had just about thrown up when he saw that shot but what could you do? He waited impatiently as paperwork was filled out and pictures were taken. He had to admit that yes, Al was *the lucky one. Tom of course had just wanted to leave after all of that but they still had one more hole to play. He knew that the next hole would not go well. The day was ruined. Nothing at this point could make him feel any better. He was at his lowest point and Al certainly knew it. That's when he remembered the indoor parachuting. This was his moment. Al was on top of the world. Opportunity was knocking. This was the perfect time to ask Al to do something for Tom.*

Tom smiled. Maybe today will work out okay after all.

After golf, the two check into their hotel room and prepare to go back down to the common area for an elaborate dinner. This was both Al's treat and *Al's choice. While Tom would certainly have chosen the swanky restaurant,* Sinatra *as promised, Al has changed his mind and selected none other than the award-winning* SW Steakhouse. *The initials "SW" is a nod to the visionary Steve Wynn.*

Wow! What a fabulous restaurant! Tom wonders to himself how much it costs to just wander through the place!

As the two head towards the bar to wait for their table Tom learns how quickly the news of "winning" travels in Vegas. A gentleman meets them at the bar, patiently waits as they order their drinks and then instructs the bartender to have the drinks brought to their table which has already been reserved for them.

As they weave their way through the dining area they begin to receive jealous glances from other patrons who were not so lucky as to have scored a much in demand table on the balcony overlooking the scenic pond.

Once the two are seated, Tom looks up and notices that there is a wavy fabric hanging from the ceiling of the portico that mimics the gentle roll of the water lapping at the pond's shoreline below them. The pond itself is surrounded with trees which are lit from below. The balcony on which they are seated has an all-glass railing affording an open view of the crystal blue water. It was almost impossible to remember that they were smack dab in the middle of a desert.

Al and Tom are sipping their cocktails when the sommelier arrives at their table.

'Good evening gentlemen. In appreciation of your fine play today,' he winked at Al but not at Tom, 'we would like to offer a bottle of our finest house wine courtesy of the management.' He pauses momentarily before adding, 'Or you may choose a selection of your own if you prefer, which shall be added to your bill.'

'No worries my good man,' said Al. 'I am going to be a millionaire soon. Perhaps we should celebrate!'

'Hold up there, cowboy,' said Tom. 'You're a long way from that!' He looked to the sommelier and shared that while Al may have made a hole in one, that only served to get him entered into the million-dollar playoff where he would still need to make yet another hole in one. Tom nodded to Al saying, 'Tiny little detail, you haven't made that shot yet and you sure as hell don't have a million bucks.'

'True, true, but still, I think we should celebrate. My friend here,' Al is pointing at Tom, 'has suggested that we try this French white that you have listed—' Al is floating his finger above the wine list in search of a particular vintage. 'Ah, right there!' Al's finger lands on a bottle which is certain to capture Tom's attention.

'I *suggested a bottle of wine?!' asks a befuddled Tom as he hurries to open the wine list and locate the bottle that Al is relating to the sommelier.*

'Yes, this French number from 2018. I'm not sure if I'm saying it right, 'Montrachet, Domaine de la Romanee-Conti'? Is that pretty tasty? Not too dry?'

Al is asking this question in the same manner as though he were asking about paint colors. Do you prefer this *neutral gray? Or* this *neutral gray?*

'Sir!' *The sommelier attempted to keep the tone of his voice in check as he said, 'That is a* $35,000 *dollar bottle of wine.'*

Tom spewed a stream of not cheap Manhattan cocktail from his mouth when he heard that. Bad timing to take a sip.

'But it's a good one, right?' asks Al.

'Yes,' the sommelier continued, 'it is an exceptional *wine but I feel it my obligation to ask if you are, um, financially* comfortable *with that purchase?'*

'Is it because of how my friend here is dressed?' Al points to Tom accusingly. On Tom's behalf, when he was preparing for this trip to Vegas, all he thought of was the blazing hot sun and lots of walking so he had packed only shorts. Jean *shorts to be exact. Al did not know that they still even* made *those anymore.*

The sommelier spoke. He had a deep resonant voice like you hear on the radio. 'Style and fashion sense are not judged here at the Wynn. *If you are comfortable wearing* that, *then I celebrate your diversity and, what is that phrase? Oh yes. 'You be you.' As for the wine—'*

Al, after having had his fun with Tom by getting exactly *the reaction he was hoping for, looked to the sommelier and said, 'You know what? I think I prefer the California stuff. We'll take you up on that house wine offer. How's that sound?'*

'Very good sir,' replied the ultra-professional sommelier and left the table. Al was really hoping that he would pop his mouth with his hand like he had seen in an old Jerry Lewis movie but of course that didn't happen.

After the sommelier had left Tom was all over Al. 'Are you freaking crazy?!' exclaimed Tom. 'You don't have that kind of money. What the hell were you doing?'

'Just having a little fun, that's all. Cool your engines and get ready to enjoy the meal of a lifetime.'

'Looking at these prices I might just stick with the dinner rolls,' grumbled Tom.

'Are you forgetting that tonight's meal is my *treat?'*

'Oh yeah,' said Tom as he hurriedly picked the menu back up to look closer at the menu items with the larger dollar amounts. 'This is *a steakhouse. I should get a good steak.'*

'Please do,' encouraged Al. 'Get what you want. That's why you come to a place like this, to get what you want.'

'Okay, fair enough, I will *get what I want. What is that* you *want?'*

Tom surprised himself by asking a question that sounded so genuine and caring. It was not *in his character.*

Al chuckled lightly. 'What I *want nobody offers, at least not in* this *country.'*

'What do you want?' prompted Tom.

Al leaned back in his chair, his eyes drifting off to the distance as he replied, 'Seafood.'

'Seafood!?' *Now it was Tom's turn to laugh. 'Excuse me but duh, we do have seafood in America! How about tomorrow night we go to* Red Lobster *and you can have a freaking seafood platter!'*

'My fault, I should have been more clear. It's not just any *seafood that I want.'*

'Yeah?'

'Yes. What I want is something very special.'

'Special, huh? What is it?' Tom was becoming irritated with this back and forth. Just say it already!

'Takifugu rubripes, or to be more specific, the torafugu.'

'What the hell is that?!'

'A torafugu is a tiger pufferfish.'

'Sorry, still lost.'

'Also known as blowfish?'

'Oh! A blowfish! Why didn't you just say that? But wait, aren't those poisonous?'

'Not all species are but the tiger pufferfish just happens to be the most poisonous.'

'I don't get it, why would you do that?'

'Do what?'

'Take a chance like that.'

Al smiled. 'To live my friend, to truly LIVE.'

Al closed his eyes and swept his arms out in a gesture to further express the emotion he was attempting to convey.

Just then something rang a bell in Tom's head. Quickly he reached out and grabbed the Tokyo Vegas pamphlet from across the table. 'Now where did I see that?' he said as he was running his finger along the print and perusing the marketing piece.

'THERE!' Tom exclaimed. 'There is it is! Al, check this out!'

Al took the pamphlet from Tom paying particular attention to the spot where Tom's finger was pointing. And there it was, 'A sample menu of what to expect when dining at Tokyo Vegas...' As Al scanned the menu items, his ears heard an angelic chorale sing as his eyes settled on what he would never have dreamed possible, 'We proudly present our signature dish, freshly prepared Tiger Pufferfish.'

'How about that?!' prodded Tom.

'I could just cry right now. No lie. I could shed tears of joy.' Al was beside himself with euphoric bliss.

'And don't forget,' Tom said with gusto, 'you will be staying there for free!'

'That's right! Oh my gosh, this is SO exciting!' Al was giddy now. 'Hey! Guess what? You're coming with me!'

'No, that's okay. That's your trip, you won it. One is enough for me.'

'Please?'

This was the moment. Don't miss it!

'Okay,' agreed Tom. 'I'll go with you.'

'Yes!' shouted Al.

'On one condition.'

'Oh, what's that?'

'That you take indoor parachuting lessons with me and then do the SkyJump from the Strat.*'*

Al looked suddenly very confused. 'Why would I want to do that?'

Tom was prepared for this answer.

'To LIVE, my friend, to LIVE! You said about that this pufferfish thing. For you it was how you can truly know that you are alive, right?'

'Something like that, yeah.'

'Well that's what this is like for me. Let's make a deal that I do the pufferfish thing with you and you do the jump thing with me. Deal?' Tom held his hand out to shake. Al gave this a moment of serious consideration before he shook Tom's hand and said, 'Deal.'

That is when the server arrived at the table.

Al did not even allow him to say his name or go through his spiel. 'We'll start with this 'Seafood Spectacular.' I am in a serious seafood mood now and this has just about everything I like from the sea. Maine lobster, king crab legs, jumbo shrimp, oysters, tuna, scallops and more! Yep, bring us that!'

'Very good, sir. I will be back soon to take your entrée orders.'

The 'Seafood Spectacular' was exactly that, spectacular. As Tom was eyeing the selections on the tower of seafood, (and yes, it was a tower!), Al busted out with his already well-worn expression of, 'Aren't I the lucky one?!' *Tom could only "groan" and bear it. Soon the server was back to take their dinner orders. Tom went first.*

'Just give me a New York strip, you know like the ones they have at Longhorn.*'*

'I will check our stock on those, sir,' replied their server sans expression. He was not writing anything *down. It was one of* those *places. Nothing would be missed or forgotten and everything would arrive correctly and on time.*

Al touches the server on the arm and says, 'Pardon me, before you commit that order to memory, could you enlighten me as to this 'WAH-GOO' stuff that you have here on the menu?'

The server maintained a perfectly stoic expression as he politely shared that they served Japanese Wagyu with a quality score of A5 and marble score between 8-10. He then explained what all of that actually meant. Al shook his head up and down the whole time as though he understood what the server was telling him. When the server finished with his explanation Al pointed at Tom and said, 'Bring him one of them Japanese 'Wagooey' type New York Strips. I'm buyin'.'

'Very good, sir. And what may we prepare for you?'

This server was smooth, he didn't miss a beat. He was smooth in appearance as well. He looked like a Hollywood actor. Maybe a few years from now he would be, who knew?

Al still has the large menu in front of him, propped open and handling it much like the tablets of the Ten Commandments as he proclaims that he will have the butter poached Maine lobster. He winked at Tom and added, 'When in Rome–.'

Tom thinks to himself, what the hell does that *mean? They were in Las Vegas, about as far from the Mediterranean as one could get! Tom lifted a corner of his menu up so that he might sneak a peek at the price of the lobster.* Holy crap! $150 bucks! *Al was living this trip up for sure. Tom could only hope that he had enough cash left in him to get them both home. Tom chuckled to himself when he considered the fact that one of them would be going home in a box with the luggage.*

Unaware of Tom's dark thoughts Al chuckled along with him which made Tom laugh all the more. Al laughed out loud now and it was immediately obvious to the diners around them that these two must just be the best of friends. Ha! A perfect alibi! Who would think to plot the death of their best friend?!

When their dinner arrived Tom did his best to savor every bite of the amazing steak placed before him while Al looked as though he were doing his best to devour the lobster as fast as humanly possible. With Tom's rough math, he calculated that Al was eating at a rate of $30 per minute. The lobster bib that he had eagerly accepted was indeed serving him well.

Tom was still enjoying his steak as Al's plate and drawn butter exited the table. Al picked up the Tokyo Vegas *casino resort marketing pamphlet once again. A dual conversation took place as Al talked about* Tokyo Vegas *and Tom talked about indoor parachuting.*

As they are finishing up an absolutely incredible meal, Tom is getting a bit sentimental, possibly even nostalgic. Truth be told, most of the fabulous things he had done and experiences he has had, both here in Vegas and earlier in Lake Tahoe, were thanks to the generosity of Al. Perhaps he should show just a bit more kindness to Al? Maybe even say he was sorry?

While still mulling the gesture over in his mind, Al excuses himself to go to the restroom. Tom has time now to give some careful consideration to what he might say to Al. Whatever he says will need to sound genuine. Tom chuckles and asks himself if that is possible. Tom only half notices that the server has brought him a cup of rich and bold coffee which he languishes over while thinking his thoughts and enjoying the serene view of the pond and the trees and the delicate music in the background which he realized now that he had somehow missed previously.

Tom has finished his coffee and waved off a refill. It is at this time that it dawns on him that Al has been gone for quite a while. Tom actually starts to worry. A little.

During the time that Al is away, the server brings the check to the table. Tom thanks him and states that his buddy is picking up the check. With that in mind he thinks to himself that the night is young so he orders another drink. The drinks are expensive but hey, Alex won a bunch of money today, it's all good.

What Tom does not *know is that Al, the server, the manager,* and *the camera crew (which have just now materialized out of thin air) are in cahoots together and are playing a mean trick on him.*

The restaurant is closing now and Al has not returned. This is Tom's first inkling that perhaps he is being stuck with the check! And of course he has NO money. Suddenly the beauty of his surroundings is turning gray.

Tom calls out to the sommelier, 'Have you seen my friend?' He shakes his head no and continues on. Tom points at his server and asks the same question, 'Have you seen my friend?' The server also says no and then adds that there is the matter of the dinner check to be settled. 'But you don't understand, my friend Al is buying!'

'Perhaps today sir, you are his *friend and* you *are the one who is buying.'*

With that the server slides the check to Tom's side of the table. Tom is aghast. He ventures a quick look at the check. It looks like the sales sticker on the window of a car and now Tom without a doubt has sticker shock.

What can he do?

Tom suddenly has a great *idea. He will charge it to the room. But wait! A signature is required. In this moment, for the life of him, he cannot recall Al's last name. Nice try. Tom doesn't even know their room number!*

Tom pulls out his phone and tries calling Al. No answer. Of course.

The manager has now arrived at the table. The camera crew is clustered around him and filming (of course) as he is asking that age old question, 'Sir, do we have a problem?'

Tom is in full panic mode now and begins to actually beg the camera crew for money. They of course stay in character and behind the scenes unable to help.

In his very worst moment Tom hears those three dreaded words—

'Well, well, well.'

Al has returned, all smiles of course, and throws down a wad of money, sufficient to cover the bill plus a rather generous tip. Tom looks up to the smiling faces of Al, the sommelier, the server, the camera crew and the manager. All collaborators. All willing participants in this evil trickery. Suddenly ALL of Tom's angst and anger towards Al has returned with a vengeance as he realizes that he is once again the butt of Al's joke. Tom's adrenaline is flowing and he could literally smash the glass railing with his foot and throw their table into the pond and Al along with it but–

Tom thinks of the big plans he has for the two of them tomorrow. The indoor parachute training, the SkyJump at the Strat *and the safety check with his new best friend, "Part-Time." An incredible calm settles over him as he considers that pot of gold waiting for him at the end of this rainbow, knowing in his heart of hearts that come tomorrow, this trip will end very badly for Al.*

It takes a very dark heart for something like that to bring a smile to a man's face but Tom is now not only smiling but actually laughing along with Al's group of merry men. As he gets up from the table Tom celebrates his newfound optimism by whispering to himself, 'Tom, you are one sick puppy.'

"Have you considered counseling?"

"What?" Benny is caught off guard by the question.

"Yeah, that sounds like a good plan." Mike added, nodding to Adam who had proposed the idea.

"Counseling for *what?!"* Benny fired back indignantly. "This is *just* a story fellas! What the *hell?!* You tell your stories and I don't get all freaky about you guys, thinking that you had something to do with somebody finally getting what's coming to them."

The four friends looked at one another, uncertain of what they should or should not do next. That comment somehow sounded very *damning*.

Tom interrupted their thoughts by saying, "Can I at least *finish* my story?!"

"Sure, yeah of course. We were just trying to help."

"Yeah? Well, *stop* helping." This last comment came out sounding mean. And angry. Kinda scary too. None of the four friends could ever remember seeing Benny be cross or even lose his cool for that matter. This was a side of Benny they did not know.

A collective chill went up the spines of the four friends as they listened to the remainder of the story with a different mindset. They all wondered if what they were hearing was simply a 'tall tale' or a true confession.

Day Three: **The Vegas Story, "Pack your own chute."**

Waking up at the Wynn *with the feature of floor to ceiling windows was something Tom had been looking forward to as the view of Vegas should be absolutely amazing from the vantage point of his hotel room.* The Venetian Casino Resort *was their closest resort neighbor. Tom had meant to peek out last night when it was dark to see the city alive with neon but the anxiety of the evening had caused him to go right to bed instead.*

This was a bright new day and Tom felt certain that this morning he would be afforded an awe-inspiring view of Vegas with the incredible diversity of structures on display, all designed for that visual "wow" *factor. He pulls open the curtain of their hotel room and then literally* screams *at what he sees.*

A 360-foot-high monster-sized eyeball is staring right back at him.

WTF?!

Tom's scream awakens Al who rushes to the window to see what has alarmed Tom. What he sees causes him to break into uncontrollable laughter. Tom is now looking at Al so he does not understand Al's reaction until he looks out the window once again.

The eyeball is gone!

It has however been replaced by the internationally known and loved bright yellow "happy face."

'That wasn't there a minute ago!' Tom says, pointing at the window and pleading his case for why he had panicked.

Al could not help but laugh at Tom's initial reaction to seeing Vegas' new toy, known as "The Sphere." *He had no idea what Tom thought he saw but* The Sphere *was quite an extraordinary structure, celebrated by all who saw it except of course, Tom.*

But-- Tom was Tom. And Tom was a strange bird.

“What is that damn thing anyway?” Tom asked with some insistence.

“Calm down my friend, it comes in peace.” replied Al in a mocking tone.

“Ha ha, very funny. Seriously, what the hell is it?!”

Al had read quite a bit about the new marvel which had been added to the Las Vegas landscape and proceeded to share what he had learned with Tom.

“The Sphere*, is both an outdoor visual experience and an indoor immersive experience.”*

“You can go inside*?”*

“Yep! It is actually an event venue with over 17,000 seats.”

“What?!”

“Yep. They have concerts there. Pretty incredible.”

“I’ll bet.”

Tom fought to stay awake as Al then launched into a twenty-minute fascinating but dry recitation on the making of the “sphere.”

“They used both centuries old mathematical formulas as well as cutting edge engineering and technology to build that thing. For example, they used geodesic math to work out the hundreds of triangles used to form the 360-degree shape and structure of the exoskeleton. They had to determine the area of a sphere in order to understand the correct placement of the 580,000 square feet of LED’s that were used. The ‘Law of Sines’ *was employed to calculate architectural angles across the building. Stereographic projection aids in capturing ultra-wide imagery and then translating it into what the human eye is comfortable viewing.* ‘Fanger’s Equation’ *comes into play when determining how to create immersive effects through the slight alteration of temperature. By employing the use of the* ‘Venturi Effect’ *air flow can be introduced*

as an additional experience method. Of course the simulated effects of the force of the air used, as it can replicate anything from a breath to an explosion, is determined by relying on the 'Linear Stress Constitutive Equation'*."*

Tom, not wishing to appear stupid after such an exhaustive elucidation exclaimed, "Well, hell yeah! I mean, it would be freaking crazy to do it without using that *equation, right?!"*

"I know, right?" replies Al while nodding his head excitedly. He was in his element and energized by the fact that Tom seemed so interested and engaged in what he had to say. But—then it hit him. The operative term there was 'seemed.' *'Let's face it,' Al said to himself, 'Tom was* never *interested or engaged in what he had to say.'*

"Your mocking *me, aren't you?"*

Tom's first thought was to keep the ruse going but then he realized that he had had enough.

"Look Al, that is a LOT of math first thing in the morning, don't you think?"

"It's not ALL math. There is a great deal of science involved as well."

Tom looked at Al with an apathetic expression. "Are you done?"

"Well there is *more. Like the use of the* 'Shannon-Hartley Theorem' *to make it possible for more than 10,000 people to interact wirelessly in real time from their seats with the actions on the screen."*

"Yeah? Well, how about this? Are you familiar with the 'Thomas-Al Proposition'*?"*

Al pondered the question before replying, "No, I am not but I am very *eager to learn."*

Al was all ears and leaning forward.

"Yeah? Good. So, the 'Thomas-Al Proposition' *is simply this;* Thomas*, which is me, proposes that* Al*, which is you, cut the math and science bullshit right now before you put me in a bad mood for the day. Does that compute?"*

Al looked hurt by Tom's rebuke. "Sorry, I was just trying to enlighten you a bit but I promise I will stop."

"Thank you," Tom said expressively, then chuckled as he stole Al's new catch-phrase by adding, "now, aren't I the lucky one*?!"*

"You're just a mean person." Al was pouting as he made this comment.

"Yeah? Well at least I'm not boring."

"I'm not boring."

Al said this defiantly while standing in the middle of the hotel room with arms crossed.

"Sure you are." Tom fired back, more out of habit than actual intent.

"Not."

"Are."

"Not!"

"Are!"

This was SO childish. Tom needed to put a stop to this ASAP before this *became the reason for his bad mood of the day. Then a clever thought came to me mind so he declared, "Oh yeah? Well then, prove it."*

"What?"

"Prove to me that you're not boring."

"Okay, I will." Al stated this with full confidence then followed up with, "Wait. How do you expect me to do that?"

Tom already had a plan in mind. "Simple. Indoor skydiving followed by the SkyJump at the Strat*. We're going there later anyway, right?"*

"Yep. That's where they're doing the Elvis impersonator contest which I'm beginning to have second thoughts about by the way."

Tom shook his head and said, "You might want to get your shit together regarding that contest since that whole contest deal is what is paying the bills for our stay at the Strat *tonight, don't you think?"*

Al was the type of guy who sometimes just needed a swift kick in the ass to get moving. Apparently Tom had done just that as Al resigned himself to getting ready for the day both physically and emotionally.

Al said, "I might throw up you know."

"Where? At the skydiving place or the Elvis contest?"

"Both if I get enough to eat at the buffet."

"Ew!!!"

The two took turns using the bathroom to ready themselves for the day's activities. Tom was ready first and spent his time looking out at The Sphere. *He didn't care what Al said, he was using the word "the" before saying the word, "sphere." It sounded too weird if you didn't. He was watching from the hotel room window as the image changed once again, this time into-- a car commercial. Tom shook his head and said, "Come on. Really?!"*

When Al came out of the bathroom Tom exclaimed, "What the hell?!"

"What?!" asked Al, whipping his head about thinking a spider had landed on him.

"Why do you look like-- that? *"*

"Look like what?"

"You know what. You look like frickin' Elvis Presley! Not a lot obviously but enough.*"*

Tom didn't want to give him too much credit. Al already had a big ego as far as Tom was concerned.

Al said with an Elvis-like drawl, "Why, thank you. Thank you very much."

"Stop it. You look and sound silly. You're not actually going out dressed like that, are you?" Was there no end to the many ways that Al could possibly annoy Tom? "And why *would you go out dressed like that?"*

"I wasn't sure if I would have time to change at the Stratosphere *later so I wanted to be sure that I was ready for the Elvis competition."*

"Al, that competition is nine hours *from now! You could have* grown *those sideburns for real by then."*

"Shut up, Tom!"

"Whatever. Let's just go."

Just when Tom thought that Al was finally ready and the two were exiting the room Al shouted, "Wait!"

"What now?" Tom said with a strong level of indignance.

Al felt about his person which of course now included an Elvis cape. He nodded his head then and said, "Yep! I almost *forgot my backpack."*

"Yep!" parroted Tom in a whiny, irritating voice. "I almost forgot my backpack!"

"Shut up, Tom. You're just jealous."

Tom eyed the backpack which was covered with military style camouflage imagery. It looked bulky, heavy and hideous. And *uncomfortable. There was absolutely nothing to like about it.*

"You nailed it," agreed Tom. "I'm just jealous."

"I knew it!" Al said smugly. "Maybe later we can go shopping and get one for you!"

"Aren't I the lucky one?!" *Tom said this with tongue firmly in cheek. "Come on let's go, Elvis. I think your limousine is waiting."*

The two exited the hotel room with their suitcases trailing behind them. Tom could have just as easily carried his as it was quite small and designed to fit in the overhead bin of an airplane. Al's suitcase, however, was like a steamer trunk from the 30's. While Tom packed just enough clothes for three days, Al might have brought everything that he had. No doubt Al would be sweating profusely by the time they made it to the street to hail a taxi.

To be fair, once outside, Tom would probably be sweating too. The blast of heat that hit you when you left the air-conditioned comfort of the casino resorts was a stern reminder that you were actually in the middle of the desert. Tom suddenly found himself *worried about the integrity of the power grid.*

***LATER** that day...* as Al and Tom were **LEAVING** the skydiving place

"Al! Don't forget your backpack! Again!" Tom grabbed what he believed to be Al's backpack and handed it to him. "Here, put that damn thing on so we don't have to come back to retrieve it!"

"Oh my goodness! I would forget my own head if it wasn't attached!"

'I wish you would,' muttered Tom under his breath.

"What?" asked Al.

"I said you did good," lied Tom.

"Oh gosh, thank you!" Al was beaming with pride.

Tom was thinking to himself, whatever it takes to get Al on that damn SkyJump was worth doing. The indoor skydiving session had gone incredibly well. Much to Tom's surprise Al had loved it! Tom had prepared himself for a truly bad experience but that was not to be. From the moment they arrived Al was enjoying himself. Things started off well when each of them were given the opportunity to choose a parachute vest from the display counter. Al was excited when he saw a vest that looked almost *exactly like his backpack.*

EARLIER *that day...* when Al and Tom **ARRIVED** at the skydiving place

"Check it out! You know *I'm getting that one!" Al was super excited.*

Al and Tom were standing at the counter where you can pick out the vest you will wear which holds your chute.

"Of course. Why am I not surprised?" Tom was snotty as usual.

"Do you have anything in "bland" for my friend here?" asked Al in an uncharacteristically snide tone.

"Sorry," said the man behind the counter. "Will gray work?"

"Sure! Give him GRAY. It will match the healthy tone of his face!"

Tom fired an angry look at Al. What the hell? He was being a real ass. Oh well thought Tom. I guess two can *play this game.*

After the two men received their parachute vests they were escorted into a room where they were taught how to "pack" their chute. 'This is the most important part of the exercise,' declared the instructor. 'There is no one you trust more than yourself in this world, which is why you should always, always, always *"pack your own chute".'*

Al had winked at Tom during that part of the instruction. Later Al made the comment, "You know I could be trusted to pack your chute but I think we both know what would happen if you packed mine!"

Al thought this was hilarious and laughed heartily. Tom, however, took that as a sign that he needed to be all the more diligent in his efforts to keep his plan of action clandestine. Tom thought again in his mind's eye of Al plunging to his death from the

top of The Stratosphere *with a tangled-up mess of a chute trailing behind him.*

Each of them took their turn in the vertical wind tunnel. Tom flew right to the top on his first go. Al, who was watching in the spectator area, jumped up and ran to the glass surrounding of the enclosure to see if he could see where Tom had gone. Tom had ascended so rapidly that he even thought for a moment that he might have to go look for Tom in the parking lot!

Finally Tom floated down from the ceiling of the wind tunnel and gave Al a thumbs up. Better to be at the top than the bottom thought Al. Even though there was a massive fan below capable of *generating wind speeds up to 170 mph, separated only by a net* of *what looked like bungee cords, indoor skydiving is completely safe and a wonderful introduction to the sport of skydiving.*

Now it was Al's turn. It took him several tries to get airborne (he was quite nervous) but once aloft he was like a balloon in flight. That sounds like a beautiful image but in truth poor Al spent much of his time bumping off the walls of the wind tunnel.

Tom was certain that Al would leave the tunnel with no desire to attempt the SkyJump. He could not, however, have been more wrong. Al was incredibly excited about the indoor skydiving session calling it the second-best *experience of his life.*

Tom was naturally curious about what the best experience of his life had been so he posed the question. Without missing a beat Al smiled and exclaimed, "why that Olympic swim from the deep end of Lake Tahoe to the shore of course!" Al paused then added, "with my good buddy Tom on the beach cheering me on!"

Tom's blood ran cold when hearing that but he recovered quickly and said, "Just you wait. This SkyJump *experience at the* Stratosphere *will be totally* life-altering *for you."*

"Well that's *an odd choice of words," said Al. Tom simply smiled. It was actually the* perfect *choice of words. He was already thinking ahead of how he would spend his evening alone.*

Before they left the skydiving place Al asked the instructor if he could pack another chute just for the experience. He was given a thumbs up. Al took this "pack your own chute" message both literally and figuratively. It was almost like a mantra to him. This was how you should live your life he thought to himself. Every day you should "pack your own chute."

When Al had finished with the literal part of packing his chute he set the packed chute just next to his own backpack. Al *knew the difference.*

But did Tom*??*

Later that afternoon...

When the two "experienced" skydivers checked into the Stratosphere, *Tom could have sworn that they were celebrities. The camera crew was once again on board. Their presence alone managed to summon the attention of a lot of people. As the cluster of interested onlookers grew Tom became progressively more annoyed with the desk clerk. Apparently there was a problem with the room. Al was trying to calm Tom and urge patience while Tom just wanted 'to get to the room already.'*

Tom is thinking that since the cost of the room was being covered by the radio station hosting the Elvis contest, that it was probably a crappy room anyway. Tom checked the time growing more impatient by the minute. He still had a lot to do in order to be ready to execute his plan of action for poor Al's demise.

As it turned out, the exact opposite regarding the room was true. Al was supposed to have a junior suite and it appeared that unfortunately none were available. A rather intense discussion was happening behind the front desk as the clerk and the manager exchanged comments. Tom thought he might even have heard the name "Wayne Newton" *mentioned. That was entirely possible as his name was emblazoned on the huge lighted marquee outside the hotel. Whatever the discussion had been about it now seemed to have been resolved. Al was handed a card key for the room and instructed to follow the bellman.*

Tom's first inclination that he might be wrong about their room came when the bellman entered a code on the elevator keypad to take them to an exclusive floor. The next clue came when the elevator door opened and magically it was like they had been transported to another world. They stepped from the elevator into a vast circular lobby with a massive floral arrangement as the centerpiece. There were four doors at compass points in the lobby area. There was also a Concierge on duty to assist them as needed. He nodded and smiled at them as they left the elevator and made their way to the door of their "room" which Tom now realized would actually be an "executive" *suite.*

The Concierge opened the door for them, bowing as he did so. The bellman followed with their things.

As they entered the lavish suite, both Al's and Tom's jaws dropped. The suite was Vegas-like incredible. There were windows all around with one side showing off the glitz and glamour of Fremont Street *in the distance, the way the strip used to be in its former glory. On the other side was the Vegas strip of today with luxurious resorts reaching to the sky, sporting the facades of the great architectural achievements around the world.*

Tom took his eyes away from the view outside and focused on the suite, which was basically a palace with every extravagance available to them. He noticed first the fully-stocked bar with four stools. He thought he might make a drink for himself but was put off by the fact that there was a cocktail already sitting on the bar with the ice shifting inside as it melted. That is rather odd he thought to himself.

The grand living space in the room offered two overstuffed couches and a love seat centered around a large hand-carved oak coffee table. A grand piano separated the living room space from the exquisite dining area which featured an incredible twinkling chandelier hanging above a twelve-chair dining table. The chandelier deserved a second look as, who knows, it might have once hung in Tara, the plantation home in the film "Gone with the Wind."

Tom's eyes came to rest on yet another oddity, a half-eaten bowl of spaghetti and meatballs at the far end of the table. 'Stick a fork in it,' was what came to mind but Tom could clearly see that there was already *a fork stuck into it.*

Someone must have left this room in quite a hurry.

As the bellman showed Al and Tom about the suite he completely passed by the kitchen area without saying a word. That is strange, thought Tom. Was there something there that they weren't supposed to see? He made a mental note to check out the kitchen the very moment that the bellman left the suite.

The bellman continued their tour by opening a couple of doors to show Al and Tom their sleeping quarters. These were two immense bedrooms, each with king-size beds covered by coverlets ornately embroidered with what oddly appeared to be a-- family crest? *Each bedroom of course had its own bathroom with the highlight being an expansive "rain-shower" with space large enough to accommodate four to five people.*

The tour was now complete and the bellman was preparing to leave. Tom realized that they had reached that "tipping moment" so he was artful in how he moved about the space making sure that it would be Al *who the bellman would look to for his tip.*

The suite was absolutely fabulous and better than anything that either Al or Tom could have imagined. The bellman snuck a peek at the tip that was pressed into his hand by Al. The tip was quite generous, possibly more than he might have imagined. The bellman smiled, he was thankful that it was the "Elvis"-looking guy that had tipped him and not the nerdy dude wearing the (wait for it) ... "jorts" *aka jeans shorts.*

As the bellman was leaving Tom swore that he heard him say under his breath, "Glad I'm *not the one that has to tell Mr. Newton that they gave his room away..."*

Thirty minutes later...

The time has come for the big event, the Elvis impersonator contest. This contest, however, is unlike any other because this contest, hosted by radio stations in both Las Vegas and Reno, was not looking for the best *Elvis impersonators. Nope. In this contest, they were searching for the* worst. *Whether or not the contestants were in on the joke was of no concern to the radio station personnel. They had a job to do and they would do it with both gusto and enthusiasm. A camera crew was on hand to capture every embarrassing minute.*

The contest is taking place in the hotel ballroom. The room is already nearly full of audience members eager for a good time. They were eager to enjoy this Elvis version of Karaoke gone horribly wrong. The excitement of the crowd was palpable. This was going to be awful!

Like watching a house on fire.

Al and Tom find their way to the Registration Table. This should just be a formality as Al has already signed up online. The two waited in line as there were two others before them. 'These dudes don't look anything *like Elvis' Tom thought to himself. Hmmm, maybe Al has a shot at this after all...*

"Next!!"

The lady behind the table shouted this loud enough for the folks on the strip outside to hear.

Al stepped up to the table.

"Name?!"

Al shared his name and indicated that he had signed up online. The lady behind the desk did not bother to look up but rather continued on with her litany of questions.

"Young Elvis? Or old Elvis?"

"Um—" Al was stuck with the very first question. Tom was immediately irritated.

"Okay," the lady marked something on her list, "let me ask it a different way. Are you going with 'skinny' Elvis or 'big' Elvis?"

Tom leaned down to the lady and whispered, "If you look up I think you will have your answer."

The lady looked up to see Al already suited up in a fully sequined, and fully stretched *bodysuit with cape. Al was now sporting Elvis sunglasses as well. She replied curtly, "Ready to go I see. Well that checks several boxes for me. Here you go darlin,' this is your name badge and contestant number. Be sure that you wear those on your person where the judges can see them during the competition. Should you win, there will be some additional forms to fill out so don't leave the property. Good luck Elvis!"*

"Thank you. Thank you very much."

Al said his Elvis catchphrase again in his slightly slurred and casual Elvis drawl. It did not sound any better this time.

"Next!!" *bellowed the lady.*

Al and Tom enter the ballroom and head towards the stage. They are met by a stagehand who asks if they are lost. Apparently they have not followed the directions given to them by the lady at the registration desk. Al tries to explain that nothing had been shared with them regarding the stage or—

The stagehand just wasn't hearing it. He told Tom to take whatever seat he could find and then escorted Al to the dressing rooms backstage where the other "performers" were getting prepared for their shot at stardom.

Once inside the dressing room Al wandered about stealing a glance at each of the performers. He was contestant number 15 and he soon realized that they were in order of appearance and he must have been the last to check-in. Was that good or bad? Who knew? He probably shouldn't worry about it, leave that to Tom who worried about everything.

As Al sauntered about he noticed how much more elaborate the other costumes were compared to his own. These people really took this thing seriously. Al looked at himself in the mirror. He didn't look too *bad. He could definitely pass for Elvis on the street, what with his cape, sunglasses and sideburns but was that enough? That was the question.*

As Al soon learned, the costumes were only window dressing. This competition was all about performance. Some of it was stage presence but nearly all of it was vocal performance.

At some point (Al had lost track of time) the lights had dimmed in the ballroom and the competition had begun. He heard contestant number "1" belting out "Hound Dog". It was actually pretty good he thought until he heard the boos from the crowd. Wow, that hardly seemed fair. The bar must be set pretty high. Al was starting to get cold feet. There was one thing he was absolutely sure about himself and that was—he cannot *sing. Oh boy.*

Al peeked out from behind the curtains to look at the crowd. It was a full house. One more thing to get him nervous. He searched for Tom but couldn't find him in the audience. They had been separated before he had located a seat so he really had no idea where he might be seated. For all that Al knew, Tom might have gone out to play 9 nine holes of golf. He wouldn't put it past him.

Oh wait, there *he was, only about six or seven rows back. He looked like he was enjoying himself, that was good. Contestant number two was shaking his hips and tearing it up to "Jailhouse Rock." Al hadn't paid much attention earlier but now it made sense. The list of available songs to choose from were relegated to either "young" Elvis or "old" Elvis. That was actually a rather clever idea. It made for the audience a natural timeline transition of both fashion and music styles.*

Contestant number three had taken the stage to sing "Love Me Tender." It is actually a woman with a deep voice. The crowd liked her at first, maybe because they got a kick out of the fact that her sideburns were obviously drawn on with black magic marker, but once she started singing (and was good!) they just weren't buying it. More boos.

The next three contestants sang and performed quite well actually but—that's not what this competition was about and soon they too were heckled and booed by the crowd. Al heard quite passable versions of "Blue Hawaii," "Teddy Bear," "Can't Help Falling in Love" and "Don't Be Cruel."

The last of the "young" Elvis impersonators has taken the stage and delivers what Al thinks is an absolutely horrible take on "Blue Suede Shoes." The crowd LOVES *it! What the heck?! Of course this is when it dons on Al that it's not how* good *you are that matters here but rather how* awful *you can be in an Elvis suit. This epiphany just gave Al a* boatload *of confidence for he* knows *how awful he can be.*

There is a brief intermission between the "young" and "old" Elvis sets. Al has a few ideas that just might help him look and *sound worse than he already does. The question is, does he have enough time to pull it off?*

Al will need a tight belt and a bean burrito as his secret weapons...

Help a brother out

"Psst! PSSSSST!"

"Hey buddy!"

"What?" Tom turned around to see some guy poking him in the back. "What do you want?"

"I think that Elvis up there on stage is trying to get your attention."

"What? Which one? Ha, ha." Tom then caught sight of Al and said, "Oh, yeah right. Thanks man." Al was motioning for Tom to come up to the stage. Tom mouthed a soundless, 'What do you want?' but that wasn't enough to get Al to stop beckoning for him to come to the stage. Finally Tom got up from his seat and walked to the stage.

"Hey Tom!"

"Yes, Al." Tom's only thought at this moment is that Al was probably going to say that he was bailing out of the contest. He was resigned to the fact that quitting on this would also mean quitting on the SkyJump. *Tom was truly surprised at what Al had to say to him.*

"Hey man, do you want me to actually win *this thing?"*

"Sure," said Tom, still not believing, "I mean, why not?"

"Did you know that the winner gets more *than just the* Tokyo Vegas *stay?"*

"More, what do you mean more*?"*

"I didn't read the whole list of stuff besides the free stay. There's also a couple of T-shirts, game tokens, blah, blah, blah..."

Tom has tuned out Al. None of this crap mattered to him. Why was he bothering him with this drivel about –

"Wait! What?*!!"*

"What, what?" asks a confused Al.

"That last part you just said, what *did you just say?"*

"The part about the gift shop stuff? Or the part about the show tonight?"

"The show, you idiot! The show!!*"*

"I'm not sure that I like your tone." admonished Al.

"My what? Oh yeah, I'm sorry Al, that wasn't nice. I think I'm just excited you know. That's it, I'm just overly excited."

"I knew you would be. I wasn't going to tell you because I didn't want you to be disappointed but now I think I could actually win *this thing!"*

"Al! The show*?" reminded Tom.*

Al looked at him strangely for a moment and then said, "Oh yeah! The show! The winner *gets two tickets for the* Wayne Newton *show tonight, here at the* Stratosphere. *With dinner and drinks included. Plus–"*

"Yeah, get to the "plus"! I am dying to hear about the "plus"!!"

"The "plus" *is that the winner, which would be* "me"*," Al bats his eyelashes like a prima donna, "and a* "friend," *which would be* "you," *if you're nice to me, get to go up on stage with* Wayne Newton *when he makes the formal announcement of the winner."*

"Oh my gosh, that would be AH-MAZING!"

"Yeah, I know how much you like Wayne Newton. *So-- do you want me to* win *this thing or not?!"*

"Of course I do! But how can I *help?"*

"Let me borrow your belt and go grab me a bean burrito from the taco stand in the Food Court."

"What the heck do you need those things for? That's—"

"Come here," said Al. He whispered his plan into Tom's ear. Tom's eye got HUGE. He immediately stripped off his belt, handed it to Al and said, "I'll be back in a flash!"

"Bring me a Diet Coke too!"

"You got it!" shouted Tom as he weaved his way quickly through the crowd that was coming back into the ballroom to reclaim their seats. The lights had flashed off and on signaling the beginning of the second set. Tom was certain to miss a portion of the show but he really didn't care.

Al was right. With Tom's help Al was *going to win this thing.*

This was SO exciting!

While Tom was away, several performers had caught on to the game and when they hit the stage were now doing their best to do their worst as they performed songs made famous by Elvis. "Always on my Mind," "Mustang Sally," "A Little Less Conversation," "In the Ghetto," and "Suspicious Minds" were performed for the crowd.

Al was enjoying himself now. None of these performers could be considered serious contenders. Al, who was peeking out from behind the curtain, caught sight of Tom returning to the side of the stage.

"Glad you could finally make it," said Al as he grabbed the bag and received a roll of the eyes from Tom.

Al then made quick work of the bean burrito and then seconds later downed the Diet Coke. He was able to make both items disappear before the usher had time to ask Tom to return to his seat.

Contestant number 14 walked on stage and was met with thunderous applause. 'Uh-oh,' thought Al. 'Who's this guy?' Al turned to watch and knew right away that his sure thing was now in jeopardy. The performer on stage was a local cat best known as "Obese Elvis." Al thought this might just be against the rules. All the other contestants were amateurs. This guy was a well-known professional comedian turned Elvis impersonator. Part of his schtick was his plus-plus size and his unabashed willingness to wear an Elvis bodysuit stretched way too tight in ALL the WRONG places. As he gyrated to the tune, "Burning Love," (give him credit, this cat could move on stage), the audience was now eating out of his hand. He would definitely be tough to beat!

The crowd was cheering as "Obese Elvis" was taking his bows as best he could in his skintight outfit. Al passed him on the stage as he headed out for his time under the lights. The "king-sized" Elvis (pun intended) winked at Al and said, "Beat that, sucker!"

'Well that wasn't very nice,' thought Al. Usually he would just get his feelings hurt and mope around a bit but he wanted to win this competition so badly that that little bit of trash talk actually got him pumped up! Al shared a quick pep-talk with himself.

'Come on Diet Coke. Come on overstuffed but quite tasty bean burrito. Do your worst!"

Viva Las Vegas!

The crowd gets silent as Al takes his place on stage. He is a big guy but looks small in comparison to the man who just left the stage. It is the belt though that makes the difference. With the way too small for Al belt as tight as it was--well just imagine if you were to put a belt on a water balloon.

And that was just the visual part of his act. Wait until the crowd gets a load of what else *Al has in store for them!*

One interesting point about the competition. In order to prevent the contestants from performing too well, the songs are being chosen for them *at the time of their performance. Each contestant would needed to have rehearsed a good portion of Elvis' catalog of hits to have prepared for the song they might be given to sing.*

As Al hears the first few chords of the song chosen for him he can't believe his incredible luck. This song by itself is a showstopper! Add in the performance he was about to give and how could he lose?

Al heard the announcer say, "Ladies and gentlemen, all the way from O-HI-O*, please give a warm welcome to "*AL*-vis" doing* his *rendition of "Viva Las Vegas"!*

The moment between the announcement of his name and the start of the song was perfect timing for the bean burrito/Diet Coke "poo-poo platter" to announce that they too *would be part of the show as Al ripped one quite LOUD and serious fart!*

In his mind Al challenged "Obese Elvis" to beat that one!

The crowd reacted with strong appreciation for such an outburst. And outburst it was as "AL-vis" had pointed the live microphone directly at his backside at just the right moment. After that Al's performance was all horrendous singing and truly painful to watch dancing interspersed with amplified bean burritos/Diet Coke farts and hiccups.

When Al left the stage there were calls for encores from the crowd. They absolutely LOVED *him! Al went back out on stage, took a couple bows, let go of few more farts and then he was done. It was time now to wait for the votes to be counted. Tom showed up backstage as happy as Al had ever seen him.*

Tom actually gave Al a HUG! What a great day!

Nearing dusk...

The sun is beginning to set in the western sky. Al is pressing Tom to head up to the SkyJump *before it gets dark but Tom it seems is now having second thoughts. He truly believes that Al has a legitimate chance now at winning the Elvis contest but the announcement won't be made until* Wayne Newton's *concert later this evening. If something "bad" were to happen to Al, Tom's one and only opportunity to meet his idol,* Wayne Newton, *would be smashed to mush!*

Much like Al will be on the Vegas strip pavement when the cord snaps on the SkyJump.

Tom is losing the battle with Al who, now that he has discovered this incredible newfound confidence, actually seems eager *to conquer his acrophobia by using the* SkyJump *to leap from the* Stratosphere. *Tom's only hope now is that his friend "Part-Time" will be his ADD self and forget to change the cable when Al steps up to make his jump. The more he thought about it the more Tom was convinced that he could count on "Part-Time" to get it* wrong *which would now actually be getting it* right*!*

Al and Tom are riding on the elevator up to the rooftop. Just when Tom is thinking to himself, at least we don't have the camera crew around, Al chooses that moment to share that another reason why they need to get moving on doing this SkyJump *thing is that the camera crew is losing light for their shoot. They are set up at the landing zone and waiting.*

This whole event will be captured LIVE!

'Oh no,' thinks Tom. "What have I done?"

"You haven't done anything," says Al. "What are you even talking about?"

"Did I just say that out loud*?"*

"Uh, yeah. Are you alright? You look a little queasy."

"I'm fine," replied Tom. "Let's just get this over with."

"Alright, alright." The two had reached the rooftop of the tower. "Let's find an available spot at the SkyJump*."*

"Over here!" shouts "Part-Time." He is waving his arms frantically to get their attention.

"Hey, look there! Perfect timing!" Al heads directly for "Part-Time's" station.

"That guy looks a little too anxious don't you think? Maybe we should go to the other station." Tom is pointing to the other SkyJump *station where there was a line of about 10 people waiting their turn.*

"Why would I go wait in line when this guy is ready to go?"

"Because the view is better over there?" suggests Tom.

"Good solid answer," said Al, chuckling to himself. "But I'm thinking that 15 feet is not going to change the view enough for me to wait in line. Besides, you don't want to be late for Wayne Newton*, do you?"*

"Of course not." Tom knew he was out of excuses. Why did you always have to sacrifice one thing to have another?

Al steps up to the safety platform for "Part-Time" to get him rigged up with his safety harness. Tom is thinking that "Part-Time" must have remembered to take his pills today because he is doing exactly *what they had discussed.*

"I hope you don't mind my dude if I take just a minute to change the cable on this bad boy," says "Part-Time."

"No, I don't mind," replied Al. "Do what you need to do. By the way, why do they call you "Part-Time"?"

"You know what? People ask me that all the time! Best I can figure out is that they see it on my shirt, right? And they're curious, right? So they ask me."

Al is looking at "Part-Time" like he has never seen a human before or at least not one like that. That was certainly a bizarre answer. He glances over at Tom who looks panicked. Al is wondering, why should he *be worried?* I'm *the one taking the jump.*

Tom on the other hand is wondering how he might be able to stop this before it is too late. Just then he hears "Part-Time" say something that just might get him off the hook.

"Hey man, I'm not too sure if you are allowed to wear that backpack when you jump, you know what I mean?"

"Oh good point!" shouts Tom. "Maybe you should wait until later when we can leave the backpack in the room."

"Then again," said "Part-Time, "It does look pretty sweet. Maybe you are *allowed to wear it. How would I know, right?"*

"Let's do it then!" said Al.

"Yep, that's the spirit my man, let's DO IT!!"

Al is all hooked up and ready to step off the rooftop of the Stratosphere. *The only thing between him and the unforgiving ground below is a cable which Tom has altered so that it will SNAP! the moment that Al's full weight at the end of his fall is upon it.*

The good news? *Al will be able to enjoy about half of his drop before he will know that he is in serious trouble.*

The bad news? *The second half will be absolutely terrifying to Al, the crowd below and the camera crew as well.*

Tom tells himself that he better start working on those fake tears!!

Tom is looking at Al and a myriad of thoughts are racing through his head. He will of course never see Al like this *again, and like* this *he means,* alive. *Tom thinks of the multitude of annoying moments the two have shared. Tom likens Al to a parasite and he (Tom) has become the unfortunate host. Whether or not that was true was immaterial to Tom as he was being ruled by emotion more than logic.*

Poor Al. He looked like a stuffed turkey what with his backpack and all that safety gear strung about him. Tom is shaking his head. Al and that stupid backpack! That thing went everywhere *with him! Almost like it had become fused to his body. He would probably be buried with it. Oops! Careful. That might actually be* true.

"Part-Time" says, "You're all set man! At least I think *so. I mean I might have missed a few things but you should be good. I* think. *Anyway, enjoy the ride!"*

Al has a huge smile on his face as he looks at Tom and mouths the words, 'Thank you.'

Tom shrugs his shoulders as if to say, 'for what?' Al would have answered 'for helping me to conquer my fear' but it was too late for that as Al takes a leap off the edge of the Stratosphere *tower. Tom is struggling with an odd thought in his head as he rushes to the edge to watch Al fall. For some reason that backpack just didn't look right...*

Just then "Part-Time" clamps him on the shoulder and says, "I sure hope our boy makes it! That is totally *the* wrong *cable for a guy his size."*

Tom looks at "Part-Time" considering the implications of such a statement. "As the safety monitor you *should know better, right?"*

"Yep! You're right about that! BIG *mistake on* my part *hooking* that *dude up to* that *cable. Hope he makes it! Alrighty then. Next in line? Hello little lady, ready to jump off a tall building for no good reason?"*

"Yes! I am SO excited!" screams a 15-year-old girl who has lied about her age to get to do the jump.

Tom steps away as "Part-Time" gets to work on the safety harness of his next victim. He leans over the edge and watches as Al is "falling" 855 feet to the ground below.

In actuality Al was not falling at all. The way the SkyJump *works is to control the rate of descent much like an elevator. More than 200,000 jumpers have safely enjoyed the experience.*

The moment has arrived. Tom is pounding his head with his fists. Any second now the cable which is Al's lifeline will have the full weight of Al's body, plus the force of gravity upon it, and it will *SNAP!*

Al is exhilarated. This experience is WAY better than the swim back to shore at Lake Tahoe. That was a challenge. This is FUN! Little does he know that he is just about at the end of his rope. Literally. He is only seconds away from proving the math written into both the laws of gravity and the tensile strength of a cable.

Al waves to the camera crew and the eager spectators below getting ever closer with each second of his harrowing fall.

Tom is busily working on an alibi which he has already determined will of course be "Part-Time." With his propensity for forgetfulness, Tom is thinking that it would be in his best interest to leave the rooftop and head for the landing zone. Better to have a totally confused *"Part-Time" for the authorities to question rather than have Tom on hand for him to look to for support.*

And that's when something ***good*** happened...

Something has caught Al's eye. Something different about his backpack. It hadn't felt right ever since they left the indoor skydiving place. Something was just off. It felt too heavy for one. And there was this metal handle-thingy. He didn't remember that being there and what was it even for anyway? Wait! That looks just like the ripcord on the parachute pack—

And that's when something ***bad*** happened...

The cable snapped *just as Tom knew it would. Had "Part-Time" been watching he might have said, 'bummer dude.' Al's descent was about to increase as gravity was now* fully in charge.

But, what happened next made absolutely NO sense to Tom for all of three seconds.

And then he could not stop laughing.

A huge colorful balloon *was suddenly just—there.*

Of course it was not a balloon at all. It was a parachute*!*

Al had left the indoor skydiving place with his parachute *pack instead of his* backpack*! What an idiot! The parachute of course would save his life! The ever-devious Tom quickly determined that he would take credit for switching the two bags and ultimately saving Al's life which would make Al indebted to him.*

The crowd below was reacting now to the opening of the parachute and the gentle glide to the ground which Al was executing beautifully. The weird thing was that he would have had zero training in actually using *a parachute. At the indoor skydiving place all you did was "fly" in the air above the fan. You never actually* opened *your chute. There was never a need for that. Regardless Al was executing a flawless landing to the cheers of the growing crowd. One thing was sure, with the camera crew on hand, Al was about to become famous!*

Tom has arrived at the landing zone and jostles his way through the crowd to be with his friend on camera. He wanted to be seen as the caring friend, not the plotting arch nemesis. Hundreds of selfies were being taken in addition to the live shots from the camera crew. Now Al, being his ever-gracious self, is hugging Tom. After all, it was Tom *that got him to do this in the first place.*

What a great friend!

Only an hour has passed since the historic jump from the tower but for Tom it felt like an eternity. The two are preparing to leave their suite for the Wayne Newton *show. Both have had time to clean up and compose themselves. Al is anxious to hear if he has won the Elvis contest and Tom is eager to know if he will possibly meet his idol. This is one of the very few times where the two of them are in step with what the other is thinking. This of course won't last.*

Al and Tom have arrived in the lobby and immediately they are escorted by hotel security through the area and into the showroom where Wayne Newton *will be performing. Not only are they receiving* VIP *treatment but it appears as though Al has gained quite a bit of notoriety both from his incredibly bad portrayal of Elvis as well as his unplanned parachute jump. He might even have gained his own fan club. As he and Tom make their way to their front row seats they can hear shouting from the upper deck. They turn their heads to see a group of about thirty people, women and men, chanting, "AL-vis! AL-vis! AL-vis!"*

Al immediately begins to encourage them by doing a "raise the roof" gesture. He has no idea if this will help him clench the winning spot in the Elvis contest but he also can't see how it could hurt.

"My people love me," Al says to Tom.

Tom would normally have a quick retort but he is still in shock over the way this day has turned out. He is certain that there will be investigations regarding the snapped cable. With any luck "Part-Time" will do what he does best and that is to be genuinely confused. Tom is expecting (hoping) that the switching of the cables will just be written off as a bad mistake. "Part-Time" will probably lose his job but that isn't something that Tom will lose any sleep over. As a matter of fact he just might have saved some future jumpers from falling to their deaths.

The moment has finally arrived. The house lights dim and the band on stage kicks into high gear. Multicolored lights are flashing in time with the music above the stage and out into the audience as Wayne Newton *stakes the stage to great fanfare. The crowd is immediately on their feet, clapping and singing, showing their love for this performer as he struts his stuff from stage left to stage right. This is 'Mr. Entertainment'! This is 'Mr. Las Vegas'!*

"He's still got it!" shares the woman standing next to Tom.

Does he need to respond to this woman? What should he do? No one else would ask themselves those questions but that's just how Tom is wired. He actually thinks about those kinds of things instead of just moving on. Tom is too easily bothered by just about everything. For example he is bothered by Al constantly bumping into him as he sways to and fro to the music being played. 'Must you?!' Tom wants to ask but doesn't.

Wayne Newton *is performing his many hits with gusto, each time inviting the crowd to sing along. He launches into "Daddy Don't*

You Walk So Fast," a million selling hit from 1972. This is one of Tom's favorite songs. He starts singing along. Al looks over at Tom and just has to chuckle. Tom knows every word. And he seems to be having a great time!

As the set continues Tom almost begins to let go of his reticence and just let go. Almost.

And then Wayne spoils it all by taking a moment to converse with the crowd. And what is on his mind? Well that near fatal jump from the tower of course. Tom is clenching his fists and gritting his teeth as Wayne describes the scenario which has taken place only hours earlier. Then he makes the statement that the gentleman who made that daredevil leap will actually be joining him on stage soon. How about that? Of course the crowd loves *that idea! Tom, however, does* not.

"Let me take a moment here to speak with all of you on a personal level. Please. Take your seats." The room grows quiet as the audience are seated, eager to hear what the great Wayne Newton *has to say. "First of all, I thank you all for coming out this evening to spend a little time with me and sing along to some old songs that are near and dear to my heart."*

Wayne paused to allow for applause.

"As many of you know, the Strat *hosted an "Elvis Presley Impersonator Contest" and they have asked me to announce the winner. This announcement will be simulcast on local radio and TV stations for all those individuals who could not be with us here tonight."*

More applause.

"Let me tell you, I am quite honored to do this as I had much admiration and respect for Elvis. For whom he was as a person, as a performer and for what he did for music." Wayne stopped for a

moment, looking pensive as he continued, "Mr. Presley was a legend and an icon but—he was also just a man, a regular person just like the rest of us with insecurities of his own. I wrote a song about him, about dealing with loneliness when you're at the top and everyone seems to know you but they don't really *know who you are inside, about how sometimes you feel like you have no one you can turn to. This song is called "The Letter" and I would like to perform it for you now. Thank you."*

Wayne performed the song with heartfelt poignancy. When he hit the last note there was not a dry eye in the house. Tom would never admit it but out of pure emotion he gave Al a hug. Al hugged him back, keeping the hold for just a bit too long which in turn made a special moment awkward.

As the applause died down Wayne said, "Well, here we are. It's time for the big announcement. I have the card with the name of the winner in my hand right here. Is everybody ready?"

Wayne waited for a crowd reaction. It didn't seem eager enough.

"I said, is everybody READY?!" This time the crowd reacted appropriately with loud yelling and cheering. "THAT's what I'm talking about!" said Wayne. "Maestro, may I have a drum roll please?"

The drummer complied and a drum roll sounded as the crowd quieted down for the big reveal. Wayne opened the envelope carefully and then gave a chuckle as he read the name. The spotlight was fully on Mr. Newton as he said, "Ladies and gentlemen, your winner of the W.H.O.A. Elvis Impersonator Contest is..."

Wayne shook his head as he looked at the card, a baffled expression of disbelief on his face. Whatever misgivings he had were set aside as he was a professional. He continued on by allowing the drum roll to build to a crescendo. Wayne then stopped it short with a simulated karate chop as he shouted out the winner's name, "Obese Elvis!"

The room was silent. Wayne was bewildered and confused by the reaction, uncertain of what to do next. He had his answer quickly as suddenly there were boos echoing throughout the crowd. Obviously, they were not happy with the choice of the winner. The booing grew louder as "Obese Elvis" began to make his way to the stage. People actually started throwing things angrily onstage.

Wayne exclaimed, "Hey folks! Don't blame me! I'm just the messenger!"

A fervor swept over the crowd as the booing intensified.

"Oh well," said Al. "I gave it my best shot."

"No!" replied Tom. "That's not right! I heard that guy is a local professional. He shouldn't even be in the competition! Somebody needs to do something! This isn't fair! You won't get to go to Tokyo Vegas *and I won't get to meet* Wayne Newton*!"*

Tom is burning mad now. Just then two things happen simultaneously. A man rushes onstage to whisper something in Wayne Newton's *ear while Security stops "Obese Elvis" from joining the performer onstage. Wayne is handed another envelope which he reads carefully, nods to the man who nods back and then leaves the stage. An irate and disgruntled "Obese Elvis" is escorted away from the stage and lead out through a side door. Once that happens order is restored. Wayne waits patiently until the crowd is focused on him once again.*

"Ladies and gentlemen, it appears that we have some new information to share with you. The envelope I was handed earlier and read to you—was a FAKE! *Apparently somebody* really *wanted to win this thing!" The crowd laughed uneasily clearly uncertain as to what was to come next. "I have here in my hand the* real *envelope with the name of the* real *winner. Ya'll ready to hear his name?"*

The crowd erupted with excitement. Tom and Al are both in shock looking to one another with eager anticipation. Could it be???

*"Ladies and gentlemen, I am hoping that you are happier with this name than you were with the last one. I give you the uncontested winner of the W.H.O.A. Elvis competition, and folks, I am reading exactly what it says here, **'AL-vis'**!!!"*

"What are you waiting on?! Go on! Get up there!"

Tom is shouting to an utterly shocked Al. The crowd is cheering. Wayne is shading his eyes from the spotlight so that he can look out into the audience to find the new winner.

"Go on up there, Al. YOU WON!!" Tom is exclaiming while patting Al on the back.

"You're coming with me!" says Al.

"Oh yeah," replies Tom suddenly realizing that he almost gave up his golden opportunity to meet the one and only Wayne Newton. *Now that the two have a game plan they quickly make their way to the stage. Everyone in the audience wants a piece of them now if only to reach out and touch. Al is a celebrity now with his fifteen minutes of fame beginning to click down. That peculiar little thought encouraged him to hurry up on stage.*

This is Al's big moment. He is not only standing on stage with the legendary Wayne Newton *but he is also the newly crowned winner of the WHOA Elvis Impersonator Contest. Life just doesn't get any better than this, right?*

Wayne puts his arm around Al and asks, "So tell me Big Winner, what's your name?"

Al replies but his response is immediately lost in the chorus coming from the crowd, "AL-vis! Al-vis! AL-vis!"

Wayne laughs and says, "Well I guess we can't argue with that, right? We don't want these folks turning on us now, do we?" Al nods his head up and down vigorously. "Well congratulations to you son. I am eager for you to give us a little taste of what your *Elvis sounds like. You* will *do that for us, won't you?"*

The crowd cheered loudly at this suggestion.

"Before we do that though, please introduce me to your little friend here."

A miffed look crossed Tom's face as he repeated under his breath, 'little friend'*?*

"Sure, Mr. Newton, this is—"

"Please, Al-vis, call me Wayne. We're friends now." Wayne gave Al a friendly hug affording the audience another reason to cheer.

"Okay, Mr. Wayne," the crowd loved this, "please allow me to introduce you to Tom who is a BIG FAN by the way."

"Hello Tom."

"Hi Wayne, it's a pleasure—"

"Please. Show a little respect. Address me as 'Mr. Newton' if you don't mind."

Tom is shellshocked with his mouth wide open and nothing coming out. In a few seconds Wayne Newton *has managed to destroy his world. Tom wants to run from the stage, find a rock to hide under and have a good cry. He is suddenly consumed with the fear that he will pee his pants.*

"Hey Tom, why the long face? I'm just having a bit of fun with you. Why not be like your famous friend here and enjoy the moment?" The crowd cheered for Tom to cheer up. "You're proud of your friend here, right?"

"Um, I-, I-" replied Tom, stumbling over his words.

"Well said, my friend. Well said." The crowd laughed along with Wayne as he poked fun at Tom. "So Tom," Wayne continued. "I think I may have a bone to pick with you."

"Wha--, what?"

Big gulp from Tom as all eyes in the audience were now laser focused on him.

What did he *do?*

Wayne turned his attention to the crowd. "For those of you who don't know, I actually live *here in Las Vegas. I have a really nice ranch not too far from here. That's pretty nice, right? I can commute back and forth to work, right? Well, it's not* always *that simple. Often I will do multiple shows in a given day and what with the crazy traffic, it's not always convenient going back and forth. Alvis knows what I'm talking about."*

Wayne points to Al who is vigorously shaking his head in agreement.

"So with that being said, here's the deal. The casino, in this case The Strat*, generously offers me the use of a suite during my residency." The crowd is applauding. "Nice gesture, right? A friggin' suite!" More applause. "And let me tell you something: IT. IS. NICE!"*

The crowd continues to show their appreciation.

"BUT!" The crowd quiets down. "When these two showed up without a reservation—" Wayne pauses, allowing for a handful of *boos. "And... there is no room at the inn---" More boos. "Do you see where this is going?" Wayne is pandering to the crowd and they are beginning to get riled up. "That's right. You figured it out. The hotel gave my room away---" The booing has intensified. "To* him*."*

Wayne is pointing at Tom who has his hands up like he is under arrest.

"It's not just me. *They gave the room to* both *of us!" Tom is pleading now. "The room is actually for* Al. *I mean AL-vis. He's the reason why we are even here. It's not me. Don't blame* ME!*" Tom is picturing an angry mob with torches chasing after him like the scene in Frankenstein.*

Wayne is chuckling. "Alright now, alright. He does have a point. The room was given to both of them and truth be told, it is Al's name on the sign-in card. Fair enough. My mistake. It happens. Sometimes the hotel is overbooked and they have to give the suite away. I get it. That however--- is not *my beef."*

Wayne puts his arm around Tom's shoulder. Tom starts to relax as the crowd has shown signs of settling down as well.

"Then we're good?" asks a meek Tom.

Wayne smiles and hugs Tom a little tighter. "Oh no. I still have a bone to pick with you.*"*

"What? What did I do?" Tom is clearly anxious and uneasy being both in the spotlight and in the grip of his idol who seems to be at odds with him in full view of his adoring fans. Now what?

"Tell me something, Tom."

"What's that, Wayne?"

Wayne points at Tom and laughs. "The memory is the first to go, right?" The crowd laughs. "It is 'Mr. Newton' to you."

"Sorry, Mr. Newton." Tom looks like a man who has just been slugged in the gut. "What did I do?"

"Tom, tell me, while I was stuck in traffic, anxiously hoping to get to my show on time, and you were relaxing, enjoying the comfort of my suite---" Wayne paused, in effect setting the mood. "Did you happen to see a bowl of spaghetti on the table?"

Tom looked at Wayne and said, "Yeah, I saw it."

"You saw it." Wayne is getting confirmation.

"Yes. Yes, I saw it."

"Spaghetti. AND meatballs, right?"

"Yeah, that's right."

"And you saw it where? On the table?"

"Yeah, that's right. It was just left on the table. Almost half a bowl of spaghetti just left on the table."

"Uh, huh. Is it fair to say that whoever left that bowl of spaghetti there must have been in a hurry?"

"Sure," agreed Tom. "That makes sense. Why else would you just leave it there? Why not put it away in the refrigerator?"

"Yes! Yes! Why not just put it away in the refrigerator. What a great idea!"

Wayne is pacing the stage, walking back and forth around Tom. Tom is eyeing him warily.

"What did you do with the spaghetti, Tom? Did you *put it in the refrigerator?"*

All eyes were now on Tom. He felt what it must feel like for the accused man in a courtroom trial. All eyes were upon him and they wanted vengeance. He was already convicted.

"I, um—" Tom swallowed but the lump in his throat would not go away. "I did not."

"Did not, what?" Wayne placed a hand to his ear to hear the answer clearly.

Al hung his head down and said, "Oh no, here it comes."

"I did not place the spaghetti in the refrigerator."

Tom is appealing to the crowd with his body language. So what? So I didn't put the spaghetti in the refrigerator. I'm not the one who left it on table in the first place!

"So, if you did not place the spaghetti in the refrigerator, the what did *you do with it?"*

The entire audience waited with bated breath as Tom stood still, fidgeting with microphone in hand.

"Tom?" Wayne prompted.

"I, um, I–"

"Yes, Tom?"

"I ate it." whispered a now frightened Tom.

"I'm sorry, what's that? Please speak up so we all can hear."

"I said, I ATE it."

Wayne was shaking his head as the audience once again began to boo.

"You ate MY spaghetti?"

"I didn't know it was yours!"

"Well, that may be true but certainly you knew that it wasn't yours!"

"Um, yes."

"You ate the meatballs too, didn't you?!"

"I offered one of them to Al."

"And did he take it?"

There was no response.

"Well, did he?"

"No. No he didn't."

"No? And, why not? Does Al not like meatballs?!"

"Al loves *meatballs!"*

"Hmm, then I wonder why Al did not accept your kind offer of a meatball?"

"Because he said they didn't belong to us."

"What's that?! I'm sorry, I did not catch that, could you repeat what you just said?"

"I said, because they do not belong to us." Tom said this in a louder tone for the crowd.

"Exactly." Wayne was shaking his head. "Wow, can you believe that folks? This cat ate my spaghetti. AND my meatballs. Al, if I

were you I would not trust him as far as I could throw him. Let me ask you this, whose idea was it to jump off the tower today?"

Al points to Tom.

Wayne looks to the crowd and says, "You saw that one coming, right?"

"Okay, enough about spaghetti and meatballs. Let's get to our friend, AL-vis here and chat about his BIG DAY." Tom snuck away and returned to his seat. "First, let's talk about the contest. YOU WON!"

The crowd was once again on their feet cheering for their new winner. Al took his bows, enjoying his time in the spotlight. Wayne handed Al a microphone and said, "What do you say? Let's see what this boy can do! Ladies and gentlemen, please welcome "AL-vis!" as he sings the song that won him the contest, "Viva Las Vegas!"

Wayne stepped away, then left the stage for Al to do his thing. Everyone was moving and grooving to his off-key and painful rendition of an Elvis classic. Tom was doubting the fact that everyone knew what they were in for as their new king, "AL-vis" belted out his winning song. Wayne came back on stage but before he had a chance to speak the crowd began chanting something new. Wayne's brow was furrowed as he attempted to discern what they were saying. His eyes lit up once he caught on.

"Do you want him to do one of my *songs?" The answer was quite obvious as the crowd went wild once again. "Alright, alright, which one?" That answer came back quickly and was unanimous. It was the most notable song of Wayne's storied career, "Danke Schoen." This German-titled song translates to "Thank You Very Much" which was a fitting send-off for "AL-vis."*

"Okay, Al." says Wayne. "You heard your fans. They love your Elvis but the question is: can you do me*?"*

"Of course," answers Al with a bit of a swagger.

"Very well then, have at it! Ladies and gentlemen, here by popular demand I give you "AL Newton!"

Cheers and laughter were mixed together as Al stepped up once more to sing. The band kicked into gear and then that fingernails against chalkboard voice of Al's could be heard singing, "Donkey Stains, darling, donkey stains. I thank you for all the mess you made..."

"Wait! Stop the music, stop the music!" Wayne walked over to Al and placed a hand on his shoulder. "Son, what the devil are you singing? Are you saying, "Donkey Stains"?!

"Yes sir. I'm sorry but I really don't know the words."

"You don't know the words." Al nods his head yes. "So you came up with "Donkey Stains." Al nods his head in the affirmative once again. "I'm sure that I am going to regret this but what is the song you are singing about?"

"Well, it's the first thing that came to mind. I remember going into Tom's bedroom this morning to make sure that he was up and there was his underwear on the floor and all I could think of was 'those stains could not have been made by a human'—"

Wayne places his hand over Al's microphone and says, "That's enough. This is a family show. Ladies and gentlemen, please applaud for our new friend, "AL-vis!" and let's wish him well in his future career as an Elvis impersonator."

The audience clapped.

"And let me give Al a piece of advice. Learn the words my friend, learn the words!"

Laughter filled the auditorium.

"One more piece of advice and then I'm taking this show back over. This is for poor old Tom. It is actually two *pieces of advice. First, if you're going to eat another man's spaghetti, get your* own

damn fork! And second, from what I heard about your underwear my meatballs were just a bit too spicy for you, am I right? Okay, Maestro, "Danke Schoen" done my way. *Hit it!"*

The band launched full swing into the song as Al left the stage in search of Tom. He found him off in a corner red-faced and embarrassed.

"This is the worst night of my life. Let's go."

"Aw Tom, he was just messin' with ya. C'mon, be a good sport."

"Let's GO!" Tom was angry and just wanted to leave. Unfortunately, there was one more thing that must be done before they could leave. By contract Al had to do a quick promotional interview for the radio station. The DJ from WHOA radio was standing nearby waiting patiently to get Al's attention.

Al and Tom walked over to the DJ and the camera crew. Al and the DJ spoke for a few minutes before they both seemed to agree on what would happen next. Tom did his very best to shrink away from the lights and cameras.

The cameras were rolling. The DJ stood next to Al as he said, "First of all, congratulations to you for being our first ever winner of *the "WHOA Is That Elvis?!" You were clearly a crowd favorite and you were great fun to follow around Vegas. You and your friend there who is camera shy. I suppose you will want to take him with you on your all-expense paid stay at* Tokyo Vegas*!"*

"Absolutely! It wouldn't be a vacation without my good friend Tom!"

"Don't say my name!" said Tom in a whispered shout.

Al laughed. "Never a dull moment with that one!"

"Let me tell you something, Al. You two guys are the most exciting thing to happen to Vegas since Dean Martin and Jerry Lewis."

"Thank you," replied Al in his trademark Elvis slur. "Thank you very much!"

"Hey, one more thing before we let you go."

"Sure," replied Al, motioning for Tom to join him. Tom refused.

The DJ said, "Not only did you win the contest but you also survived a fall from The Stratosphere Tower. *What do you think you will do now? Go to* Disneyland*?"*

Al laughs and moves over to join Tom. He gives Tom a huge bear hug and says, "This guy gave me the time of my life on Lake Tahoe and then upped the ante here in Vegas. Disneyland*? Hell, no! I got only one thing to say, "Tom, take me to* Tokyo!*"*

The Four Friends

The four men, not including Benny, each went their separate ways to their cars in the parking lot. Once inside they each waited about 10 minutes, time enough for Benny to have left on his own, then the four of them got out of their vehicles and met up once again. They wore troubled faces as they stood in a darkened area of the parking lot to compare each man's takeaway from their time with Benny this evening.

"What should we do?" asked Trevor, the mother hen of the group. "Call his parents?"

"He's not a child!" retorted Adam. "He's a grown man."

"That's true but he *does* still live at home. The question is have they noticed these changes in Benny? Or does he put on an act when he's around them?" Trevor, an avid golfer, always looked at things from every possible perspective. Like reading a putt.

"That would be a tough act to maintain," said Mike. "Don't you think?" Mike was always the pragmatic one. Being in the landscaping business he couldn't just let a problem fester. He had to provide solutions to get positive results.

"I think he needs help," said Jimmy. "Professional help."

"Well that kind of goes without saying," Adam stated, never once to mince words.

"Hey, I *care* about the guy. I'm just trying to help." Jimmy responded defensively.

"Come on, guys!" declared Mike. "We *all* care about Benny. Let's not fight amongst ourselves here. The question should be what can we do to help? Adam, you're an attorney. Do you know someone in the medical field that you could call?"

"What? Only *attorneys* know people in the medical field?" fired back Jimmy.

"My bad, sorry for that, alright who do *you* know?" asked Mike.

"Uh, me? I don't know nobody. I was just sayin'..."

"Anybody."

"What?"

"Anybody. You don't know *anybody*."

"Yeah, that's what I just said."

"No, you--, never mind. How about we take tonight to sleep on this and we do a Zoom call tomorrow to share ideas?"

Jimmy said, "That sounds good to me, Mike."

Trevor said, "Count me in."

"Okay," Adam chimed in, "how about I be the one to start the call from my office? You guys tend to be out and about more so than me."

"That makes sense," said Trevor and the others shook their heads in agreement.

"Okay, 10 am work for everyone?"

Once again they all shook their heads in unison.

"One last thing," said Adam. "Do you think he is a danger to anyone? Including *himself?*"

That was not a question which any of them truly wanted to answer but Mike stepped up and said soberly, "I sure hope not."

Part Three

Take Me To Tokyo

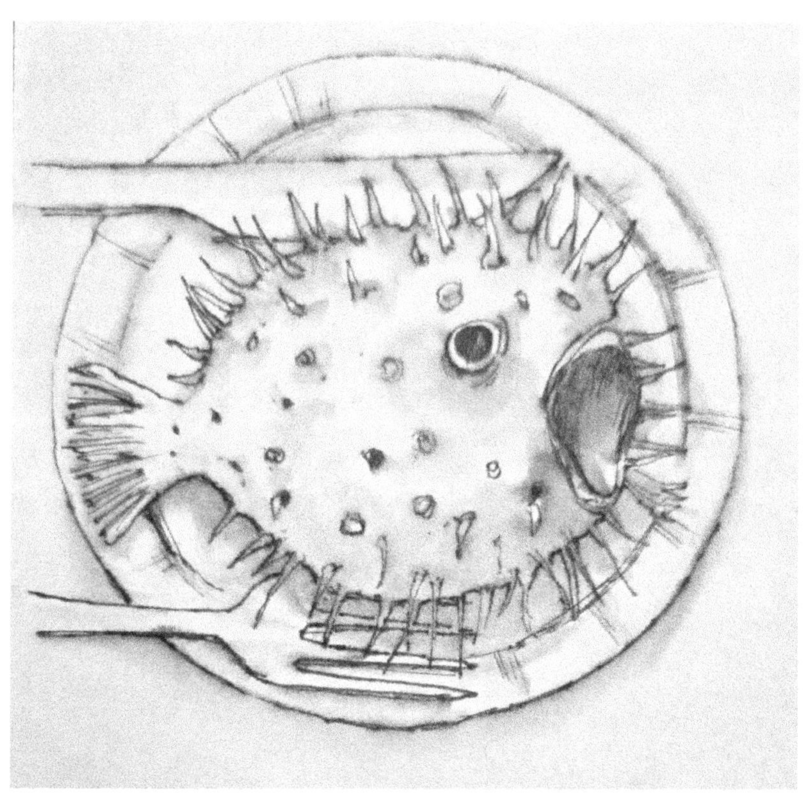

Tokyo Vegas - Day One

Al & Tom

'No rest for the wicked' Tom is thinking to himself as he trudges through the lobby of The Strat. The fact that he is leaving one incredible complimentary Vegas hotel suite for another seems to be lost on him. As a matter of fact he is so caught up in feeling sorry for himself that he doesn't catch sight of the incomparable Wayne Newton in civilian clothes waiting to return to *his* suite.

Al of course saw him and waved. Wayne, ever gracious, smiled and gave a hearty wave back. There was a side-eye glance directed at Tom which of course never landed. A handful of intrepid fans from the night before were on hand to offer fanfare to the new and now undisputed Elvis Impersonator Contest Winner. Al took the ownership of his new crown quite seriously and bowed to his admirers. This did nothing to allay Tom's irritation with Al.

Al had told Tom that he had called an Uber for them but that was a lie. He told Tom that mistruth for two reasons, one so he would get moving and not bitch about having to deal with public transit and two, because he wanted to surprise him. **Tokyo Vegas,** the all-new Tokyo themed casino hotel resort, had actually sent a limo to pick the two up and whisk them away to their all-expense paid stay. This would be something really special.

Meanwhile, there is a 10 am Zoom Call with the "Four Friends"

Jimmy clicked on the JOIN icon and then Adam's face filled the screen.

"Hey Adam," said Jimmy.

"You're muted," said Adam.

Jimmy went to click on the microphone and then realized that Adam was just pulling his leg. "That joke never gets old for you, does it?"

"Nope!" said Adam and he then proceeded to do the same to Mike and Trevor.

"How is everyone feeling this morning?" asked Jimmy.

"'No worse for the wear,' as my Grandpa used to say." This from Mike.

"Mike, I have not heard that idiom in years!" said Trevor.

"Yep, it's an old expression," said Adam.

"I thought it was a phrase," said Jimmy.

"It's actually all of the above. Guys, you ready to get moving on this Benny thing?"

The other three gave a thumbs up as they had now muted their microphones to allow for Adam to start their meeting.

"So," Adam began. "I called Benny's parents."

The three friends leaned in towards the screen once they heard that, eager to know what Adam had learned. Adam already knew that his answer would disappoint but he had to share it anyway.

"There was no answer. As a matter of fact, there was no *service*. Benny's parents might have been the last people in America to still have a landline." He paused while they all chuckled. "But no more."

There was a muted response from the group as they considered how they might somehow get in touch with Benny's parents without his knowledge.

"Guys." Adam had everyone's full attention. "I also called the school."

Adam allowed that to sink in for a moment. Benny of course worked at the high school they had attended. It seemed like a rather bold move on Adam's part but hey, he was an attorney and he could talk his way out of anything.

"And?" prompted Jimmy, wary now of the look of concern that had come over Adam's face.

"I spoke with Principal Tharp."

"What?!" exclaimed Trevor. "He's *still* there?!"

This remark went without additional comments as this was not new news. Trevor had a tendency to forget things and then be surprised when he heard them again.

Mike got the call back on track.

"Is everything okay? What did Tharp have to say?"

"Well," Adam began, "this is quite troubling. He said that Benny walked in a few days ago and just quit."

"He quit?!" The three friends said this unison.

"I figured he would be there forever!" said Jimmy as the others nodded their heads in agreement.

"Yeah, well that's not all. This is even more disturbing. Principal Tharp said that Benny seemed somehow *different* to him. He said he was surly, disengaged and even rude."

"That doesn't sound like the Benny we know at *all*." Mike paused, then added, "but it sure *does* sound like the Benny we were with last night."

"Yeah it does," agreed Jimmy. "Why would he not tell *us* that he quit his job?"

"Yeah, what's up with that?!" chimed in Trevor.

"That's not all the Principal said."

Everyone was now quiet with their full attention being given to Adam and what he was to say next.

"Principal Tharp was quite concerned about Benny's behavior. When he came in that day to, well, quit, I guess he upset several students by not seeming to know who they were and brushing them aside like they were just annoyances to him. He even cursed at a few of them to leave him alone."

"That's *not* Benny," said Jimmy.

"Yeah, that's what Principal Tharp said as well. So *he* called Benny's parents."

"What did they say?" asked Trevor.

"He had the same problem I had. Their number is no longer in service."

The three friends were shaking their heads and showing their disappointment fearing they had reached a dead end.

"That's not the end of it."

Everyone's ears perked up.

"The principal went down to their house. No one was home. And by that I mean *no one*. The place was cleaned out. Empty. Vacant."

There was a shared gasp from the group.

"Principal Tharp said that as he was peering through the windows a nervous neighbor approached him to ask what business he had at the house. The principal said that after explaining who he was and his association with Benny the neighbor opened up and said that it was the 'strangest thing.' One day Benny was personable and chatty, the next he seemed like he had a chip on his shoulder and was moving his parents out of their home to an extended care facility."

"What the hell?" exclaimed Jimmy. "What happened to them? I thought they were pretty healthy for their age. Certainly not in need of a care facility!"

"That is almost verbatim what the neighbor said. You know, *something* about this, no, actually "*everything,"* about this, is just not right. I'm worried about Benny if that *is* Benny. And I'm worried about his parents."

"Adam, how could it *not* be Benny? We saw him ourselves!"

"Yeah we did and we all thought the same thing. We all *know* Benny and that *wasn't* Benny." Since that thought seemed like it did not square up with reality he added, "It sure didn't *seem* like him anyway."

"So what do we do now?" asked Trevor.

Adam responded. "I say we keep digging until we find an answer. Let me know if any of you hear from Benny. If you do, don't say *anything* about what has just been shared but please, *please* try to find out where he is if at all possible. Call me right away if that happens."

They all agreed to the plan as they signed off. Once Adam's screen went blank he whispered to himself, 'Benny, what *have* you done?' It was a question to which he feared learning the answer. Adam was a worst-case scenario thinker and he was already doubting the true whereabouts of Benny's parents. While he believed that wherever they had been moved to that they were at rest now, a nagging thought somewhere in the back of his mind suggested that "at rest" might mean something *else* and they might be somewhere *other* than an extended care facility.

Al & Tom - Magic Carpet Ride

Grumpy Tom's eyes lit up when he caught sight of the limo and then saw the chauffeur walk up to Al to take his luggage. Tom eagerly surrendered his own meager stash next and then there he was with Al, comfortably seated in the lap of luxury as though this were a magic carpet ride. The limo pulled away from The Strat and the onlooking gawkers eager to get a peek at the "celebrities" inside the limo. Soon they were leaving the strip and heading east towards Henderson and Lake Las Vegas.

The glitz, the glamour and the high-rise hotels were fast behind them as the limo headed north on Interstate 15 and then southeast on Interstate 11. It was an unexpected sight for Tom to see the sprawling growth of suburbs which now cradled the Vegas Strip. There was not much of interest to see beyond that at the moment so Tom settled back in his seat. Much to his surprise, Al suddenly produced two cups of Starbucks coffee for them to sip on for the duration of the trip. Tom was now feeling like royalty.

Tom and Al were in full relaxation mode so they did not notice that the scenery outside the window had changed once again no longer hiding the fact that they were fully ensconced in the dessert. Inside this world of leather luxury, the limo was comfortable with the air conditioning efficiently doing its work. Outside the temperature was hovering around the 100-degree mark. They would experience a blast of that sweltering heat the moment they stepped out of the limo. For now though they were just enjoying the ride.

The Four Friends - Their first lead

The email read, 'Guys, I think I found Benny.'

The others were quick to reply, 'How did you find him?'

Adam replied, 'I have a buddy who can track down credit card purchases. He told me this one was easy because the purchase had been flagged for a funds issue. "Benny" charged a flight to Reno.'

'Wow, that's great!' wrote Jimmy. 'Wait, isn't that the airport that you fly into when going to Lake Tahoe?'

'Oh yeah, that's right,' wrote Adam. 'Why Tahoe though? Do you think there is a connection here with Al? Or Tom? I mean at this point, who knows? There is still much more work to do to get to the bottom of this but at least we have a lead.'

'Do we though, really?' typed Jimmy.

'Do we really WHAT?' Adam wrote.

Mike had already been typing so his comment came in out of place. 'Reno? Lake Tahoe? What the hell? Why would Benny go to any of those places?!'

'Have a lead.' Jimmy responded to Adam's earlier question.

'At this point it is really ALL that we have so yes, I am calling it a "lead." What is causing you to question it?' Adam pressed.

'Did you check the date of travel?' Jimmy wrote.

There was a pause of only a few seconds but it seemed longer as they all waited for the reply, each of them coming to roughly the same conclusion.

'Gentlemen,' Adam wrote. 'The date of travel matches the date of travel in the tall tale Benny shared with us about Al and Tom. And–'

'And??' prompted Mike.

'And a buddy of mine just sent me a follow up email. You're not going to believe this'

It was so unlike Adam to miss anything in his grammar or punctuation so the missing period at the end of the last sentence was kind of a big deal.

'Try us.' wrote Mike.

'That same credit card was flagged at the Reno Airport Car Rental place for lack of funds. No surprise there because I think Benny only used that card once in a blue moon. He never went anywhere or did much out of his usual routine.' There was another pause. 'And yes of course, the card being flagged at the rental car place matches up with the date of the tall tale fiasco. Damn! I am beginning to think that Benny's story was REAL.'

Trevor had been typing furiously to put in his two cents worth. His message eerily blinked on the screen the moment the others had finished reading Adam's message. 'Think about it for a minute,' wrote Trevor. 'What have we been talking about? Maybe Benny *isn't* Benny.'

No one responded. They all knew where he was going with this so Trevor decided that he would go ahead and call out the 800-pound elephant in the room.

'Maybe *Benny* is really *Tom*.'

No one was quite sure how that could truly be or how it could even be possible but none of them could discard the idea either.

'I have an appointment I need to get to,' shared Adam, 'but we can't allow this to get away from us. Should we do another Zoom call?'

The other three members of the four friends quickly typed, 'YES!'

Al & Tom - *Tokyo Vegas*

Tokyo Vegas was intentionally perched on the side of a mountain slope at the northeastern ridge of Lake Las Vegas to be in harmony with its surroundings. As though that was even possible. While it might seem like it was an odd juxtaposition of a Tokyo themed resort to be placed so near to the Tuscan inspired private homes on the South Shore and the taste of Italy to be found when walking about MonteLago Village, one need only consider that within a few city blocks on the Las Vegas Strip, you can experience the ambiance of a castle at Excalibur, the sphinx and a pyramid at the Luxor, the Eiffel Tower at Paris Las Vegas and the skyscrapers of New York City at New York New York.

Tom was fascinated with how much the view from the limo changed along the way of their journey to Tokyo Vegas. First there was the towering, themed casinos with scores of pedestrians making their way along the Strip and then they were on a short stretch of highway. Moments later they were crossing a remote desert far from civilization. And then, just like that, they were entering another mystical and magical world.

Lake Las Vegas is a shimmering oasis in an otherwise forbidding landscape. Dotting the surrounding hills are private Tuscan-inspired homes to the south and vacation villas to the north. Both sides featured incredible golf courses with palm trees waving in the arid breeze. A massive hotel complex occupied the shoreline of the northwestern portion of the lake which was as blue as one could possibly imagine.

Just then it came into view, the jewel of the crown, the sparkling all-new Tokyo Vegas Hotel & Casino. And it was simply... breathtaking.

Once Al and Tom stepped out of the limo they braved only a moment of intense heat before the air-conditioned cool of the casino hotel welcomed them into a land of enchantment. The General Manager of the hotel greeted them as they entered, which meant there was no need for them to visit the Reception Desk. The two would later learn that a trip to the Reception Desk would require a brief walk across a replica of the famed Niju Bridge to the heralded rampart of the Imperial Palace as a backdrop. The effect would have been well worth the journey.

Al and Tom glanced down to see that the GM had handed them both a proximity key card to their room as well as a Rewards Card to use while gambling. During the brief interchange with the GM a server from the bar had approached to hand each of them a complimentary cocktail from the bar.

"What is this?" asked Tom. He took a sip and his eyes lit up. "Oh my! This is SO refreshing!"

The GM stated with elegance, "That sir is a Yuzu Highball, one of our most popular offerings here at Tokyo Vegas. I hope you enjoy. Please call upon me should you need anything, anything at all." He then actually bowed before stepping away.

"Wow!" Tom said. "This is amazing! I feel like a king!"

"*I AM the King*, thank you very much," stated Al with his now overused Elvis slur. "The King of Rock and Roll."

"You are–," Tom began with several choice words in mind but did not finish his thought. None of this would be happening right now if not for Al.

"I am what?" pressed Al.

"You are–*so right*," said Tom a bit cheekily. 'Nice scramble there' he thought to himself.

Al smiled smugly and the two headed off to their room. The Japanese gardens that they passed through on their way seemed to have a calming effect on both. The wallpapered hallways featured a mix of Yoshino cherry trees in different states of bloom.

When Al and Tom stepped into their room both gasped. From the view through the windows to the incredible opulence all about them there was no describing their initial reactions. Both stood in awe for a moment just taking it all in.

"How did our luggage get here before us?!" asked Tom.

"You're so weird!" exclaimed Al.

"Why do you say that?" Tom fired back.

"We're here, in the lap of luxury, surrounded by all of - THIS! And the luggage thing, THAT'S what impresses you?!"

"Shut up," Tom said glumly.

"Whatever," responded Al. "I'm going down to the casino to play some blackjack and WIN SOME MONEY!!"

Tom loved the idea of losing Al for a while. "Sounds like a plan. I'm going to hang out in the room for a few minutes then go check out the resort."

"Okay, I will see you later!" Al said as he was leaving.

"Yep. See ya."

Tom. Alone at last. Bliss.

The Four Friends - Go West Young Men!

The following day the four friends jumped on a Zoom call which was once again initiated by Adam. Each of the four men were dressed appropriate to their business. Adam was in a suit and tie. Trevor sported a golf shirt with the stitched logo of his golf academy prominently displayed. Mike was wearing the uniform of his landscaping business. He always wore what his guys wore whether he was cutting grass or at a business meeting. His comment when asked about his attire was always, 'I *work* for a living.' The odd man out at this session was Jimmy who seemed a bit more stressed than usual. He was generally a bit high strung but today his focus was not all there.

"What the *hell* are you wearing?" asked Trevor.

"Me?" asked Jimmy.

"Of course *you*! Everyone else on this call looks *normal*."

The other three laughed as Jimmy pinched his shirt to pull it closer to the camera for a better view. His shirt was the uniform shirt worn by his employees at the drive-thru burger kiosks which he owned. Thirty plus locations to date. The shirt, like all uniforms, was an odd blue fashioned from colors not found in nature. Jimmy always said that they were from the "mistake mixes" that they sold cheap to uniform companies. Jimmy's uniform also had an overly large logo printed, not stitched, on it to save a few pennies on cost.

"Yeah, I stopped by one of my lower volume units for a quick visit and they put me to work!"

"Seriously?" asked Adam, not containing his laughter. "What? Are you working drive-thru today?"

"Hey guys, I WORK for a living, alright!" Jimmy said in jest.

"Um, excuse me, but that's MY line!" Mike had jumped in.

"Is that what you call it? *Work?*" joked Adam.

"You really want to go there? 'Mr. Never Gets His Hands Dirty'?" Jimmy jibed.

Trevor piped in. "Go easy on Adam fellas. As an attorney his hands are *always* dirty!"

"Alright, alright, let's get back on track. I have an appointment in ten minutes and Jimmy has a grill order to attend to."

Adam's comment brought a chuckle out of the other three and then they got to the matter at hand. Adam quickly brought them up to speed with what his investigation had brought to light. There were a few comments back and forth but it was Trevor once again that cut right to the heart of the matter.

"You know whether we were talking to "Benny" or to "Tom" is not the issue at this point. What matters most is what happens next---"

"Trev, what do you mean?" asked Adam.

"I mean, if this Al fella is a real person and Benny is not who we think he is, then Al may be in danger. *Real* danger."

"What are you suggesting? asked Mike.

"Well, if the story he was telling is true..."

The other three leaned in waiting for Trevor to continue.

"Then I think that they are both still in Vegas. Most likely they are at that swanky new resort **Tokyo Vegas**."

Jimmy jumped into the conversation. "Are you saying that we should contact the authorities out there? What would we even tell them? They're not going to believe the crackpot story that we have to tell."

"Nope! I think you're absolutely right, it's a crazy story and too hard to explain. No, I say that we *go there* and *find them* ourselves. Whatever Benny, or this Tom, is up to, we need to put a stop to it. Can each of you get away for a few days?"

Each of the four friends looked at their phones, checking their appointments and calendars. Within minutes they agreed that yes they could find the time to fly to Vegas to track down their friend Benny. He was a lifelong friend. They at least owed him that much.

Al & Tom - Ticket to Tokyo

Tom leaves the room to take a grand tour of the fabulous Tokyo Vegas. He finds the casino to be almost boring. Everything was in red, which is interesting but other than that it was ALL business. This was a serious casino. That's not to say that the patrons were not enjoying themselves but rather that it was a more "civilized" atmosphere than that of other casinos he had visited. No screaming, yelling and jumping up and down.

The hotel section was beautifully adorned but not ostentatious. So far Tokyo Vegas was possibly a bit understated for all the hype it had received, or so thought Tom thought until he arrived at the main courtyard.

It bore the name ***Tokyo Nights.***

And it was--- **WOW**.

Tom had never been to Tokyo. Until now. Ane even though he was not REALLY in Tokyo he could not help but mutter to himself, *'could have fooled me'!*

This courtyard space was, no other way to describe it, the bustling city of Tokyo with shops and food stalls aplenty. If one were to look off into the distance they would be greeted with the grandeur of Mount Fuji some 60 miles away.

There was a gentle breeze in the air which Tom felt quite comforting. As he walked about he was quite taken with the cleanliness of the space. And though he knew that he was in a building rather than an actual city he remembered that he had heard that Tokyo was a very clean city. Unlike Americans the Japanese people did not walk about with food or drink in hand. These items were consumed at the place where they were purchased which greatly lessened the opportunity for loose trash to be cast aside.

As Tom meandered about the various "streets" of Tokyo he suddenly realized that he was famished. Because this version of Tokyo was in America there was English subtitles to be found everywhere so he easily located a restaurant.

The restaurant is called "Unagi." Tom scanned the lighted menu board outside of the restaurant and found that he liked many of the items he saw. Tom, however, would be the first to admit that he did not have much of a daring palette. The stir fry and California Roll were at the extreme end of his taste. He went inside, found a table and had a *fantastic* lunch.

Al & Tom – Winning Streak

No surprise, Al is winning again! He has been at the same craps table for hours and surely enough his luck had changed. The hootin' and hollerin' which Al was making could be heard all about the casino. Soon he had amassed a crowd of onlookers urging him on to keep the streak alive. Additional security arrived but held their positions discreetly so as not to disturb or offend their patrons. Winning was allowed here as long as one did not overdo it, lol.

Al was having the time of his life and lost in the moment, not realizing that he had missed lunch and it was nearing dinner time. He had just begun to give back some of his winnings when the pangs of hunger urged him to leave the table in search of food. The pit boss was clearly disappointed that Al was leaving before he could return more of his good fortune.

When Al stepped away from the table the crowd dispersed to find other pursuits. Al need only an upward glance to see signs which would direct him to restaurant row which was nestled in the heart of downtown "Tokyo." Al headed in that direction with gusto and a pocketful of the casino's money.

The Four Friends - World Wide Web

Within 48 hours the four friends, Adam, Mike, Jimmy and Trevor had each boarded a plane in their respective cities, all of them headed for Las Vegas. Adam flew first class while the others flew economy. For each of them it was by choice. This shouldn't paint Adam as uppity or snobbish. He was every bit as grounded and humble as the others. The difference maker for him was the simple fact that he had the longest flight and the most work to do while on the flight. With first class he would gain free Wi-Fi and this would give him access to that all too easily now taken for granted miracle creation known in its early days as the world wide web. Now it was simply the internet.

The plan was for the four of them to meet up at Tokyo Vegas where they would all be staying. That was the most pragmatic and simple plan. But–simple isn't always easy. What they quickly discovered was that Tokyo Vegas was currently the hottest ticket in town. The resort had been booked months in advance of their grand opening.

The next best thing was to book their rooms at The Westin Lake Las Vegas. This was a sprawling resort which for years had looked out upon a serene lake and a sparse mountain range with a brilliant blue sky as the backdrop. Over time the shores became populated with Tuscan-inspired homes on one side and million-dollar Italian-influenced villas on the other. The lake became home to recreational kayakers, paddleboarders and the more serious folks who belonged to the Lake Las Vegas Rowing Club.

Adam was not looking that far ahead at the moment. He had settled into his seat in first class on the plane and they had just reached cruising altitude. He waved off the complimentary champagne in favor of a cup of black coffee. This airline served Seattle's Best which conveniently was his preference for coffee.

Adam logged on to find an internet connection eager to take him wherever he wished to go on the world wide web. His plan was to do a deep dive into Benny's life but a little voice inside his head told him to start with the parents. He listened and the voice was right. As Adam looked back further through the years what he discovered quickly brought clarity to the foggy situation which Benny's friends had found themselves in.

A few of the other passengers in first class were also engaged in work on their laptops so the gentle tapping that Adam made on his keypad was not at all an annoyance to them. There was, however, *three* times where Adam emitted an unexpected gasp at what he was seeing on the screen. The first two times the passengers closest to Adam in first class looked over at him with the "excuse me" look given when one is out of place. The third time their gazes were less forgiving and he was forced to apologize before moving on. He now had the attention of the flight attendant as well. But Adam said to himself, if these folks only knew what he had just uncovered they too would be making an audible gasp. This information was nothing short of life-changing.

Potentially *lifesaving* as well.

Al & Tom - Menu Find

Tom had just finished his meal and was heading out of the restaurant "Unagi" when a familiar face caught his eye.

"Part-Time?!"

The young man Tom knew as Part-Time laughed as he heard the name and said, "That's funny! They call *me* Part-Time *too!*"

Tom shook his head in befuddlement. What was *with* this guy?

"I know that! I was talking to *you!*"

"Oh, well hey! How are you? Wait! I *know* you!" Part-Time suddenly seemed eager to carry on the conversation.

"The guy from The Stratosphere, right?" Tom supplied the answer.

Part-Time looked confused. "Nope." He shook his head and said, "Sorry, I thought you was somebody else."

Rather than go down that road Tom made small talk, "So you work here now?"

Part-Time replied, "Yeah, I got *fired* at my other job so I work here now part-time.."

"Like your name?"

"Ha ha, yeah. What? I don't get it."

"The name on your shirt---. Never mind."

"Yeah, they call me 'Part-Time' so they gave me this shirt..."

Tom tuned him out. He has seen this movie before. Too many times actually. Just then Al showed up. He looked ravenous. Tom was thankful that he had already eaten. Like most things watching someone else eat *bothered* him. He would try to evade Al if at all possible.

Too late.

"There you are!" shouted Al.

Tom's shoulders sagged and his head pitched forward. He found himself suddenly in Al's grasp with no other alternative but to join him for his meal. Tom would have to endure an hour's worth of hearing the story of how Al commanded the craps table and how the crowd had cheered him on. Blah, blah, blah. And then---

"Wait! *What* did you say?!"

Al gave him the side-eye before repeating, "I can't believe that they have pufferfish on their menu. That has been on my bucket list for years!"

"Pufferfish you say? Let me see that." Tom reaches for the menu. Sure enough there it was, a picture of a "prepared" pufferfish but–the description of the item was written in Japanese. Tom wasn't sure that he would have recognized it had Al not pointed it out. "How did you find this? I looked all over that menu and didn't see it."

"That's because you looked at the *American* menu. This is a specially printed menu for Japanese tastes." Al was beaming with pride with having put one over on Tom.

"Whatever," said Tom as he scanned the menu realizing now that *everything* was written in Japanese. He changed his tone as a new thought occurred to him. "So you actually *like* the taste of pufferfish?"

"I don't know. I have never tried it. But I want to!!"

"Hmm," said Tom, "isn't that, um, *poisonous*?"

"Sure, it can be but I would *definitely* trust it in a place like this."

Al looked up and around indicating the Tokyo Vegas resort. Then Tom thought to himself, '*Of course* it would be safe in a place like this because it would be prepared by a *certified* chef who was *qualified* to prepare such a meal.

But---, *what if* a lesser qualified cook prepared it?

Perhaps someone who only worked *"part-time"*?

"That's a devilish grin. What *are* you thinking about?"

Tom smiled, "It might surprise you but I was just thinking about treating you to a great meal."

"But I just ate!"

"Not now! But hey, we will be here for a few days. It is *my turn* to treat *you.* And trust me." Tom said this as he tossed the menu onto the table. "This dinner, *my* treat, will be *incredible.* Honestly, it will be-- *to die for!*"

The Four Friends - Follow Al, *not* Benny

A severe weather system was in the works in the Midwest which meant that there were flight delays for the other three and a course diversion for Adam's flight. The news shared by the captain over the intercom was met with instant moans and groans from most of the passengers of the fully booked flight.

At this point in time Adam could not have said with absolute certainty that a life hung in the balance and that every minute counted but he was reasonably sure that it was true and that was enough to scare the hell out of him. Upon hearing the news he immediately emailed his three friends to let them know that he would not be arriving in Vegas until the next day. His friends were quick to respond stating that with the exception of Jimmy who was flying from Utah *their* flights had been either delayed or cancelled as well. Adam set about to changing the room reservations for all four of them.

Once on the ground as his plane was taxiing to the gate Adam felt the compulsion to text the guys one last thing. He needed them to be on the same page as him regarding the situation they were now facing.

Adam texted:

'You won't believe what I have found out about Benny. And Benny's parents! *I will fill you in on everything when we get together. One thing I think I can say for sure is that Benny is* NOT *Benny! Not the one* WE *knew anyway. Also, at this point, if we have any hope of saving Al (and I* DO *believe that there* IS *really an Al), then we need to follow* Al's trail, NOT Benny's. *After all, it is this Al fella who is actually paying for everything and Benny, well, he---.'*

The text ended abruptly, then a new text followed:

'Sorry about that, anyway, I have my credit guru sniffing the trail of Al's credit card charges as we speak. Get yourselves emotionally ready for the news that will--. Suffice it to say that it will at the very least shock you and most likely upset you. It's that, um, disturbing. See you all soon in Vegas.'

Mike fired back with a text of his own. *'Is Benny okay?'*

Oddly, at the same moment, each of the three friends responded exactly the same with *'What the---??!!'* as they read the text on their phones from Adam that read:

'Guys, so sad to tell you that with what I know now, I think it is a safe bet (no Vegas pun intended) to say that Benny, AND his parents, might well be – deceased.'

Al & Tom - Tokyo at night

When Al and Tom left the restaurant something was *definitely* different. Tom stopped dead causing several people to walk right into him. He did *not* apologize, which was no surprise to Al who did the honor for him.

"Do you notice anything *different*?" Tom asked Al.

Al looked around and then replied complacently, "Well it *is* nighttime."

"THAT'S IT!" exclaimed Tom. "WOW!"

Tom now took the time to really look around and truly gather in what he was seeing. The "sky" had turned dark. No big deal, right? That always happened when day turned to night except--- they were inside! The ceiling which previously had been projecting a blue sky with wisps of clouds moving about was now a black night sky with twinkling stars. And yes! An occasional shooting star for good measure.

All of the "city" was now lit up with the typical lights of a city with neon banners grabbing the attention of pedestrians. And there were "street sounds" in this city although there were of course no vehicles present. Still though, the effect was incredible.

This was the shopping and dining district in the Tokyo Vegas Resort and it was true to its namesakes. The glitz and glamour of Vegas, the charm and intensity of Tokyo wrapped into one. Tom could spend a whole week here. Tokyo nights with *so* much fun to be had.

"Well, well, well."

The dream vanished in an instant. The effect of Tokyo city was still omnipresent but the thought of enjoying himself had disappeared with *that* voice speaking *those* three words.

"Glad you could finally make it."

"Thank you for killing the moment." Tom said desultorily. "Like always."

"Well, someone had to do something. You were standing in the middle of the walkway with your arms outstretched looking like a fool. People were having to find their way around you."

"Oh yeah Al? Well people have to find their way around *you* all the time."

"Nice comeback, repeating my own words. *So* clever. Hey, which way would I look to see Mount Fuji?"

Tom pointed and said, "It's right there..."

But it wasn't.

Tom was certain that he had seen it earlier and then he realized that you would not be able to see it at night. The two continued walking through the streets of Tokyo. Al busied himself with telling of his good fortune at the craps table while Tom concerned himself with the formulation of a plan involving a bucket list dinner *poorly prepared* by a "part-time" chef.

Tokyo Vegas - Day Two

Al & Tom - To each his own

The next day found Tom playing golf on an exclusive golf course with incredible scenery all around. He should be having the time of his life. He wasn't. The fact that the temperature had hit 104 degrees had not swayed him from taking advantage of a free round of golf, courtesy of the hotel. This was an ultra-private club and a Jack Nicklaus Signature golf course. Tom was not passing up this opportunity no matter what the boys in the Pro Shop tried to tell him about the potential for heat exhaustion.

Al had other things in mind. He parked himself inside a cabana at the pool, safe from the scorching heat of the sun but in close proximity to the bar. The Yuzu highball was his drink of choice and with no thought given to the time of day, (it's 5 o'clock somewhere), he told the attractive pool server to get them coming. He was out by his third drink.

To get the *full* experience, Tom teed off from the tips. This lasted for all of two holes. He had only twelve golf balls in the bag and he had already lost four of them just trying to get to the fairway. There were five sets of tees on this course. By the time he made the turn Tom had advanced to the senior tee. He was playing by himself so there was no need to make up a story about some prior injury which *forced* him to hit from that tee.

"Wakey, wakey."

Al's heavy eyelids fluttered open with some amount of effort. "Yes?"

"Sir, your time here at the cabana has expired. There are other guests waiting to use this amenity."

"But I just got here," argued Al. "I have until 11am."

"You are correct sir. It is now 1pm. The hotel has been gracious enough to allow you to sleep through *lunch*. We have not needed this cabana until *now* so there was no need to rouse you." The hotel manager paused for a moment before continuing. "Will you need assistance in finding your way to your suite?"

Al blinked his eyes several times, looked at the couple waiting anxiously for their time in the cabana and then said, "No, that will not be necessary. I'm up. And I'm fine."

Al stood up, wobbled unsteadily for a moment and then gingerly made his way through the pool complex to the doors of the hotel. The hotel manager and the young couple who now occupied the cabana might have been making bets under their breath as to whether Al would end up in the hotel or in the pool.

It was the hotel.

Once inside the hotel room Al collapsed on the bed and was out like a light.

The heat was oppressive. Tom was unable to drink enough water to offset what his body was losing. Any normal person would have turned their golf cart around and headed towards the clubhouse. Tom, however, was stubborn as hell and refused to let the course and the elements win. He lost five golf balls on one tee box just trying to get over the expanse of a canyon. Tom was not opposed to cheating so he finally just dropped a ball on the other side. Without taking a stroke. Even though he had just hit five penalty shots.

Note to self: You can't shoot 80 if you count all the *bad* shots. Just count the *good* ones!

This was a sprawling golf course with generous fairways and well-manicured greens. All of that was lost on Tom as he trudged through his round. If asked he would be unable to describe the final four holes of the course. He was so close to passing out that he had no memory of them. When he arrived back at the clubhouse the kind man in the Pro Shop dispatched the caddie (which Tom had refused earlier, he had no money with which to tip him anyway) to escort Tom back to his room safely.

Just like Al had done only an hour earlier Tom collapsed onto his bed. Before the caddie could leave the room Al stirred in his bed. He looked around sleepily, saw Tom crashed out in his bed and a young lad who had no doubt brought him here preparing to leave.

"My wallet."

"Sir?" said the young caddie.

"My wallet there next to the TV. Go ahead and pull a fifty out." Al saw the surprised look on the kid's face. "For you troubles." Al pointed a finger at Tom.

"You don't have to do that sir."

This kid was way too kind. Al snorted and said, "Look at it this way kid. Fifty bucks is nothing compared to what you're saving me if it had been necessary for Security to bring him in here. Grab a fifty. You earned it."

"Thank you sir. Thank you!"

There was no further response from Al. He was already snoring. The caddie let himself out of the room thinking to himself that this errand had actually paid off. Sad but true, the guy that gave him the fifty was probably *always* bailing out his loser buddy.

Al & Tom - It will be *my* treat

A few hours later both Al and Tom were up and moving about their hotel room. neither could say that they were rested. Al had a killer headache and Tom felt like all the strength in his body had been sucked out of him. It was fair to say that neither was in a particularly good mood. Such was the onset of a perfect storm.

Al and Tom looked like two drunken sailors as they made their way down the hotel hallway to the elevator. They were headed down to the food court for some salty food and gallons of water. Both were still a bit unsteady on their feet. Al from sucking down three highballs and Tom, whose skin was now bright red from soaking up a nuclear reactor's share of ultraviolet rays from the sun. Tom is speaking heatedly (no pun intended) with Al about an as yet unresolved issue.

"Listen, Al. I'm about to give you the greatest meal experience of your life."

"And I thank you for that! What a great friend!"

"Yeah, right. About that "friend" business. How can I call you a friend if you won't release those papers? Just notarize them and hand them over to me. No big deal. It will take all of two minutes and our work is done. Then we can enjoy being in this amazing city at this fabulous resort!" Tom is doing his best to sound both convincing and sincere.

"But I already AM enjoying myself! Those papers can wait. Besides, I still have not heard from Benny yet. I need *his* approval before I can finalize those papers."

"THAT'S what you have been waiting on?! A call from Benny?! I can arrange *that* with no problem. Just give me a time that works for you. I will have him call the room and I promise to be *somewhere else* so that you will have the room to yourself with NO distractions!"

There was a new urgency to Tom's voice now. It was tinged with just an edge of eager anticipation.

"Well, I would prefer to meet with Benny *in person.*"

"That's impossible." Tom said flatly.

"Impossible?" inquired Al. The two had stopped once again. Al moved them over to the side to allow for patrons to walk freely past them. "Impossible *why*?"

Tom seemed flustered by the question. "Hello! We're in Las Vegas and he's in Ohio! Duh!"

Al crunched up his face while reading Tom's facial expression. There was much to be gained by reading a person's face. But right now Tom was a closed book. He was hiding something. This releasing of the papers (documents) he had been asked to notarize was a very big deal to him. Knowing this Al had admittedly dangled that need as a carrot to get Tom to go along with him to Lake Tahoe and now to Vegas but–something was decidedly not right about the whole "papers thing" but he just couldn't seem to be able to put his finger on it.

"Okay. Deal."

"What?!" Tom's demeanor changed in an instant like a crying child who has just realized that there is no parent around to see the "boo boo."

"You have Benny call me tomorrow at, let's say 3pm which would be 12noon in Ohio and I will get what I need from him and *then* I will be able to have the papers finalized."

"Really?!" Tom asked eagerly.

"Really," said Al with a soothing calm in his voice. "And then maybe *you* can relax and enjoy yourself for once."

"While you're having your bucket list dinner of exotic pufferfish I will be perusing the documents to be sure that all is in order. You go on and do, whatever. I'm going to run back to that restaurant and get us a reservation for tomorrow evening. I can't read Japanese but it looked like there was a 24-hour notice required for that dish like they do with duck. This is one dinner that you will never forget!"

With that Tom was off in a flash.

He did not hear Al say, 'but I won't have the papers *with* me...'

The Four Friends - The Truth About Tahoe Tom

It is late in the day when all four friends finally meet up in the courtyard area of The Westin Lake Las Vegas. On the horizon the early evening sky is already showing the spectacular colors found only in this part of the country. The four men have found seats for themselves in overstuffed chairs circled about a stone fire pit which was already giving off heat to ward off the cool night air.

A server arrived only moments after they were seated to take drink orders. They ordered reflexively although each of them would have argued (if asked) that they were famished and in need of food. The cocktails, however, would be the appropriate choice for all that they were about to hear. The restaurants at The Westin were fantastic but since their destination was the fabulous new Tokyo Vegas, they all decided to eat there because... *'when in Rome'* which only made sense because grammar had lost its place in social discourse.

Before Adam began with his oral treatise about all that he had learned about Benny and his parents, the four of them took a few minutes to relax and soak in their surroundings.

The air was crisp and cool but not cold. The night sky was fast approaching from the west and they were all in awe of how black the sky would become. There was so little "light pollution" around them that the gallery of stars above took one's breath away.

Before the final light of the sun had faded below the horizon the guys had taken in the sights available to them. The pool was in view and it was a virtual paradise surrounded as it was by towering palms. The hotel was perched higher up on the edge of land which presented the courtyard as something of an amphitheater to all that was below.

A small but active marina was off to the right with boats rocking gently to and fro in the mild chop. Further right was a pedestrian bridge and beyond one of the greens of the golf course skirted this area of the lake. There were no golfers at this hour of the day. Looking to the left was a growing collection of homes that by design gave credibility to the feel of an authentic and vibrant Italian countryside community.

Across the lake there was the incredible newly opened Tokyo Vegas. As fabulous as it was those who chose to make their life here in Lake Las Vegas saw it as a stain on their landscape. They had fought hard to prevent its construction but like other new ventures before this one their valiant fight lost to the irrepressible force of progress.

There was still a bad taste in the mouth of those residents who could remember the loss (by way of a hedge fund manager from New York City) of "The Falls," an incredible golf course designed by the legendary professional golfer Tom Weiskopf.

"The Falls" was particularly known for its back nine which had dramatic elevation changes from start to finish. The signature hole featured a green surrounded almost entirely by rock. An intriguing element to that green was the oddity of the auditory experience. One could whisper and still hear a pin drop from across the green.

Adam broke the pensive mood of the group by asking the question, "Is everyone ready for what I have to share?"

The other three men looked up and each nodded their head. The place where they were seated was on a stepped courtyard leading down to the lake. There was a wall behind them and they were gathered around a fire pit facing one another. The benefit of this was that Adam could speak openly without concern of anyone eavesdropping on their conversation.

For the next twenty minutes Adam explained how he wove his way through the tapestry of information available to the public. The weave was tight but once he was able to discern the pattern of the fabric the navigation began to make more sense.

Two minutes into Adam's comments Trevor urged him to "lose the area rug metaphors" and just get on with the story. They all had a laugh at that and Adam got serious.

With only enough detail to accurately describe each step taken Adam revealed how his search into Benny's background had been a dead end from almost the very start, which urged him to look instead into the history of Benny's parents. That is when he struck gold.

Five minutes into his story came the first bombshell.

"Benny was adopted??!!"

Trevor exclaimed putting into words what the others were thinking.

"That's right." Adam replied.

"I didn't know..." said Trevor.

"None of us knew," responded Adam. "There was no way for us TO know because Benny himself didn't know that he was adopted."

"Oh."

"Exactly. His parents never wanted him to question his place in the world so they determined never to tell him that he was adopted."

"Seems a bit selfish to me but okay. I may be getting ahead of myself here but does that have anything to do with what else you have discovered?" asked Jimmy.

"It absolutely does!" exclaimed Adam nearly shouting.

"Something tells me this is going to be a jaw-dropper." This was from Mike.

"And you would be right on target with that statement."

"Let's hear it," said Jimmy.

Adam looked from one guy to the other allowing a moment of direct eye contact with each. Whatever it was that he had to say it was obviously of great import. That is when he dropped the second bombshell.

"Benny has a *twin.*"

"What???!!"

The four friends said this in unison, their voices erupting loudly with the incredulity of the shared information.

Trevor was the first to put two and two together. He said, "Is it a boy?"

Jimmy had done the math as well and quickly went beyond that to ask, "The bigger question is, is it *Tom*??"

All eyes were on Adam as he responded.

"So, yes to your question Trevor. Benny's twin is a male. To your question, Jimmy, and I'm guessing that everyone has jumped to the same conclusion, I can't say for sure. I could not find anything on his history. Presumably, he is alive as there was no record of infant death. Benny's parents had a meager income so I draw the inference that they could only afford to adopt one of the twins.

Where and how they adopted Benny seems to be a bit nefarious so it is also possible that *they* didn't know that a twin existed."

Adam let this sink in before he continued on with sharing the information he had collected.

"My supposition is this; that Benny has an *identical* twin."

Adam paused.

"And that this twin must have somehow discovered that Benny was out there and went to find him. Any search he might have started for his birth parents would have gone nowhere. That was a dead end for me. It would have been for him as well."

"So what you're telling us is that *'Benny,'* who for the *first time ever* had a tall tale to tell, might actually have been *'Tom'*?!" Trevor asked.

"That is my guess, yes. The twins were not named at birth. Benny's parents named him *after* the adoption. I have no idea if "Tom" is the other twins' *real* name. I also have no clue as to what his last name might be either."

"Follow Al, not Benny. That's what you said in your text." stated Mike.

"Or Tom for that matter since we don't have a last name, right?" asked Jimmy.

"That is correct," Adam replied.

"So, are we back in limbo again?" Mike wanted to know. He was in good company as there were resigned looks also from Trevor and Mike. And then Adam surprised them.

"No, not at all. As a matter of fact, I know exactly *where*, and *how*, to find both Al and Tom."

"*Really?* How?"

Adam seemed pleased that he had this opportunity to put all the pieces of the puzzle together for them. This is often what he did in his professional life as a trial attorney. Put together the pieces of a puzzle to determine what is legally fair and just.

"Everything, and I do mean *everything*, on their trip together, when not covered as an expense by the radio station 'WHOA,' was registered under *Al's name. And* paid for by *Al*."

"But you don't know his last name?"

"Oh but I do! When he won the Elvis contest his first AND last name was posted on the radio station's website. It was easy to track him from there on."

"Fantastic work Sherlock. Is that it?"

"Nope! There's more."

"More?"

"Yep!"

"What more can there be?"

"How about the "why" behind Tom masquerading as Benny. What motivation is there to do that?"

"Oh yeah. You know that TOO?"

"Yes," said Adam. "Yes I do."

Al & Tom - A fish to die for...

The planning of a murder was turning out to be all too easy. As it turned out, Part-Time was *already* scheduled to be working tomorrow evening at the "Unagi" restaurant AND the Executive Chef was off for a few days. Although there were implicit instructions that pufferfish was **not** to be sold on days when the Executive Chef was not present, those instructions were written in Japanese and therefore (according to Tom anyway) simply did not exist since Part-Time could not read them.

Part-Time was all too eager to try his hand at cooking a fish dinner. While he knew nothing about the "pre" preparation of such a deadly creature as the pufferfish he felt quite confident about how to pan fry the thing. He had watched on several occasions how *other* fish had been prepared and figured that he could easily do the same. To him this was just a *fish.* Like any other. If he was being honest, Part Time probably would not have been able to tell the difference between a trout and a salmon.

The Four Friends - The Big Reveal

"Is it time now for us to lose the melodrama and find out the motivation behind why this Tom character is masquerading as Benny?"

"Yeah, and why he seems to have a death wish for Al who seems to be a quirky dude but a genuine friend?"

"Both fair questions," answered Adam.

"Well?" pressed Trevor.

"Can I share that part over dinner?" replied Adam.

Their eagerness to have their questions answered came second to their gnawing hunger so the search for a restaurant became their top priority. The four friends were now in the Tokyo Nights section of the Tokyo Vegas resort. They too had walked about the complex with their mouths open in awe of what they had seen. The attention to detail in this replicated version of Tokyo and its surroundings was incredible. The urgency of their quest to find Al & Tom was slowed by their natural curiosity of things unseen.

"There!" shouted Jimmy. "That's the place!"

Jimmy was pointing to a restaurant with a neon sign stating the name in both English and Japanese, "Umami."

"You know what that means, right?" asked Adam.

"It means flavor!" replied Jimmy enthusiastically.

"It means," Adam began as though he were speaking to a child, "MSG, or in other words, salt."

"Yeah, Mr. Know-It-All? Well let me tell you something. I sell thousands of pounds of French fries every day and you know what our secret "flavor" ingredient is? That's right my friends, salt!" Jimmy stated all of this with great pride and conviction in his voice.

"Hey! They have ramen too! I'm in." Mike chimed in and was now heading towards the door of the restaurant.

"Wait guys! Don't we want to see what other Japanese cuisines might be available here?" Adam was always the one to appreciate and enjoy other cultures.

Trevor took a few steps to his left where he could see the sign for the next restaurant available to them in restaurant row.

"Guys, what is "Unagi"?"

"Did you say 'unagi'?" asked Mike.

"Yeah, Unagi, what's that? Is that better than Umami?"

Trevor has his hands up with palms open and shrugging his shoulders with that 'don't ask me' look.

Adam chuckles and says. "I think we're good with this place." He is pointing at Umami.

Trevor says, "I'm still curious what "Unagi" means, if you know."

"Eel. Unagi is eel." Adam states matter-of-factly.

"Ramen it is then!" bellows Mike as he slips inside the Umami restaurant. The others are quick to follow. They find a table in the courtyard area where they can people-watch as they eat.

The food is incredible, the service impeccable. Japanese beers and sake litter their table as the dinner seems now to have pushed them off course from their shared mission to locate Al & Tom.

Adam senses this and waves off their remarkably attentive server who is seeking to bring them yet another round of beverages.

"Gentlemen, we need to talk." Adam says this gravely in hopes of garnering the attention of the group.

"We are talking!" laughs Mike.

"I mean about our situation," responds Adam. "You still haven't heard the motivation behind why Tom may be impersonating Benny."

"Oh yeah," said Jimmy. "I almost forgot. What's the deal?"

Adam now had the full attention of the group and their server had wisely read their faces and determined this was a good time to disappear.

It was nighttime in "Tokyo" now and there was a new energy in the air in the "streets" of the city. This buzz served to heighten the moment as the other three friends waited with bated breath to hear what Adam had to share.

"Okay guys, you are *not* going to believe this!" Adam began. The other three leaned in eagerly anticipating what Adam had to say. "Benny's parents won the lottery!!"

Jimmy, Mike and Trevor acted as one might expect with eyes and mouths wide open in shock. None of them had ever actually *known* someone who had won the lottery. Benny's parents? That was fantastic! Although not poor they were certainly not well to do. It couldn't happen to a nicer couple. These thoughts were shared unspoken by the group.

Mike was the first to comment. "How much did they win??"

Adam talked with his hands as he exclaimed, "Ten million dollars!"

The reaction from the group was not at all what Adam would have expected.

"What?!" he said to them.

"That's it?" said Mike. "Ten million?"

"Yeah, well I guess it's actually closer to 7 million since they elected to take the lump sum amount so after taxes 7 million." Adam explained.

"Seven million." This came as a statement from Trevor.

Adam is now perplexed. "Guys, you are making it sound like they *owe* 7 million. They WON 7 million!"

"That's good but *only* 7 million? I mean it's the lottery and you always hear about these people winning like *300* million, you know what I mean?" Mike is trying to explain his reaction to the figure Adam has shared.

"Yeah, I agree with Mike," said Jimmy. "Why only 7 million?"

Adam is beside himself with bewilderment.

"Guys, raise your hand if you have a million dollars."

No hands were raised.

"Now, tell me this, if you *did* have a million dollars, would you feel rich?"

All three heads moved up and down.

"Alright then, well get this, Benny's parents won *seven times* that amount! Get the picture?"

A shared "wow" passed through the group.

"Now that I have your attention," Adam began.

Trevor challenged Adam. "Don't get salty on us now. You know that's a natural reaction. You probably thought it too."

Adam laughed. "You know what? You're right which helps to explain Benny's, I mean Tom's, motivation. You see, Benny's parents of course had never had that much money in their life so they had no idea what to do with it so they did what any set of loving parents would do, they gave it away."

"They gave it away?" asked Mike incredulously.

"To Benny! They gave it away to Benny in the form of a trust fund."

"Oh yeah, of course. To Benny."

There was a moment of quiet as this news was disseminated amongst the group. No conclusions seemed to be at hand as they considered what they had heard. Adam sensed this and spoke for them.

"Guys, the money, the seven million dollars, THAT is Tom's motivation."

The guys shook their heads in agreement but it wasn't all there just yet.

Adam continued on.

"There is just one little wrinkle to that problem of stealing the seven million dollars from Benny's parents though isn't there? That seven million dollars now belongs to--- *Benny.* In a *trust fund.*"

"Yeah? So?" Mike prompted.

Adam smiled. He was eagerly anticipating that 'oh my god' look that would cross their faces as he placed the final puzzle piece in place for them.

"Guys, only *Benny* can access that seven-million-dollar trust fund, right?"

They all nodded their heads yes.

"ONLY Benny. Or---," Adam waited for the group as they all leaned in closer to hear more. "Benny's IDENTICAL twin."

"TOM!" They shouted in unison.

"Yes," said Adam. "Tom. The one and only Tahoe Tom."

Al & Tom - The faceoff and the ultimatum

Tom tells himself that he has every intention of preventing Al from eating the deadly fish. He will simply question the server as to *who* has actually prepared the meal, which is a fair question when dealing with pufferfish.

'It *was* the Executive Chef, correct?' Tom will ask. The server will say, 'No, I'm sorry, our Executive Chef is off today but give me a moment and I will check for you.'

Tom will caution Al not to take a bite until they are certain that the fish is safe to eat. The server will return in a panic screaming, 'Don't put that fish in your mouth!'

Fortunately, thanks to Tom erring on the side of caution, Al will not have not taken a bite just yet.

'What is wrong?' Tom will ask. The exasperated server will say in between halting breaths that, 'I don't know HOW this is possible but our DISHWASHER cooked that fish!'

Where things would go from there who knew but Tom would come out smelling like a rose, acting as the good friend that Al believed him to be. At that point in time he would eagerly offer up the papers to sign over the ownership of the trust fund from the recently deceased Benny to his only living heir which of course... is his twin brother Tom.

What might become of Part-Time was probably just good karma. That guy was *bound* to kill somebody sometime through his reckless way of going through life. Tom allows himself a bit of credit as this most likely will save some lives.

Al & Tom - Death by Seafood

"But I don't *have* them."

This comment brought Tom crashing back down to earth from his light-hearted daydreaming.

"What? Are they locked up in a file cabinet at work or something?"

"Actually my *bro* has them." Al smiles broadly as he mentions his brother.

"I think that you're stalling. Who says *'bro'* these days anyway? Just give me the papers to sign. *Now.* Or *else.*"

"Or else *what*?" Al finds it difficult sometimes to take Tom seriously.

Tom looks around nervously at the other diners and then steals a glance back at the kitchen. Their meals are not yet on the way to the table. Tom has no idea how long it takes to prepare a pufferfish but he didn't think time was on his side.

"Look, just know that time is running out for you to get your shit together and get me those papers."

"What does *that* mean?"

"It means that I'm good for my word. No papers and you're getting a pufferfish dinner now for sure!" Tom is sporting a rather smug look on his face.

"Thank you!" says Al thinking at first that this sounds like a great deal for him. But then Al's smile starts to fade as his sixth sense kicks in warning him there may be danger ahead. He thinks to himself that that was such an odd thing for Tom to say just then. Was there some hidden meaning?

Ah, perfect timing!

Before Al is able to put any thought into his concerns the truly delectable smell of a freshly prepared pufferfish dulls his senses and the alert signals he has received are simply ignored.

To Part-time's credit the pufferfish is wonderfully seasoned.

Al happily enjoys---

Every...

Last...

Bite.

The Four Friends - A day late and a dead guy short

Adam, Jimmy, Mike and Trevor are relaxing for a few minutes after having a truly delicious dinner. Each of them ordered something unique and exotic from the menu. The dishes were incredible. This *place* was incredible. This trip of course was no vacation but it would be easy enough to turn it into one if they could complete their mission this evening.

The next steps were to start asking employees around the resort if they had seen Al & Tom. Although they had only a cursory description of Al they surely knew what Benny looked like so they could just as easily describe his twin, Tom.

Just then there was a commotion in the courtyard. Paramedics raced past with a gurney. Security personnel appeared out of thin air to take control of the situation to keep curious onlookers from getting in the way of the paramedics. The four friends had just started to get up to leave but Security encouraged them to remain seated until the situation, whatever it was, had been resolved.

Only moments later the paramedics rush past in the opposite direction one on either side of the gurney. There is a large man on the board gasping for breath. Another man, just out of their view, is running alongside of the gurney and calling out to his friend to "stay with me!" and "don't give up!"

The four friends look at one another gravely, feeling for both the man on the gurney as well as his great friend who is hanging with him until the bitter end.

Moments later an employee from the restaurant where the "food-poisoned" victim, (as they are referring to him now), has just been taken. The employee is in handcuffs. The four friends are able to catch snatches of what the employee is saying as he is escorted past them in the courtyard.

"*Part-Time!?* That's funny! That's what my friends call me. Don't know why. How about that fish I cooked, huh? Pretty good for my first time, right? Wow! Check out that fountain over there..."

The four friends would discover too late that their mission to save Al's life and possibly bring Tom to justice had all been in vain. Too soon they would track Al and Tom back to that very restaurant where Al had been served a poisonous fish at the direction of a greedy friend.

No doubt Tom would disappear now to avoid the attention of law enforcement. The four friends agreed that Tom surely would not attempt a visit to Al's funeral.

That would simply be too risky, even for Tom.

They would be wrong.

Day Four - Rest in Peace Al

Al is lying at rest in the funeral home. Tom is standing at the coffin looking down at the body of his dearly departed-- *friend?* Tom, nostalgic but *not* teary-eyed, is thinking back on his time with Al. He tries to focus of course on the *good things*. One or two memorable moments come to the surface but all too quickly the waters of his memory become murky with what were the *annoyances* of being with Al. The list was long and soon Tom is once again in a dark place and thinking only of himself. He is not being *in the moment* to say the least.

Tom has drilled down to one particularly bothersome habit of Al and that was the phrase, *'Well, well, well.'* Those three words, spoken by Al in the absolute *worst* situations, would cause Tom's hackles to rise and he didn't even *know* what that meant until he looked it up. Turns out the expression fit perfectly. As did nails on a chalkboard.

Those three words, *'well, well, well,'* spoken in that drawn out gotcha monotone that Al had just set Tom on edge every time he heard it. And it seemed that every time he heard it good old Al was *sneaking up* behind him to say it. Never to his face.

Now *that* was creepy, it almost seemed as though he was hearing it now---

"Well, well, well."

Tom gritted his teeth and balled up his fists. He scrunched up his face into a mask of fury. The deceased body of Al lay before him and yet *somehow* he could *clearly* hear Al speaking those three vexing words directly behind him. The worst possible scenario came to Tom and he said, "No! That's simply *not* possible."

Had Al managed to come back from the dead to haunt Tom? It would be *so* like him!

"Glad you could finally make it."

That phrase made Tom shudder with trepidation. Slowly he turned away from Al's casket towards the sound of the three haunting words and looked directly into the eyes of---

Al????

"Hey buddy!" said a person who looked, and sounded, *exactly* like Al.

Tom nearly fainted. The version of Al standing before him was *not* a ghost and fortunately for Tom was quick to catch his fall and support him. *Was Tom dreaming all of this?*

"You must be Tom," said the ghost. "My bro' has told me all about you."

"Bro?" Tom managed to say weakly. "You mean your *brother*??!!"

"Yep! *Twin* brothers I might add. Sorry to spook you there! You okay? You look a little pale."

Tom had now regained his composure and was looking at this "new" Al with fresh eyes. He was less than polite as he walked around him, peering at him, sizing him up, evaluating his posture, judging his body structure. Tom got right up in this version of Al's face, squinting as he stared directly at him with unbelieving eyes.

This *was* Al. But it also was *not.*

"Aldo and I are identical twins. You see there are two types of twins: identical and fraternal. Fraternal are–"

"I *know* that" declared an annoyed Tom. Damn, the voice of this version of Al sounded *exactly* the same! "Wait! *What* did you just say?!"

The new version of Al stopped in midsentence then repeated, "Fraternal twins are---"

"No, no!" stammered Tom. "*Before* that! What *name* did you say??"

"Aldo. That's *his* name." The new version of Al was pointing at the deceased. "Did you not know his name? I thought you two were close friends."

Tom scrunched up his face at that notion suddenly finding this new version of Al just as irritating as the last. "I *didn't* know. I just always called him Al. So it's Aldo, huh? What is he, Italian or something?"

The new version of Al laughed at this. "Yes, I guess you could say that. Our father was Italian and our mother's heritage was Chinese. Aldo received a name in honor of our father. My name is in honor of our mother."

Tom nodded his head with understanding. Things were now starting to make sense.

"Okay, so you and Al–"

"Aldo."

"Sorry. You-- and *Al*-DO," Tom made a point of expressing the second syllable, "are twin brothers. *Identical* twin brothers. So, what is *your* name?"

The new version of Al smiled sweetly and said, "My name is *Al*-SO."

Tom burst out laughing much to the chagrin of the assembled mourners in the funeral parlor. To be respectful, "Al-so," the other version of Al, took Tom by the arm and moved him away from the casket.

"I don't understand," said Also softly. "What is so funny?"

Tom can hardly catch his breath. "You don't think that's hilarious?!"

"What? What is hilarious?" Also is demonstrating patience.

Tom gathers himself and is trying *not* to laugh as he says, "You two are twins."

"Yup," states Also.

"So, they name one Al and the next one Also. You don't find that hilarious? They might as well just named you *'Next'!*"

A stone-faced Also said simply, "I don't get it."

"You being serious?"

"Yup."

"Wow. No sense of humor. You two *are* identical."

"That's not funny either."

"You're right about that," agreed Tom. "That's just sad."

Al-SO, the *new version* of Al as Tom kept thinking of him seemed to be almost as good-natured as Al-DO. *Almost.* There was something just under the surface though that had Tom a bit on edge. Tom wondered if Also might have another side to him with a temper, possibly even an anger management issue. Time would tell.

"So tell me, Also," Tom said in a mocking tone, "how would I tell the two of you of apart?"

"Well, that's easy. I'm the one that's *not* dead."

Also laughed at his comment and then laughed even more at Tom's reaction.

"I *do* have a sense of humor alright and so did Aldo." Tom looked curiously at Also urging him to continue. "By the way, in his will he left something for you."

"He did?!"

"Yes he did."

"Was it–some *documents*?" Tom implored. This could be that big moment that has eluded him for so many months.

"Documents, huh, is that what you're hoping for? We'll see. I'm not sure. Whatever it is it's in a box. But all in good time. For now, I'm famished. Would you care to grab a bite to eat?"

"Sure!" snickered Tom. An image of Al's face as the poison of the pufferfish made its way to his heart came quickly to mind. "Tell me, Al-SO, do you like *seafood*?"

Part Four

Take Me To Yellowstone

Same Sh*T, Different Day?

The invitation comes from Al-So for Tom to travel with him to Yellowstone of all places. Had it been just about *anywhere* else, or with *anyone* else, Tom most likely would have declined. But he had never been to Yellowstone and it was not a place to which he cared to venture alone. Plus, Al-so had mentioned to Tom that Aldo had left him some money for just such an adventure so it seemed like the right thing to do. Not just taking advantage of the money but spending time with Al-So also (pun intended) while he dealt with his grief. Tom after all (according to him anyway) was a very caring man.

Several things had happened after Al-so and Tom's first meeting at the funeral home. The two did go out to dinner that evening but not at Tom's preferred place, Unagi at Tokyo Vegas. Al-so chose a plate of spaghetti over the seafood dinner which Tom may have had in mind. It would be an understatement to say that Al-so was wary of Tom. Besides, the "poisonous pufferfish" plate would *never* happen again at Unagi. Not only had Part-Time been fired (immediately) and removed from the restaurant in handcuffs, the dish itself had also been removed from the menu.

As for Part-Time, he did not serve any jail time but was directed to do fifty hours of community service. As was customary for Part-Time, he only showed up to serve his community service "part" of the time so strike that no jail time comment from earlier. Part-Time is now *doing* time. *Full time* doing time. Word is that he has made a lot of friends in his cell block.

When Al-so's plate of spaghetti arrived Tom's head cleared and he realized then that he might still have a shot at gaining access to his dear brother's trust fund. He couldn't use it where he was now anyway. Al-so had now become Tom's ticket to getting his hands on the legal papers which he must sign to transfer the trust fund into his name. By fate it would seem, Tom was now the only surviving heir to the lottery windfall experienced by Benny's adoptive parents.

Tom, much like he had done with Al, felt that he needed to ingratiate himself with Al-so. Accepting the offer of this trip was the first step. All too soon, for Tom anyway, it just felt like the same shit, different day.

Yellowstone Sojourn - Day One

Tom's flight had just landed and he was preparing to deboard the plane to meet up with Al-So in the airport terminal. This was all Al-So's idea. Had it been left up to Tom he would be meeting up with Al-So at the Yellowstone Airport and taking an Uber directly to Old Faithful. Apparently it doesn't work that way. The closest large city to Old Faithful was Bozeman, Montana which is why Al-So chose to fly them both to—*Minneapolis???!!!*

'Don't worry,' said Al-So. 'I have a plan.'

As Tom waited impatiently for his turn to get up from his uncomfortable seat in Economy Class, he thought of smacking himself in the head for accepting Al-So's invitation in the first place. 'The apple doesn't fall far from the tree,' Tom muttered to himself when comparing Al-So to Al (Al-do). He knew that euphemism was completely inaccurate but he didn't care. He needed some kind of statement through which to vent.

During the flight Tom had taken some time to review the itinerary which Al-So had put together for the two of them. *It was atrocious!* And that *was* the perfect word. The plan called for Tom to fly to Minneapolis, meet up with Al-So at the car rental counter at the Minneapolis-Saint Paul International Airport where they would then hop into a car (whatever was available) for the remainder of the journey.

'That's not so bad,' Tom had initially thought.

Until he looked at a map.

What the hell??!!

It was no less than a 16-hour drive from Minneapolis to Yellowstone where they would finally arrive at the spot of the incredible Old Faithful geyser. Something which Tom had longed to see his entire life.

Until now.

16 hours in a *car?!*

With *Al-So??!!*

Torture. It was going to be just plain torture.

Al-So was Al's twin in so many ways. Which of course only made sense. After all, they're twins!! So, just like Tom would have expected of Al, there is old reliable Al-So, on time, and waiting for Tom at the car rental counter.

"I still have to get my bag—" Tom began to say as Al-So wrapped him up in a smothering bear hug.

"It's so good of you to come! You have a wonderful taste for adventure! I think most people would have opted for the nearest airport and an Uber, right? But not *you*, Tom! You're an *adventurer*! I know you are eager to hit the open road. Fresh air and hours and hours of driving! Well, sitting anyway. You prefer being a passenger. Well that's what Aldo told me anyway." Al-so laughed at this.

'I hate being a passenger!' Tom thought to himself. 'What an idiot I am coming on this trip. A complete and total idiot.'

Out of the blue came a crushing bear hug from Al-so and just like that Tom's murderous intentions were back in play. The decision was made. *Al-So had to go.* He had until Old Faithful to enjoy what was left of his life and then he *had* to go. The good news was that Tom had LOTS of time to dream up a clever exit for Al-So.

Tom smiled.

Like Aldo before him, Al-So would never see it coming.

Mitchell, SD

Day One of this Yellowstone trip had seen the two traveling through open country on I-90 passing through Sioux Falls to the first stop on Al-so's list which was Mitchell, South Dakota. It had been nearly 5 hours of driving with nothing for the two of them to do but talk. Al-so had opted for a vehicle without a radio. (Tom didn't know that such a thing even existed in this day and age).

'Why are we going to Mitchell, South Dakota?' Tom had dared to ask.

'Trust me,' said Al-so. 'You will thank me when we get there. This is something *pretty* special.' Tom didn't know what to think of that comment. After all, this guy's brother had thought that the world's largest ball of twine was "pretty special."

Just prior to arriving at their first "once in a lifetime" place to visit, Al-so announces to Tom that he should prepare himself to see *The Corn Palace*, the only one of its kind in the world!

Tom asks himself under his breath, 'why would they even need *one* of them?!'

Tom has no idea what to expect but it certainly isn't what he will soon see before him.

"Are we in Russia?" asks Tom with no holding back on sarcasm.

Al-so laughs and responds with an answer dripping with authenticity.

"You talking about those onion top domes there?" Al-so is pointing. "That is a Moorish design influence. I doubt that they had anything "Russian" in mind when they put those up. Interesting observation though."

'Why does he think I care?' Tom asks himself. Just then Al-so pulls into a parking lot and begins to get out of the car.

"Are we actually *visiting* this place?" asks Tom incredulously.

In the same tone of voice, Al-so responds with, "Free parking *and* free admission, why *wouldn't* we visit this place?!"

'Maybe because it's in the middle of nowhere?' Tom says under his breath.

"What's that?" asked Al-so.

"I didn't say anything," said Tom. "Come on, let's go. Wait till I tell my friends that I visited the Corn Palace!"

Tom thought he had the last word until Al-so said, "According to my brother Aldo, you don't *have* any friends."

It was rare for Tom but in this moment he was at a loss for a comeback.

Although only half-listening Tom somehow feels himself being drawn into what he is hearing. They are standing outside of The Corn Palace and a passerby, surely a local, had stopped to give both him and Al-so an overview of The Corn Palace and its history. **

Much to Tom's chagrin, he is quite interested in hearing what this older gentleman has to say.

"It was back in 1892 when this place was first conceived. It might look it but I can assure that *I* wasn't there." The man and Al-so shared a laugh. "This was built as a gathering place for folks to enjoy a fall festival. The festival was a celebration of the harvest and the end of another crop-growing season. Like all things it grew over the years. This building you're looking at here was completed back in 1921. I wasn't on hand for that *neither!* Not so as I recall anyways."

Al-so and the elderly gentleman shared another laugh. Tom thought that these jokes about The Corn Palace were "corny" but decided to keep *that* to himself.

"It wasn't until the 1930's when the decorative features you see up there, the kiosks and minarets as they're called, were added."

"Were you around for that?" Tom asked eagerly.

"Nope." The man said with finality.

Tom shrunk away as the conversation continued between the man and Al-so. Tom was disengaged now and only heard bits and pieces. This was now quite a practical structure which hosted industrial exhibits, shows, meetings and the like. It also became a home for local high school basketball. Tom heard the man say that it has become one of the *top 10* places in America for high school basketball.

Inside The Corn Palace there are murals to be seen which are made from corn. This is true of the outside of the structure as well. Tom leans in to hear this part. He hears that every year The Corn Palace is decorated with naturally colored corn, grains and other grasses to make it "the agricultural showplace of the world." Tom is amazed by the different colors of corn which adorn the exterior of the building. He sees yellow, red, white, blue, calico, orange and—green?? Incredible.

Al-so wants to go inside, which they do. The saving grace for Tom is that it is nearing 5 o'clock when the doors close for the day. He is wondering if they can make Yellowstone by nightfall.

"No way Jose," says Al-so.

"What?" asks Tom.

"No way we're making it all the way to Yellowstone today."

'Did I say that out loud?' Tom wonders to himself.

Al-so smiled at Tom and then winked as he said, "Best watch yourself Tommy Boy, I can read your mind."

Tom stood there for a moment then said, "Well *that* just scared the hell out of me."

The two got back in their rental vehicle and headed west.

* *Information regarding The Corn Palace can be found at* www.cornpalace.com

Missouri River Overlook

There had been an uneasy silence in the vehicle for nearly an hour when Al-so said, "You awake?"

"Of course I'm awake, it's not even dinner time."

"Good, because something pretty special is coming up and I don't think that you should miss it!"

"Do we have to stop?" pressed an ever-annoyed Tom.

"No we don't *have* to stop," Al-so shot back. 'For this part anyway' he added under his breath.

"Alright then, I can't wait!"

Al-so was perturbed. "Tell me something. If you couldn't be an asshole what else might you have aspired to be? I think there is still an opening for *normal*."

"Oh you're just hilarious. What is it that I'm looking for?"

"Just shut up and pay attention."

"Yes captain," replied Tom.

Just then the vehicle they were riding in crested a rise and the entire topography of the land seemed to change as a new, and welcomed spectacle, came into view. After hours of open plains with only the colors of wheat, road and sky to see, now there was a new and beautiful vision pleasing to the eye.

It was the Missouri River and the panoramic view from the open road was one of grandeur. Al-so was grinning ear to ear drinking in every moment. In minutes they were on the bridge crossing over the mighty river and then just like that they were on the other side with the same scenery as before.

Al-so turned eagerly to Tom to say, "So what did you think?!"

"Of what?" asked Tom nonchalantly.

"Of *that!*" Al-so fired back and pointing behind him.

"The river?"

"Yes, the river. Quite a spectacle wasn't it? I mean coming up out of nowhere. One minute you're on the open road with the same view for hours and then all of a sudden, wow!" Al-so was talking with his hands to express his thoughts.

"You need me to drive?" asked Tom.

"We've already covered that, no. Why bring it up again?"

"Because you can't seem to drive, and talk, at the same time." Tom made exaggerated motions with his hands to make his point clear.

"There is none so blind as he who will not see."

"Isn't that from a song back in the 70's?" asked Tom.

"Maybe. Never truer than right now that's for sure."

"Chill out Al-so. I was just kidding. That river was the *best* river I have seen all *day*! Not lyin'." The sarcasm in Tom's voice was think enough to cut with a knife.

The vehicle began to slow and Al-so was pulling off the road to his left.

"What are you doing?" asked Tom.

"Going back," replied Al-so.

"Why??" Tom was not happy with this turn of events.

"Because we missed something, that's why."

"What did we miss? I *saw* the river."

"You *glanced* at it, I'll give you that but there's more to see, just be patient."

"But I don't *want* to see more."

"Ain't *that* the truth!"

"That sounded *mean*."

"Sorry, not my intention. Just stating a fact."

Tom made a baby's sad face like when they soil their diaper. "That sounded mean too!"

"Truth hurts, what can I say?"

Tom had more to say but clammed up when Al-so made that last comment. He apparently had a line you shouldn't cross and Tom had just stuck his toe over it. Good to know how far he could be pushed.

Heading east now Al-so appears to be looking for an exit. Tom has no idea what Al-so is up to so he keeps to himself. This is the right thing to do as Al-so is just on the edge of losing his temper it would seem.

"There it is!" exclaims Al-so.

Tom is looking all around, craning his neck to see what Al-so has seen. He is soon to discover that it is an exit sign that he has been looking for. Tom steals a glance at the dashboard to see the gas needle. Half a tank, they're still good so this can mean only one thing. Yet another stop to see yet another ball of twine. Ho hum.

That was the way Tom viewed all roadside attractions. You've seen one world's largest ball of twine; you've seen them all.

They are just outside the city of Chamberlain, South Dakota cruising along slowly in search of-- something.

"Pull over!" shouts Tom.

"Pull over? Why?" asks a surprised Al-so.

"Because I *see* it! That's why. Now pull over."

Al-so pulls over and stops. Tom is the first out of the vehicle and runs over to the thing which he has spotted. He stands proudly next to it perhaps attempting to score a few points with his agitated companion and road warrior.

"Take my picture?"

"Next to *that*?" asks a surprised Al-so.

"Yes! Isn't this what we came to see? A giant rooster sculpture? Let's get it over with."

Al-so is laughing now. As he is looking at the *pheasant* sculpture (definitely *not* a rooster) he makes a snide comment, "You sure know your birds, don't you?"

"What?" asks Tom.

"You think I drove all this way to see a giant pheasant made of railroad spikes?" Al-so has his hands on his hips looking back and forth from the large sculpture to Tom.

"Sure sounds like you," Tom states with conviction.

"Nice jab. That one landed." Al-so turned to walk away. "Come on," he said over his shoulder. "I took a wrong turn. What we came to see is on the other side of the highway."

"If it's a giant frog made of railroad ties I'm not interested."

"Just get in the truck," Al-so demanded.

Tom threw up his hands and did as he was told.

Twenty minutes later, due to an unyielding flow of traffic, they have made it to the other side of the highway and Al-so is standing before the statue that he wanted to see.

"What is it?" Tom is asking.

They are at the Missouri River Overlook and standing at the base of the 50-foot-tall stainless-steel statue which is known as *Dignity: Of Earth and Sky* designed by sculptor Dale Lamphere to honor the cultures of the Lakota and Dakota people.

"I like it," Tom adds. "This is impressive. What does it symbolize?"

Al-so looks up at Tom then points down to the mounted plaque near the statue. "If you know how to read, look at this and stop asking me dumb questions."

Tom sidled up to Al-so. He had the urge to just haul off and punch the guy but decided he would read the plaque instead. Soon he was enthralled with the message as he read that the sculptor had used three Native American models of various ages (14, 29 and 55), to perfect the face of Dignity.

The statue of a Native American female whose name is Dignity stands alert as she casts a peaceful gaze across the waters of the Missouri River. Her arms are outstretched, her hands clutching a quilt emblazoned with a unique star of turquoise and diamonds. The quilt's 128 stainless steel diamonds feature color-changing pieces that glitter in the sun and move with the wind. This causes a calming rippling effect. She is ever vigilant as the statue is lit at night causing the diamonds to cast a gentle glow in the night sky. Dignity is easily visible from the interstate. *

**To learn more about Dignity: Of Earth & Sky, go to:* www.travelsouthdakota.com

Murdo, SD

Al-so and Tom walked about the statue for several minutes before Al-so glanced at his watch and said, "We'd better get going."

"You don't have to tell me twice!" said Tom.

Al-so just shook his head. Tom was intolerable.

Heading west once again there is silence in the cabin of the truck. Both men seem to be at peace for the moment. The sun has begun to settle in the western sky providing a spectacular vista of colors which was truly not to be missed. Al-so, however, decides not to comment. He will enjoy it alone.

Tom is busy on his cell phone checking messages. He doesn't actually have any but he doesn't let on. As a matter of fact, he doesn't even have cell service. Al-so knows this but *he* doesn't let on. They have another two hours ahead of them before their next stop. Why poke the bear?

It was nearing 7pm by the time they pulled off the interstate and drove into a small town by the name of Murdo.

"We need gas?"

"Yep," said Al-so. "That and some chow. You hungry? I'm starved."

"Sure, I could eat. Do you know a place? Hopefully, it has a full bar."

"Sorry to disappoint," Al-so began, "but places tend to close early around these parts. We're going to grab some grub here at the Circle E Drive-In. I hear the food is good but you had better plan on eating in the car. I think they're about ready to close."

Tom's disapproval was evident as he threw a childish tantrum. Suddenly Tom stopped and turned to look at Al-so who was grinning and shaking his head.

"I gotta be honest with you. I thought all this time Aldo was bullshittin' me about you but he was right."

"Right about what?" Tom asked indignantly.

"You're nothing but a big baby." There was no malice in Al-so's voice as he was just stating a fact. Tom huffed but said no more.

Truth be told the food was damn good and really hit the spot. Tom had just settled back in his seat for a full evening of driving when Al-so pulled up to the front entrance of a small hotel.

"What are we doing here?" asked Tom.

"We're going to see if we can get ourselves a room for the night."

"HERE?" exclaims Tom.

"What's wrong with this place?" asks Al-so. Although it is a rather small hotel it *is* a national brand. "I think it looks just fine."

"I don't mean "here" this place the hotel, I mean "here" this place, the town!"

"What's wrong with this town?"

"Nothing's wrong with the town other than the fact that it Is not where we need to be. Yellowstone is where we need to be," Tom adamantly. "And if you're too tired to drive then I can take over for a while but let's get to where we're going!"

Al-so was quiet for a moment, perhaps carefully choosing the words he was about to say. "Okay, first of all, you CAN'T drive."

"Sure I can. I have a license." Tom was being his usual defensive self.

"Well that may be so but you can't drive THIS vehicle."

"And why not?"

"Because I didn't purchase insurance for you to drive this vehicle, that's why not."

"Why the hell not? Don't you trust me??" Tom was angry now.

"No I sure don't."

"Well you trust me enough to share a hotel room with you."

Al-so laughed. "I may look like my twin brother and sound like my twin brother but I'm NOT my twin brother. No way in hell am I sharing a hotel room with you."

"But that's just crazy. That will make this trip cost twice as much!"

"You can owe me."

" *What?!* I thought *you* were paying for this trip. YOU invited ME!"

"You're a gullible one. I ain't paying for you."

"Wow. Now you *do* sound just like your brother." Tom muttered this last comment with clear disdain.

"Same shit, different brother." Al-so laughingly said as he got out of the vehicle. Tom was not far behind as they headed for the front desk to see about getting *two* hotel rooms.

Yellowstone Sojourn - Day Two

Tom was up at 6am eager to get started for the day. He had already walked down to the hotel lobby to avail himself of their free breakfast and coffee. Neither was very good but FREE was always a good price.

When he returned to the room Al-so was still in bed sawing logs. Tom nudged him and said, "Hey! Do you know what time it is? We probably want to get going, right?"

Al-so's head appeared out of the covers and he cocked one eye open as he spoke. "Nope. Still early. The place we're going to doesn't open until 9am."

"What place?! We're going to Yellowstone!" Tom exclaimed defiantly.

"Yes, that *is* true," said Al-so. "But *first*, we're going to the Pioneer Auto Museum."

"Where the hell is that?"

Al-so pulled the covers back over his head as he replied, "Right here in the town of Murdo, South Dakota. Not far at all, only a mile from this hotel but—they don't open until 9am."

Tom flung himself onto the other queen bed and screamed into a pillow. Al-so, now becoming used to these antics, just drifted back to sleep.

The Pioneer Auto Museum is everything which the name implies but also so much more. Al-so had read about it and was dying to make a visit there. Whether Tom was onboard with this plan was immaterial to Al-so. Unlike his brother Aldo, Al-so remained unmoved by Tom's wants or needs. As far as Al-so was concerned, Tom was just along for the ride and if he didn't like it he was free to walk back home to wherever the hell it was that he came from.

"What is this place? Just a junkyard full of old cars?" Tom wants his feelings to be known right from the get-go.

"You see rust, I see another form of patina."

"I have no idea what that means."

Al-so lowers his head and peers at Tom through skeptical eyes as he endeavors to enlighten Tom.

"When brass oxidizes and turns green that color is referred to as its "patina." The bronze which has weathered the elements is showing its age but there is value to what has happened to the metal. People who see rust however tend to see only decay."

"Yeah? So what does that say about me?"

"Exactly. What *does* that say about you?" Al-so shook his head with approval. "That one's on me. I did not expect you to catch on so soon."

"What?" asked a befuddled Tom. "What did I say?"

"The truth. Now come on, quit wasting time."

"*Me?!* I'm not the one wasting time, *you* are."

"I know you are but what am I?" Al-so retorted.

"What????"

The Pioneer Auto Museum was almost like being in a ghost town. It was certainly a step back in time. As the two men walked the streets of this open-air museum there was much for them to see. They began their journey in the remnants of a town pulled from

1880. There was a dentist's office complete with chair and implements of, well, they looked more torturous than medical.

There were several storefronts, a church, a post office, a stagecoach and then—things started to get a little weird. Suddenly time, and the place in which each item they saw, did not matter. There were cars, lots and lots of cars, from just about every decade. Tom's eyes landed on a model that he had coveted while in high school but could not have afforded at the time.

The more the two men walked around the complex the more the two began to believe that this was a museum of lives lived and of the material things that we long for and cherish. There is a gun collection, a doll collection, a card collection, a stamp collection, and a menagerie of vintage toys. All of this might have seemed random were it not for the simple fact that these things had mattered in someone's life. These things struck a human chord in everyone who walked through this museum. Was it a museum? Or was it a virtual photo album of how we seek to learn and understand and bring joy into our lives.

For all of Tom's bickering about how this stop would be nothing but a waste of their time, he knew that he would walk away from the experience with an odd sense of fulfillment. For the brief time that he and Al-so had walked the museum the museum had affected him in ways he did not expect possible.

*** To learn more check out The Pioneer Auto Museum at www.pioneerautoshow.com*

The time came for the two to get back on the road. Al-so of course was driving but for the moment Tom is thankful that he might have some time to himself. To look out the window at miles and miles of the same nothing and just think.

Tom became a bit somber and introspective. Much of what they had seen at the museum which had brought a smile to Al-so's face from a distant memory were alien to Tom. He had been denied the wonderful childhood that Al-so must have had living with birth parents who truly loved him.

Tom had lived in foster homes his entire life and learned that the things he wanted in life, toys and the like, must be "shared," they could not be "owned." Not by someone abandoned and alone like him in this world. Tom was bitter towards those people who had nice things, a nice life, family. He had been bitter towards Al, he was bitter towards Al-so and he had a deep resentment of his own twin, Benny who had lived a life he would never know.

Unless–he could get his hands on that trust fund...

"I could not *believe* all the things that were in that place, am I right?"

"Huh? What? What place?"

"Sorry," said Al-so. "I thought you were awake."

"I AM awake! Just daydreaming I guess." Tom felt the heat of embarrassment on his face. "Yeah, I have not seen that many random things in one place. But they were all, I don't know, *worth seeing* if you know what I mean." * *

"I know exactly what you mean. That place was incredible. Don't take this negative because I sure don't mean it that way, but it was almost like it was the backlot for the filming of 'The Twilight Zone'."

Tom laughed and said, "You nailed it. I will never forget that experience."

"Careful now, you keep talking like that and I might get to thinking that you're a normal person."

"I AM a normal person," Tom retorted with a tinge of anger in his voice.

"Sure you are," laughed Al-so. "Isn't that what all the serial killers say?"

Tom shot Al-so a look that could kill but he did not appear wounded by it nor did he even flinch. Tom let out a heavy sigh. This "Al" was made of much tougher stuff than the other "Al." *This* "Al" was actually beginning to scare him. A little.

Tom changed the subject. "Where are we going to *now?*"

Al replied instantly. Like he had a plan.

"A little town by the name of Wall, South Dakota."

"Okay," began Tom with a dose of frustration coating his words, "and *why* would we be going to Wall, South Dakota? Because it's *there?* Do they have a *Barbie Museum*? Or a *Wheat Palace* that we can see?"

Al-so shook his head and said, "Damn! 'Smartass' just runs *rampant* in your veins, don't it?"

"I, I--," Tom stammered. He had no comeback for that one. It didn't matter. Al-so had moved on.

"Wall, South Dakota happens to be the home of the famous '*Wall Drug*' which is where we're headed."

"Never heard of it," Tom shot back.

"Well, you've never heard of kindness, common courtesy or human decency either. This is going to be quite a learning experience for you."

The sullen look on Tom's face did not have the desired effect on Al-so. He just looked straight ahead at the unending highway. Tom was beginning to dislike Al-so more than he disliked Al, or Aldo as was his given name. Tom would still continue to call him Al.

Tom looked out the window allowing his thoughts to wander. Why did he dislike Al? Well for one, Al was an annoyance of the highest order. But that wasn't really it, was it? It had more to do with the simple fact that Al could have easily turned over the trust fund documents to Tom and they could have gone their separate ways. For some reason which Tom could not fathom Al saw Tom as a friend. What a poor judge of character!

Al-so was different. Tom disliked him for different reasons. While he might seem like the same easy-going guy as Al, he was only an identical twin on the outside. On the inside he was cold and cunning. Tom was more than a little worried that Al-so suspected Tom of directing the events which had led to Al's death. What a leap he was taking with circumstantial facts. How unfair! Didn't anyone care about the truth anymore? But that was the problem in this scenario wasn't it. Al-so DID care about the truth and like an evil dentist he would keep drilling until he got to the root of the problem. Which was Tom.

Tom looked over at Al-so whose eyes were trained on the road. In Tom's mind he was thinking what a James Bond villain might be thinking, 'what kind of clever death can I concoct for you?' What he actually said, "What is at Wall Drug that we would want?"

Al-so answered immediately. "You mean, what is at Wall Drug that YOU would want?" He was pointing at Tom when he said this.

"I don't know what you're talking about. I don't want nothing at Wall Drug."

"Anything."

"What?"

"'Anything,' not 'nothing.' You don't want "anything" at Wall Drug."

"Yeah, that's what I just said." Tom was adamant. Al-so decided it wasn't worth the bother of explaining.

"It's not something that you *want.* It's something that you will *need.*"

Al-so had just pulled off at the exit headed towards the sprawling façade of Wall Drug.

"What will I need?"

"Cowboy boots."

"*Cowboy boots?!* Why will *I* need *cowboy boots??!!*"

Al-so had an inscrutable look on his face as he said, "Trust me. When the time comes, you will know."

Al-so got out of the vehicle and Tom followed behind trying to unravel the word web that he had just ventured onto. A voice inside his head whispered, *'This is a trap.'* Another voice said, *'Stop being a pussy.'*

Tom gathered himself and determined that if Al-so was buying then that was just fine with him. He was about to get himself a first-rate pair of cowboy boots although he sure couldn't explain why you would go to a drugstore for boots.

Tom started thinking about all of the hand-painted road signs that had captured his eye along the highway. For twenty or so miles he had seen them and they all had one thing in common, the words "Wall Drug" at the bottom. One of the signs had stood out for him now that he was giving it some consideration. The sign had a roping cowboy with chaps and spurs and a message that read:

Cowboy Up!
BOOTS-BUCKLES-BELTS
and a whole lot more!

Mako Sica

"Do we need gas already?!"

"Nope!"

"Then why are you pulling off the highway? Restroom break?"

"You are one curious fellow, aren't you?" Al-so is shaking his head and chuckling to himself.

"I just want to get to where we're going. Geez!"

Tom attempted to sound exasperated. Al-so wasn't buying it. He had another plan in mind. Tom seemed unimpressed with the topography change of the land when they crested the hill and were met with the grandeur of the Missouri River snaking through the open plains. Al-so thinks to himself, 'Let's see what kind of charge we can get from Tom when we visit *this place*!'

Within minutes the calming "sameness" of the prairie land was gone! And then suddenly, they were on--- the moon!

The road was now a twisting and turning thrill ride as they wove their way through rock formations jutting up from the land. To both his left and right Tom could see only rock or, the absence of rock, meaning that the side of the road would just drop off into a vast canyon. The beauty of the place was completely lost on Tom.

"Where the hell are we??!!" Tom shouted. His knuckles were white with the death grip he had on the door handles.

Al-so stole a quick look at Tom and bellowed with laughter.

"Keep your eyes on the road!!" Tom commanded with icy fear lacing through his words.

Al-so has settled back to enjoy the ride. As much as Tom might want Al-so to hurry through this area both knew that was something of a death wish. The roads were completely safe and well maintained but were a distracted driver begin to venture away from it meant a certain fall to a tumbling, rocky death.

"What *is* this godforsaken place???" Tom demanded to know.

"Agree to disagree on that comment," replied Al-so. "I'd be willing to bet that the Man upstairs is quite pleased with the work He has done here. As they say though, 'Beauty is in the eye of the beholder,' and honestly, you ain't much of a beholder."

"I am too a beholder!" Tom fired back.

"No, you're an idiot."

Tom got quiet after that comment and began to pout. Al-so ignored him and set about answering Tom's repeated question.

"Tom, this here is the Badlands. They call it the 'Land of Stone and Light.' We are driving through the Badlands National Park." *

Al-so paused for a moment waiting for another smartass comment from Tom but none came so he continued.

"The name is derived from the Lakota words 'mako sica' which translates literally into 'bad lands.' It is believed that the use of the words were to describe the difficulty involved with traveling over or attempting to live off of these lands. There are many challenges here. When it rains the wet clay becomes slick and sticky. There is also the issue of navigating the jagged canyons and buttes that dominate this landscape. Winters here as you can imagine are quite cold and windy while the summers are arid with few safe water resources to be found."

Tom was being quiet, complacent and possibly attentive. Al-so could not be sure that Tom was actually *listening* but while he had an audience he was eager to continue.

"What fascinates me is that the geology of the badlands affords us a look into Earth's past as their lifespan to date is about one million years." Al-so turned to Tom excitedly and said, "Did you know that the badlands erode at about *one inch* per year??!!"

No comment from Tom.

"Scientists estimate that within the next 500,000 years the badlands will have eroded *completely*!"

"And to think that had we not jumped off the highway when we did we might have *missed* all of this!!" Tom's comfort with Al-so's cautious driving meant that his sarcasm had returned.

That comment in Al-so's mind meant that Tom needed to be taught a lesson. He swerved off the road suddenly onto a designated scenic overlook. Tom was once again jolted by the suddenness of Al-so's driving maneuver. He was further surprised by Al-so turning off the engine and getting *out* of the truck.

"Where are you going?" asked Tom. He did not get an answer.

Al-so began to walk away from the truck towards the edge of the precipice.

"I'm not getting out!" shouted Tom. "You're on your own out there!"

As though the two were still immersed in their conversation Al-so shouted back, "For perspective, the granite in the Black Hills, where you will find Mount Rushmore, erodes at the rate of one inch per *10,000* years!"

"What?" said Tom. "Who even *cares*??"

Al-so continued to walk ever closer to the edge. Beyond him were the layered rock formations of canyons which had taken a million years to form and less to tumble away.

Tom got out of the truck. He had become unnerved by Al-so's persistence in walking ever closer to the edge.

"Al-so! Stop! That doesn't look safe!" Tom smirked as he said this thinking to himself, 'keep going big boy, you already proved in Vegas that you know how to take a fall!' That was when Tom had to remind himself that this was Al's twin brother, *not* Al.

Tom was out of the truck and walking towards Al-so who looked back once and then seemed to increase his pace as he began walking determinedly towards the edge of the cliff. Tom was fraught with mixed emotions as he grappled with deciding which was the greater loss, Al-so or the documents he now had which secured Benny's trust fund money for him.

"Oh SHIT!!"

Tom yelled as he ran towards the spot where Al-so had been. He had watched as Al-so took a step onto a place where there was no rock on which to land. His body had pitched slightly forward and then Al-so had just dropped from view.

Tom could only imagine what he might see when he reached the edge of the cliff.

How far would Al-so have fallen?

How many rock outcroppings might his body have collided with on the way down?

What type of bloody mess of a human body was Tom about to see???

Tom arrives at the edge with the greatest of caution. He does not expect to rescue Al-so from his fall, only view the carnage for confirmation of death. As he peers over the edge, he sees—

Al-so only four feet below him crouching on another precipice. He was smiling and nodding his head with satisfaction as though he was proud of some kind of accomplishment which he had made.

"You're--- You're--- alive."

Al-so grinned and said, "Oh if you could just see your face right now and what I can read all over it."

"Relief?" prompted Tom.

"Nah," replied Al-so dejectedly. "I see something different. It's written in bold letters so it's easy to read. "I see *disappointment*."

Tom stammered, unable to recover from being so decidedly put on the spot.

"Let me help you up," offered Tom.

"Nope. I'm good. Besides, I wouldn't want you to confuse a helping hand with a purposeful shove."

"I was just trying to help," said Tom, moping like a child. "I know you're afraid of heights."

"My *brother,*" Al-so began, "was afraid of heights. I'm not afraid of anything. The only thing I struggle with is a severe intolerance for ignorance."

"Oh well, that–" Tom stopped midsentence. He looked at Al-so in disgust and headed back to the truck where he curled up into as much of a ball as possible to survive the remainder of their journey through the badlands.

** To learn more check out Badlands National Park at www.nps.gov*

Wall, SD

"Pull over," said Tom. "We have arrived."

"I will when I find a spot closer to where we're going," replied Al-so.

"This IS where we're going!" Tom stated his ego and bravado once again intact.

"Open your eyes Tom and tell me how much walking you're willing to do."

Tom scrunched up his face thinking that was a weird thing to say until he did open his eyes to see that the façade of Wall Drug kept going and going and going. It was like a city block long!

Finally Al-so found an open spot and pulled in. Tom started to open his door then stopped when he noticed that Al-so had not yet moved to get out.

"What?" asked Tom.

"Just thinking that it might be wise to prepare you for what you're about to see."

"It's a drug store. I think I have a pretty good idea of what might be inside."

"And you would be wrong," admonished Al-so.

"Alright then, you win. What the hell *is* this place?" Tom was a bit flustered.

"Come on, let's go. I will tell you as we walk."

After getting out of the vehicle, Al-so began sharing with Tom what he knew of Wall Drug.

"This place has been here since 1931. The city of Wall once affectionately known as "the geographical center of nowhere." One of the proprietors of this here Wall Drug back in the day came up with an idea to draw customers in."

Tom stopped walking. He was interested in what marketing ploy must have been used to turn a small drug store in a nondescript town into the thriving tourist destination it is today.

"Well? What was their genius idea?"

"You're overthinking it," said Al-so. "I didn't say that it was genius."

"Am I?" Tom fired back. "Overthinking it? Okay. What, free gas?"

"No, but you're kinda on the right track." Al-so paused for a moment before saying, "Free *water*. And they still offer free water to this day."

Tom throws his hand up in mock surrender. "That's the craziest thing I have ever heard!"

"Which tells me one thing."

"Yeah? And what's that?"

"That *you* would never have thought of it."

"Whatever." Tom is easily angered when he feels like someone is making him look stupid. "Did they offer anything else?"

"Coffee for a nickel."

"There you go," said Tom. "Now you've got something."

Al-do just shook his head and kept walking.

Once inside Tom began to get a feel for the vastness of the place as he saw the aisles and aisles of—stuff. "What is all this---?"

Al-so said, "If The Pioneer Auto Museum is to be considered the final resting place for things from days gone by then this is the end point for all things *now*. From this area of the country. And I do mean "all things"."

Tom is in awe of just how much stuff there is in every aisle and on every shelf and mounted on every wall.

"What the HELL is that?!" exclaimed Tom.

Al-so looked in the direction that Tom was pointing and chuckled.

"You never seen one of them before?" Al-so is baiting Tom.

"No! I'm not stupid. I don't think *anyone* has ever seen one of them before."

"Well it looks real enough to me."

Al-so walked over to the shelf on the wall where the item was that Tom had referenced, then reached out and grabbed it. He held in his hands an impressive display of taxidermy. This was obviously a full-grown jackrabbit. With horns.

"This here," continued Al-so, "is what you would call a jack-a-lope. Or an "antelabbit" if you prefer. Not too many around these days."

"A 'jack-a-lope.' What the *heck* is that? You've got to be bullshitting me! A jackrabbit that has *antlers*?"

"Horns, Tom. They have *horns*. Antelope horns."

"But that's not possible. That means that an antelope and a jackrabbit—"

"Anything is possible in the wild, wild west Tom. *Anything*."

Tom stood there for several minutes staring at the stuffed animal which Al-so had replaced on the shelf. "No way," said Tom. "That's not, that's just not right."

Tom left the jack-a-lope behind to search for Al-so who had managed to find what was certainly a cowboy boot mecca. If you couldn't find it here, they probably didn't make it.

"Pick out a pair that you like," called Al-so from several aisles away. "I'm picking up the tab for this one."

Tom liked the sound of that but did not like the idea of being forced to buy something he neither wanted nor needed. To spite Al-so he decided that he would choose the most offensive pair of boots that he could find. A pair that might make Al-so gag every time he saw them. There! Perfect!

"Excuse me!"

"Yes sir?" said a uniformed employee.

"I would like to try these on please. Nine and a half wide."

"Certainly, sir. I will be right back." There was no reaction at all from the employee. Tom figured that they must see weird shit like this all the time.

Al-so began to move in Tom's direction but he waved him off. "I want to surprise you!" yelled Tom.

"You do that with everything you say and do," muttered Al-so.

"What's that? I can't hear you over here."

"Nothing!" shouted Al-so. "I'll be over in the cafeteria. Come get me when you're ready to check out!"

Tom held up a thumbs up and then took a seat to wait for the employee to return with the boots he was about to try on. Ten minutes later with a box of Tony Lama boots in hand Tom went to find Al-so who was relaxing in a wooden chair enjoying a 5-cent cup of coffee.

"So what'd you get?" Al-so reached out for the box.

"If you don't mind," said Tom. "This is a very kind gesture of yours. I would rather wait until our next stop and let you see them on me."

Al-so thought for a moment considering what their next stop would be and that was Sturgis. If he knew Tom like he thought he knew Tom, he had probably picked out the most obnoxious pair of boots he could find. Of course beauty is in the eye of the beholder they say but there was certain to be a pair that would get a roll of the eyes in the town where Tom had come from. That would have been his standard.

Taking all of that into account Al-so said, “Deal. Let’s head up to the register and then skedaddle out of here.”

Tom had a big smile on his face as they headed to the front of the store. At the checkout lane Tom asked Al-so to look away when the clerk opened the box to examine the boots.

“Are these for a lady friend?” asked the clerk.

“No!” Tom replied brusquely. “They’re for me!”

“Okay,” replied the clerk. “Yeah, I can see that.”

Tom grabbed the sack from the clerk and jerked his thumb at Al-so as he said, “He’s paying for them.”

“You the boyfriend?” asked the clerk.

“What?” asked Al-so.

“Nothing. Just messin’ with ya. That will be $862.38. Will that be on your charge card today?”

Tom watched Al-so closely but he didn’t bat an eye at the price. He paid without showing any emotion at all. Tom was initially disappointed that there was no reaction to the price but then thought to himself, just wait until he sees what $800 will buy in the middle of nowhere.

Nearly an hour of uninterrupted driving occurred which was a blessing for Al-so. He enjoyed being immersed in his own thoughts. Just then Tom erupted with the statement, “Look at that! Box Elder. That’s a kind of maple tree!”

Al-so looked at the road sign to which Tom was pointing. A small town by the name of Box Elder was coming up on their left. "Boy, when you know some-thing, some very little thing, you want the whole world to know it, don't you?"

"Hey, I listen to all of your trivia." Tom countered.

"Is that right? Well, did you know this? Box Elder is also the name of a bug. A bug that people often confuse with the stink bug. As a matter of fact, I'm a little confused right now to be honest."

"Can't you ever say anything nice?" Tom pleaded.

"Can't you?" Al-so fired back.

"I--," Tom began but Al-so shot him down by stating his question was rhetorical. Silence once again in the vehicle.

They were soon passing Ellsworth AFB on their right. Al-so would have liked to have shared that this was where the training of B-17 Flying Fortress pilots had been done during the second World War but that was sure to fall on deaf ears. The two passed through Rapid City without a word between the two of them.

Black Hills, SD

"Where we going now?"

The truck had left the highway and was headed in a southwest direction.

"We're going to the Black Hills of South Dakota."

"What's in the Black Hills of South Dakota if you don't mind me asking."

Al-so glanced over at Tom to determine if he was being sincere. He was.

"There is a good-sized manmade carving there that I would like to see with my own eyes. It's something of an icon."

"Yeah?" said Tom. "Don't know that I have ever heard of it."

"Really?" Al-so was setting Tom up for an embarrassment. "You never heard of Mount Rushmore?"

Tom attempted to recover quickly. "Mount Rushmore. Of course I heard of Mount Rushmore! I thought you was talking about the other one."

"The *other* one?" prompted Al-so.

"Yeah, that other one that no one cares about because it's not very big."

Al-so is shaking his head in disbelief. "Do you live under a rock?"

"No of course not. Why?"

"Let me ask you this first. What is Mount Rushmore a carving *of*, as far as you know?"

"Duh," retorted Tom with a bit of anger. "It's the presidents!"

" *Which* presidents?" pressed Al-so.

"The, um, first four." Tom responded.

"The first four."

"Yeah, the first four."

Al-so shook his head in amazement. You just can't make this stuff up.

"And they were...?"

Tom shared an explanation with his answer. "I didn't do so good in history."

"Well."

"Well, what?"

"I didn't do so *well* in history."

"Yeah, me either."

Al-so threw his hands up in mock surrender but then decides to enlighten Tom on the specifics regarding the "other one" as Tom had referred to it.

"You're wrong about the Crazy Horse Monument by the way. The face alone of Crazy Horse is 27 feet *taller* than the heads of Mount Rushmore. You could actually fit Mount Rushmore "inside" the Crazy Horse monument."

"Whatever," said Tom not wishing to spar with Al-so any further.

"And—" Al-so is clearly *not* done with Tom. "It was *not* the first four presidents. It was Washington, ---"

"He *was* the *first!!!*" exclaimed Tom. "I'm not stupid."

"Agree to disagree. Yes, Washington was the first president. Next to Washington on the monument is Thomas Jefferson—"

"He was the *second president!*"

"No Tom, he was the *third.*"

"Oh," said Tom. "Well, nobody remembers those other two anyway."

"The other two. The ones that nobody remembers. Let's see, what were their names? Hmm. Oh yeah, Teddy Roosevelt and Abraham Lincoln. *Those* guys."

"I'm gonna take a nap. Let me know when we get there."

Al-so was thankful for once more having a bit of peace and quiet in the truck. He thoroughly enjoyed the dramatic scenery as he drove deeper into the woods towards Mount Rushmore.

Both men went in separate directions at both Mount Rushmore and then later at the Crazy Horse Monument. Both carvings were breathtaking and made one appreciate the tenacity and incredible drive in the men who made it their life's work to create such wonders from the rock face of two unforgiving mountains.

Sturgis, SD

The final stop on that day's journey was Sturgis, South Dakota. Tom knew of this place and for some odd reason seemed quite eager to get there before dark. He kept asking how long until they arrive.

"What's in Sturgis that has you so worked up?" asked Al-so.

Tom smiled as he said, "That is where I shall do the grand reveal of my new cowboy boots! I can't think of a better place."

"Well," said Al-so. "I can't wait to see 'em."

The original plan was for them to spend the night in Deadwood, SD but Al-so was feeling like a piece of deadwood right now from all the driving he had done. Better to rest for the evening plus he was eager to see the boots Tom had picked out. He seemed very excited to show them off.

After checking into their hotel and freshening up a bit the two headed out to find themselves some dinner. Tom had made Al-so swear that he would not sneak a peek at Tom's boots until they got to the restaurant. It was not easy though as the bizarre looks which Tom was receiving from folks as they made their way along the western street was almost too much to bear. Tom seemed to be enjoying every minute of it.

The two gave Tom's name at the host stand to wait for a table and then made their way into the bar for a pre-dinner cocktail. That is where everything went horribly wrong for Tom. Tom was wearing cowboy boots but Tom was no cowboy however *most* of the men in this bar *were* cowboys. And those who weren't were bikers. *That* was a bad mix.

"Hey glamour boy! Are you *mocking* me with them *'shoes'*?"

That's how it all started. Tom was elated. He had read the room and thought this was about to be hilarious. Much to his chagrin, he had *not* read the room correctly.

"These *boots* you mean?" countered Tom with displaced confidence. "Why these were a gift from my buddy here. I just took them out of the box. He has questionable taste wouldn't you say?"

Tom is pointing at Al-so thinking that he will deflect the angst that this cowboy and now others in the bar were showing towards him. It didn't quite work out that way.

"Yeah, well you're the pretty boy that's wearing them now aren't you?" The cowboy spit in Tom's face as he talked. A few of his cowboy friends were now suddenly at his side.

The choice Tom had made of these over the top both in price and design cowboy boots was intended to be a joke on Al-so. Now it appeared that the joke was on Tom. And these cowboys who were staring both at Tom and at his outlandish boots were *not* smiling.

Tom looked down at the boots. They were *perfect*, that is if you were a country singer on the rise in Nashville. Ornate brown and blue colorful stitching on the sides moving down to the blue glitter that dominated the rest of the boots. And man did they *sparkle*!

Tom was suddenly quite nervous. These boots had offended these cowboys and there was one thing he knew about cowboys was that they were good at two things: roping cattle and fighting. They were probably *best* at fighting.

Just then the cowboy got his face right up into Tom's face and said, "You're either brave or you're stupid."

Al-so decided to help a brother out.

"I can assure you fine gentlemen that he is *not* brave."

The cowboy smiled and said, "Just as I thought. He's stupid."

With that the cowboy reared back and took a swing at Tom who *somehow* managed to duck. The punch landed in the face of a biker who had walked up to see what the fuss was about. The biker was roughly the size of a Mack truck. He took the punch like it was a slap from a schoolgirl. He responded to it however as though the cowboy had sucker punched his mother. He decked the cowboy and the next thing you know it was an all-out barroom brawl.

Al-so grabbed Tom by the arm and said, “Let’s get the hell out of here before we both get killed!” They made a mad dash for the exit. Tom learned quickly that his flashy boots were *not* built for speed. He was slipping and sliding crazily as he tried to keep pace with Al-so.

The two made it safely back to their hotel room and the last thing that Tom heard before he nodded off was Al-so yelling, “You dumbass! What in the *hell* were you thinking??!!”

Yellowstone Sojourn - Day Three

Tom wanted to sleep in but Al-so just wasn’t having it. Even with Al-so relating to Tom that today was the magic day when they would actually arrive at Old Faithful, Tom just pulled his covers around himself tighter. Al-so resolved to leave the hotel room to have a relaxing cup of coffee on his own.

The moment that Tom heard the lock click in the hotel door Tom was out of bed in a flash. He unhooked his cell phone from the charging wire and went immediately to the app where he kept his notes. Tom’s understanding was that the visit to Old Faithful would signal the end of this exhaustive journey and the time would have come for him to *finally* have the trust fund documents in his greedy little hands.

Tom had been through so much to get to this moment. He was not going to blow it now. He had spent countless hours doing research on how to navigate the legalities of taking ownership of Benny's trust fund. Reviewing the checklist had become a daily routine. He had come too far to miss a single step. And he refused to let Al or Al-so stand in his way. That trust fund was *owed* to him.

The hotel door opened just as Tom was preparing to swipe out of the app and shut down his phone. He quickly set the phone aside on the bed face side down.

"Oh good! Sleepyhead has finally decided to seize the day! Up at the crack of 10:30. Don't worry yourself none, I have already milked the cows and plowed the north forty and sent the kids off to school."

"What are you talking about?" Tom asked with irritation.

"Nothing. Just random stuff other people feel the need to do before 10:30 in the morning. You're probably wanting a cup of coffee, right? Hmm, I wonder, do coffee shops stay open this late?"

"Shut up and quit being a *dick*!"

"How about *this* for a deal? I will shut up and quit being a dick if *you* will *get up* and quit being a *loser*! *Deal?*"

Tom threw off his covers and stomped into the bathroom to take his shower. Al-so hurriedly moved to the bed and picked up Tom's phone. He smiled as he saw that the phone was still signed on and the app was still live. Al-so chuckled to himself as he thought two things you can count on with Tom: to always be late and to always be reckless. *This time* it would cost him.

The reassuring sound of the shower running gave Al-so the time he needed to review Tom's checklist and commit it to memory. While his brother Aldo (Al) had been hesitant to share all of the details of what he knew about Tom's scheme to steal Benny's trust fund (Al would not have known that he was going to die at Tokyo Vegas), there was enough information in this checklist for Al-so to fill in all the blanks.

What he learned just now would seal the deal for Al-so. Old Faithful was just a waypoint. The final destination for he and Tom would be "*The Zone of Death.*"

Devils Tower

Tom was uncomfortable and quiet during the hour and fifteen-minute drive to Devils Tower. He had no idea where they were going; he presumed Yellowstone, specifically Old Faithful but Al-so was forever surprising him with his little side trips.

Tom was handling his phone nervously as he scolded himself once again for leaving it behind when he went to take his shower. Once he realized his mistake he had run out of the bathroom with merely a hand towel to cover himself in search of his phone. It was thankfully *exactly* where had left it on the bed and Al-so was perched on the mini sofa leafing through a magazine of local interests. Tom was relieved to see that the phone appears to have been untouched but Al-so was a sly one. There was no guarantee that he hadn't looked through it.

"Forgot my phone!" Why Tom felt he had to say that he had no idea.

"Do you get a lot of calls while you're in the shower?"

"Shut up!" said Tom. He wondered to himself if Al-so would have been that belligerent if he had taken a peek in Tom's phone. Maybe that was a sign that his phone had *not* been where he had left it.

Once inside the bathroom he checked it and it was shut down. He had to enter his passcode to enter and of course the app had been closed. He himself had closed the app, right? Tom could not remember and that troubled him greatly. He was counting on an ill-informed Al-so to give up the trust fund documents willingly. Tom needed him to believe that it was what his brother would have wanted.

"I'm ready," Tom had said after he stepped out of the bathroom fully dressed.

Al-so gave him the once over and then said, "I for one am a bit disappointed."

"At what?"

"I would have thought that with as much time as you spent in the bathroom this morning that you would be much prettier."

Tom gave Al-so an exasperated look as he thought to himself 'does this guy *ever* stop?!'

Just then something came into view which forced Tom's jaw to drop. His eyes glazed over as he took in the sight of what he believed to be only Hollywood special effects.

Tom looked over at Al-so and said, "It's REAL???"

Al-so laughed to himself as he thought finally he had found something that could impress Tom. The Corn Palace hadn't done it. The Pioneer Auto Museum hadn't done it. The Badlands and Wall Drug were both lost on him. Mount Rushmore and the Crazy Horse Monument both invoked the comment that they were "smaller" than he thought they would be. But this, the rock formation known as Devils Tower; *that* had Tom's full attention.

As they got closer to the actual "thing," Tom burst out, "That's it! That's the "thing" that Richard Dreyfuss made a model of! He made it out of mashed potatoes at the dinner table! It was huge! It was THAT thing!"

Al-so was still driving and getting closer by the minute. They passed a sign that read: **Devils Tower Monument.**

"What is that thing anyway?"

"We *just* passed a sign!" Al-so wanted to add the words 'you idiot' but was able to hold his tongue which was fortunate.

"I *know* it's Devils Tower. I remember that from the movie "*Close Encounters of the Third Kind*" and I *saw* the sign. My question is, what the hell is it? I have never seen anything like it! I thought they made it up for the movie."

Al-so switched to trivia mode which was his comfort zone. He began to relate to Tom all that he could possibly ever want to know about Devils Tower. Tom only half-listened (as usual) but picked up enough of what he wanted to know. He was not sure if he was surprised by the fact that there was not a solid answer.

What *is* Devils Tower? One thing that geologists agree on is that it began as magma (molten rock) beneath the Earth's surface. What they cannot agree on are the processes by which the magma cooled to form the tower, or its relationship to the surrounding geology of the area. Numerous theories have been suggested to explain how Devils Tower was formed. One thing was certain though and that is that it was one crazy looking rock formation.

Tom was deep in thought when Al-so posed his question.

"What?"

"I said, did you notice that Devils Tower is spelled without the apostrophe?"

"A better question," Tom said, "would be why would I *care*?"

Al-so ignored his anticipated insolence and shared that 'apostrophes suggesting possession or association are discouraged within the body of a proper geographic name.' (US BGN Principles, Policies, and Procedures).

"Good to know," said Tom in a placating fashion.

Al-so once again ignored Tom as he parked the truck and the two got out to fully take in this geological marvel.

* *To learn more check out Devils Tower at www.nps.gov*

Gillette, SD

The first town that they passed through after leaving Devils Tower was Gillette. The name alone elicited a string of stupid and unnecessary comments from Tom.

"What's in Gillette?!" Tom asked followed by his punchline. "Is that where they make razor blades?"

That was only the first of many idiotic things to fall from Tom's mouth. Inside Al-so was thinking of an adage from his younger years. 'That was so funny I forgot to laugh.' Finally he had had enough and said to Tom, "We have seven and a half hours of driving ahead of us. I swear I will veer into oncoming traffic if you keep that up!"

Tom was mum the remainder of the journey.

Old Faithful

Tom was back to his old self when finally they stood and witnessed the majesty of an Old Faithful eruption. Al-so thought back to a song he recalled that had lyrics stating, 'that don't impress me much.' Shania Twain had it right if she was talking about Tom.

Al-so did not attempt to beleaguer Tom with more boring details but since Al-so was interested, he did read up a bit about the infamous geyser. Although Old Faithful* was only one of nearly 500 geysers in the park it held the distinction of being one of only six geysers that park rangers could currently predict. It had definitely lived up to its name as the length between eruptions has changed by only about 30 minutes over the last 30 years. What most people don't know or maybe had not thought to consider is that it is possible that Old Faithful may just stop erupting someday.

'Nothing to see here' might be a sign the park rangers would have to erect.

Earlier in the day, just *before* they had arrived at Yellowstone National Park, Tom caught a glimpse of something out of the corner of his eye that *really* fired him up. An airport!

What???!!! Yes, there *is* a Yellowstone Regional Airport.

Tom is quite annoyed and he makes this clear to Al-so after three days of nearly continuous driving.

'But think of all that you would have missed!' Al-so had replied.

Tom relented just a bit by saying, 'I'm not gonna lie. Devils Tower *was* pretty cool.'

Tom has been on, what he believed to be, his best behavior for some time now but his patience was beginning to wane. He believe that the time had finally come for Al-so to make good on his promise to hand over the trust fund documents. Al-so, however, was playing coy, acting as though that promise had never been extended by him.

The two men were at the Old Faithful Inn only steps away from the reliable and infamous geyser in Yellowstone which drew around 4 million visitors each year. Tom is sucking down a Deschutes Black Butte Porter while Al-so is taking his time with a smoked old-fashioned.

Tom is staring fixedly at Al-so while he is nonchalantly gazing at the massive stone fireplace in the lobby and the timbers of the log cabin style architecture of the interior of the hotel.

"Are you even listening to me?" Tom demands.

"I have heard *every* word. Did *you* listen to *me* when I told you I don't have them with me?"

* *To learn more check out Yellowstone National Park Old Faithful at www.nps.gov*

"Then where the hell *are* they?!"

Several patrons looked in their direction.

"Lower your voice please and I will tell you."

Al-so reached into his coat pocket. It looked like a map. Tom was immediately encouraged by this new development. Tom's spirits notched a little higher when Al-so unfolded the map, laid it on the table in plain view then proceeded to smooth out the creases. Al-so beckoned Tom to lean in closer as he pointed at the map.

"This trip was necessary." Al-so began. "Maybe not all the side trips perhaps but I couldn't fathom coming out this way and not getting a taste of what the old west has to offer. You get me?"

Were it not for the fact that they were at the tail end of their journey Tom might have answered differently but right now he had a sense that his pursuit of the trust fund which he believed to be *owed* to him was nearly over. He could afford to be a bit more indulgent with Al-so than he might be otherwise.

"I get you," said Tom. "And may I say that I appreciate all the planning and research you did to make this trip a grand success."

Al-so could detect bullshit from a mile away and this was some seriously magnanimous bullshit. Still though, it felt good to be shown some appreciation for all he had done, even if it was not sincere.

Tom was lost in thought already thinking of how he might spend the windfall coming his way. Just then he realized that Al-so had stopped talking.

"I'm sorry Al-so, I must have zoned out for a minute, could you repeat that?"

Al-so made the 'hmm' sound as he said, "Sure. Of course. You know, I don't think I have ever heard you apologize before now. For anything."

"Yeah, well," said Tom as he shrugged his shoulders. "I guess it's just not in my nature."

"No," agreed Al-so. "I guess not."

Al-so got down to business after that exchange and proceeded to explain all that Al had shared with him prior to Al's untimely death. The key to everything was in a box, buried in a particular place near the Idaho/Wyoming border. The map had the directions on how to get there and the coordinates on how to locate the box.

"Is the box just sitting out somewhere for anyone to take it?" Tom had asked.

"Oh no," Al-so had replied. "Aldo had taken the precaution of burying it."

"So what you're telling me," said Tom, "is that we are in search of buried treasure."

"Well that I don't know," replied Al-so in earnest, "as I have no idea what might be inside of the box. I only know what Aldo had relayed to me and that was that you are the rightful owner of its contents."

Tom had heard angels singing when he heard those last few comments from Al-so. After that he was all in. Nothing would deter him at that point. Not even the fact that the two of them were about to backpack in the wilderness for a good forty-five miles to get to the spot indicated on the map. So focused was Tom at reaching this destination that he had no qualms about where they were going even when hearing the dangers such as bears and other wildlife. Not even the name of the region, The Zone of Death seemed to deter Tom.

"What's our next step?" was Tom's only comment.

"We need to get some gear."

"Okay, let's do it."

The two clinked glasses in honor of their final expedition together. No mention was made by Tom that he had no funds to offer towards the purchase of their gear. Al-so let that pass. He knew who he was dealing with it as he had spoken with his brother Aldo on many occasions about Tom.

Al-so knew all that he needed to know about Tom. And Tom thought he had a good read on Al-so as well. What Tom *didn't* know was that Al-so had been disingenuous with Tom now on several key facts of their next sojourn, one of them being Al-so's claims that he did not know what was in the box.

Truth be told, there *wasn't* a box for them to dig up.

That was an outright lie to get Tom to travel with Al-so to—

The Zone of Death...

The Zone of Death

Population: 2

Al-so is perusing the words he sees on his screen:

The Zone of Death is defined by the intersection of Yellowstone National Park with the state of Idaho, in the southwest corner of the park. It holds the distinction of being one of the most remote areas in the country with no established residents. There is a school of thought which declares that as a result of a reported loophole in the Constitution of the United States, which guarantees that the "accused shall enjoy the right to a speedy and public trial, by an impartial jury of the State and district wherein the crime shall have been committed.' a person may be able to theoretically avoid conviction for any major crime, up to and including, murder.

Source: Wikipedia

Al-so now shuts down his phone to conserve battery as there is no cell service here. What he was reading he had copied and saved to his documents. Al-so is now quite well-read on the loophole of The Zone of Death. And he knows fully well what he is doing. Al-so understands The Zone of Death to be a place where a man may presume to *legally* commit murder.

That is *why* he is here.

The Agreement

"This is it!" proclaims Al-so. "We have arrived."

"Great! When, and *where*, do we start digging?" said an excited Tom.

Al-so shook his head back and forth in exasperation. Tom was an exhausting person to be around. His lust for riches seemed to know no bounds.

"Save that for tomorrow," replied Al-so. "We're going to need our strength. This ground is hard and we're both tired. I say we turn in early and get some good sleep before we tackle the dig for the box of documents that Aldo buried."

"But you *do* know where it's buried, right?" asked a worried Tom.

"Yes, I have a pretty good idea where it is but there may be a few false holes dug before we actually come upon the real deal."

Tom does not appear pleased with Al-so's answer but he decides to accept it all the same. Both men shrug off their backpacks and kneel down to rest their weary bones before setting up camp.

"Will you need help pitching your tent?" asked Al-so.

"No, I am quite capable, thank you." Tom fired back as though insulted.

Al-so chuckled. "You read me wrong. That was just a question. I'm not offering any help. You're on your own out here."

"Yeah? Well I'm just fine with that."

"Is that so?"

"Yes, that's so."

Al-so lowered his head and then peered up at Tom with questioning eyes.

"Do you *know* how to make a fire?"

"You have been the one making fire during this trip. I figured that's what you liked to do."

"That wasn't my question."

"No, I *don't* know how to make a fire! Not without matches or a lighter! I'm not a fucking caveman. Alright? You happy? But I *do* know how to cook! You make the fire and I will feed us. Does that sound fair?"

Al-so smiled. "Agreed. That sounds fair. As long as you're doing *something* to pull your own weight on this journey."

"I have been carrying this friggin' backup haven't I?"

"Of your own stuff!"

"Not ALL of my own stuff."

"You have a checkered past with backpacks don't you?"

"I don't know what that means," said Tom.

'Because you're an idiot,' snickered Al-so under his breath.

"*What* did you say?" asked Tom with a tinge of anger in his voice.

"I said I'm tired and I'm hungry. Let's pitch our tents and then I will make fire and you will make dinner. Agreed?"

"I don't think that's what you said."

Tom was perturbed. As usual.

"Agreed?" pressed Al-so.

"Agreed," replied a reluctant Tom.

"What are you making for us by the way?" Al-so asked as he unbundled his tent and set about to driving stakes into the ground.

"Stew."

"Stew, huh? What *kind* of stew?"

"*Canned* stew. Look around you! We're in the middle of freakin' nowhere. Show me where the kitchen pantry is and I will add some spices to kick it up a notch!"

Al-so just laughed. "Will it be safe to eat?"

Tom stopped his progress in pitching his own tent to fire back at Al-so.

"You're just like your brother. You don't trust me. How's this? You watch me prepare it and then we both ladle our portions from the same pot. I will even offer to eat first."

Al-so nodded his head. "I think we have reached an agreement."

"Thank the gods! We have an agreement to eat dinner!"

Boots On

Al-so and Tom are finishing off the remainder of the stew. It was a canned product but to be fair it wasn't bad. Besides just opening the cans and heating up the stew Tom actually *had* added a few spices purchased at the same time as their gear. Al-so had watched him break the seal on each plastic container as an extra precaution.

Tom realized then just how tired he truly was and began to pull his boots off.

"What are you doing?" asked a troubled Al-so.

"I'm taking off my boots."

"Why would you do that?"

"Because I have been hiking all day and my feet are killing me, that's why."

"Well," said Al-so. "I think it would be best for you to leave them on."

"And why is that?"

"Snakes." Al-so said this with conviction.

"Snakes, huh?"

"Yes, snakes. You do you but I guarantee you that I am leaving my boots ON! I don't want to wake up in a cold sweat with a snakebite on my foot!"

"Is that a thing?" asked a suddenly worried Tom.

"Hell yes that's a thing! Boots on or risk a snakebite!"

"Would that be deadly?"

Al-son waved his hand and said nonchalantly, "Nah! Just call 911 and be sure that the paramedics get to you within 15 minutes and you'll be fine."

Tom seemed to accept this.

Al-so shook his head bewildered and said, "There is no cell service! There is no 911! We're *alone* out here! In the *wilderness*! Do us *both* a favor. Just wear your fucking boots while you sleep, alright?"

"Alright I will! Geez!"

"You'll thank me in the morning."

"I doubt it."

"You're probably right. You won't but a normal person probably would."

Tom flipped off Al-so before he escaped inside his tent to settle in for the night. Tom took one last look around the landscape and then went to get inside his tent as well. He had thoughts zinging around in his head that he just knew would keep him from drifting off to sleep.

Questions like 'How could a snake get in the tent if it was all zipped up?' and 'Couldn't a snake just as easily find its way INTO his boot?' and lastly, 'What if Al-so built the fire over top of where they needed to dig for the buried box of documents?'

Finally Tom drifted off and slept more soundly than he had in some time.

Tom was snoring to beat the band, which was truly a gift for Al-so given what he needed to do. Trying to be stealthy in the wilderness was nearly impossible. Tom's freight train snoring was good cover for Al-so as he stepped on dry twigs and leaves littered on the ground.

It was difficult to suppress the loud grunt he made as he tugged open the large metal jaws of the contraption he had anchored into the ground. What he was doing was the most nefarious thing he had ever attempted in his life but he reminded himself, while it may be considered barbarous it was most certainly justified.

Moments later Al-so slipped into his sleeping bag in his tent in the middle of the wilderness with no cell service and an as yet unconfessed killer but that would soon change. And the lengths to which Al-so had taken to effect that change are what allowed him to sleep untroubled knowing that he was safe and sound.

Call of the Wild

The scream could be heard for miles.

That is *if* there was anyone about to hear it.

There was not.

Tom was crying and tugging at his leg. The pain was hot and intense. He cried out for Al-so as tears streamed down his face.

Tom's first thought was that he had been bitten by a snake! But that was crazy, he still had his boots on. His foot felt like, well it felt like it had been amputated. All the pain was north of his foot in his leg.

Tom looked down. His boot was still on and offering protection from a snake bite. He heard what sounded like water in his boot but knew instantly that it was blood. He tried to move but fell immediately. That's when Tom realized that he was tethered to the ground.

"What the fuck?!"

Zanzhi

When Al-so unzipped his tent and came out to get a breath of cold mountain air Tom was still writhing on the ground in pain. He was tugging on his leg with his right hand and pushing with all his might on the metal contraption lodged on his boot with his left hand. It was only making matters worse.

"Ever play with a Chinese finger torture toy when you were a kid?"

Al-so allowed some time for Tom to answer but he was too caught up in trying to free himself.

"You see, you put a finger in each end and tug. You can't pull your fingers out and the more you try the more trapped they become and the more pain you inflict on yourself. It is referred to as "zanzhi" and it seems you have created your own version of it. I wouldn't do that if I were you."

"You son of a bitch!" Tom screamed at Al-so. "You put a bear trap in front of my fucking tent!!?? What were you thinking?!"

Al-so throws out a quip he thinks to be quite clever.

"Well, you really *stepped* in it this time!"

Al-so is crying from laughing so hard.

"Sorry but you have to admit, *that* is funny!"

Al-so has busied himself kicking at the embers of the fire hoping to get a spark. He is successful and soon has a fire going and is able to boil some water for the instant coffee his brain is craving. Can't start the day without coffee.

"I made coffee if you want some. Help yourself." Al-so waved a hand casually at the pot. Laughter followed this comment as Al-so bore witness to a helpless Tom attempt to struggle to his feet.

"I see you're still wearing your boots. No snake bites right?"

"Yes, I'm still wearing my boots and thanks to YOU, this one is filled with blood from this fucking bear trap you set!"

"See? I was right. I told you that you would thank me later for those cowboy boots! Without them, that bear trap would have taken your foot clean off!"

Tom is aghast at Al-so's comment. "You're taking credit for *saving* my *foot?!* YOU set the fucking trap!"

Al-so said, "That sounds a bit harsh when you say it like that. Remember that I was the one who encouraged you to get those cowboy boots. I did it to *protect* your feet."

"Wait!" exclaimed a panicked Tom. "You said FEET. Plural. Why did you say FEET???"

Al-so chuckled as he said, "I think you're getting a little ahead of yourself, don't you?"

The Standoff

An hour has gone by with no resolution for either man. Tom is hoping that Al-so will help him to remove the bear trap which is clamped onto his leg. He can't do this alone. All of the tugging and pulling he has done has allowed the teeth of the trap to penetrate the boot further and now sink deeply into the flesh of his leg. At this point Tom was fearing that the teeth of the trap were now perilously close to touching bone. He was attempting to remain as immobile as possible.

Tom's prayer is for the bear trap to be removed and the buried box to be recovered so that he might finally set his eyes upon the document naming him as the rightful heir to Benny's trust fund.

Al-so is set on discovering the truth behind the lies. He believes that Tom has murdered his twin brother Al and possibly others. It is his plan to place Tom in an impossible situation to force a confession. Unbeknownst to Tom, Al-so has brought along a camera to record all that Tom has to say.

Turning the tables

Al-so is sitting on a rock near the fire and sipping on his coffee. Tom continues to whine about the pain and the injustice of it all but Al-so has managed to block that out. He looked Tom dead in the eyes as he spoke.

"No more lying and deception. None of that will help you now. It's time for truth. Who ARE you? And what have you done with, or *to*, Benny?"

"Benny? Who the fuck cares? No one really gave a shit about Benny. He was a loser since the day he was born."

Al-so rolled his eyes at Tom's insensitive remarks.

"Where is he now?"

"In a better place. Does *that* make you happy?"

"No. Not if it means that mean he is dead."

"It means what it means." Tom's face is wet with tears from his pain.

"You really *are* a bad person aren't you?" Al-so is pointing an accusing finger at Tom.

Tom is indignant, "I'm just trying to get what is rightfully *mine*. And the *only* way I could do that was to assume Benny's place in the world."

"How would you do that? I mean how DID you do that? Surprisingly, you seemed to have fooled everyone! Benny's parents. Benny's friends. You said you hadn't seen him in years. What am I missing here?"

"Imitating a loser is easy peasy."

"No imitation necessary with you."

Tom ignored Al-so's sarcasm as he said, "Look, like I said before, I'm just trying to get what is rightfully mine."

"Which is?"

Tom was incensed at this discussion. He attempted to shrug it off by saying, "I think you already know all of this, surely Al *must* have told you. Benny's quote unquote "parents," well, *our* parents, came into a large sum of money. But--- not only did they not have a clue what to do with it, they also had no *plans* to share the wealth!"

"Wait! Did you just say "our" parents? Like in yours AND Benny's?!"

"Yeah, that's right. OUR parents. Benny and I are identical twins. They, those *people*, only wanted *one* child so at birth they kept *him* and gave *me* away."

"Well, that explains a lot. If it's true."

"No, that explains EVERYTHING. And hell yes, it's true. Why would I lie about that?"

Al-so chuckled and said, "I don't know. Money perhaps?"

Tom ignored the comment.

Al-so wasn't done.

"Have you no *love* for Benny? For your own *brother*?"

"*Love?* What is *love?*"

This time Al-so ignored Tom's comment.

"Tell me, even though you believe that I *already* know, how does Aldo figure into all of this?"

"That's simple. Al was a notary. He didn't blink an eye when I asked him for help."

"That sounds like my brother, always willing to help."

"Yeah, well he notarized all the documents, well *almost* all, of the documents I needed to claim my *parents* money upon their death. For some reason though he was holding out, refusing to put his notary seal on a few of them. That of course put us at odds."

"So you were friends before that?"

Tom laughed. "I wouldn't go that far. You see, I'm a loner. I don't *have* any friends. I mean, I always said hi to him when I passed by his desk at work but outside of that, no."

"I see." Al-so said. "Well, it just so happens that Aldo told me *everything*. He had suspected you were up to no good for a while. I told him it was a bad idea to play junior detective but he wouldn't listen. He kept saying that you were probably a good guy after all. But you're not, are you?"

"And you're so different? You nearly took my foot off with a bear trap!"

Tom's comment was lost on Al-so as some revelation seemed to come to light for him.

"Wait. Go back. Did you just say, *'upon their death'*?"

"Yep! That's how inheritance works. Duh."

"Oh my god. So am I to presume that Benny's parents are *dead*?"

"You can *presume* anything you damn well please."

"You-- *murdered* them?"

"You just jump *right* to your own damn conclusions, don't you?"

"What? Are you saying that I am wrong?"

"What I'm *saying* is that I approached them with um, a *business* proposition. So to speak. They had options. What can I say? They chose poorly."

"And Benny? What has become of Benny?"

"Don't be stupid. One can *only* become an '*heir*' when another one passes."

"So you murdered *him* too."

"You are building one hell of a circumstantial case here "counselor." All these accusations from a man who set a bear trap at the opening of another man's tent. What does the Bible say? Something about he who is without guilt may cast the first stone? You're living in a glass house brother."

Al-so was immediately angered and shouted back defiantly, "Don't you *dare* refer to me as *'brother.'* I *loved* my brother. Unlike *you.* And I am here to defend my brother's honor. *That* is why I set the bear trap. To hold you in place while you *confess* to the murder of my brother. You have *already* confessed to the killing of Benny and his adoptive parents. And I have it recorded!"

With that comment Al-so pointed at a small video camera which had been cleverly hidden away until now. Tom shrugged it off.

"I have done no such thing. And *I* didn't kill your brother. That loser "Part-Time" did when he improperly prepared a poisonous pufferfish."

"Not pulling the trigger does not make you innocent when you're the one left holding the smoking gun."

"That doesn't make any sense."

"It makes all the sense in the world. To *me*. Face it, Tom you're not going *anywhere* until you make a full confession to the part you played in murdering my brother. There's no way you can open that trap yourself and I'm not about to treat the wound. I know better than to try to come near you. Your only hope to get out of this situation *alive* is to tell the truth. Right here. Right now. I will take this recording to the authorities and let them know of your whereabouts out here in the wilderness. They will send a team to bring you in and because they are something you're not, which is *humane,* will offer you medical aid. And let's be honest, the longer you refuse to confess, the more at risk your foot, possibly your *whole leg,* becomes subject to amputation. Take all the time you want Tom. I have *all the time in the world.*"

"Do you? *Do you really?* You have said on multiple occasions that you can't trust me and yet you still gobbled up the stew I made for you last night."

Tom made his comeback statement with a surprising level of confidence.

Al-so is not buying it.

"*Us* you mean. The stew you made for *us*. We *both* ate that stew. And I watched your every move as you prepared it. You can't BS me into thinking that you poisoned the stew. I saw every ingredient that you put into the pot. I know for a *fact* that you didn't poison the stew."

"You got me there! I'm not gonna lie. You are *absolutely* right. I freely admit that I did *not* poison the stew."

"Alright then, you should also admit that you have no hold over me at this point. Don't try to make this seem like a standoff because it's *not*. You are the *only one* over a barrel. You are the *only one* at risk out here."

"Am I though? The *only one* at risk? Let me tell you something smart guy. It just so happens that I was quite aware of your mistrust in me so while you were ultra focused on every little thing I added to the stew, you weren't paying attention to what I was doing outside of that mundane task."

"What the *hell* are you talking about??"

"I *didn't* poison the stew. But I *did* poison your *bowl! Ha!* And if I have this figured right you should be feeling the early effects of that just... about... *now*. Tell me, do you feel a bout of diarrhea coming on *'brother'?*"

"You're an idiot Tom. Killing me only means certain death for you. You have no bargaining chip left."

"Oh I wouldn't say *that* Mr. Al Two Point 'Oh.' I just so happen to have the 'antidote' if you want to call it that of the bad shit that I *greased your bowl with* BUT, you will have to take the risk of getting *near* me to get it. I'm not giving it up any other way. I sure as hell am not going to toss it to you!"

"Fine, then you will lay there and die of exposure and your injury, you stubborn bastard."

"Oh so *I'm* the stubborn one? We'll see who's stubborn after several hours of flaming waste comes out of both ends of you." Tom emits an evil laugh that send shivers down Al-so's spine. "You *too* will lie there and die of exposure and dehydration."

"You're a *fool!* And a *dead man!*"

"Ha! It takes one to know one."

Al-so's face colored suddenly, then he jumped up and grabbed his backside.

"Oh SHIT!"

"*Liquid* shit you mean!" Tom laughed as he shouted his rebuttal.

Al-so had run into the woods and was now crouching painfully next to a tree as his body began to respond to whatever it was that Tom had added to his bowl.

Al-so shouted from the woods.

"This is *horrible* what you did to me! You're one sick man!"

"Oh yeah, *that's* what your defense would be in a court of law? That's what jurors will ponder coming from a man who set a bear trap outside the tent opening of the man *he* is accusing of being sick? Quite reasonable logic there. Not so sure you thought *that one* through all the way."

Al-so returned from the woods white as a ghost and holding his pants up with one hand. It was clear that he was anticipating an urgent need to return to the woods at any moment.

"I feel like I'm going to pass out."

"Yeah? Well before you do, come help me pry open this bear trap so we don't *both* die out here!"

"I don't think I have the strength..."

Al-so sank to his knees and then crumpled into a ball. He turned his head so he could face Tom. He was unaware of his own moaning. The pain in his gut was excruciating. Both his throat and his butt were feeling the aftermath of the lava that had flowed through him. At this point he could not help Tom even if he had wanted to.

Ashes to ashes

Al-so and Tom stare at one another for the better part of an hour. Hatred is in their eyes even as they both begin to fade. They are in a small clearing which nature will inevitably reclaim as its own. Their bodies will become sustenance for the wild creatures that roam this land. Their motivations for being here will be carried away by the wind as if the two had never existed.

Epilogue

The Last Word

As the two men began to lose consciousness, each one succumbing to the demons that had brought about their demise, both saw a vision of "Al" as they each had known him appear before their eyes.

Al-so saw his twin brother Al-do standing at the gates of heaven smiling broadly as he said happily, "Glad you could finally make it."

Tom saw something similar yet altogether different.

Tom saw the pearly gates before him with a handwritten sign which read: You're Not Welcome Here.

Just then Tom felt a *presence* behind him as an all too familiar voice said those three infuriating words...

"Well, Well, Well."

The Story behind the Story

Where did the idea for this crazy story come from?
This is something I am asked frequently.
Here is how it all began---

I have a coworker. Let's call him Alex.
I pass by his work area every day as I am walking to mine.
Alex *always* has a comment to make.

On one particular day, after I had been out of the office for a week's vacation, I am passing by Alex's work area and he poses the question, "Where have you been?"

I answer, "I was in Lake Tahoe with my son. He is a snowboarder."

"Hmm," he replies. And then asks, "Why didn't you take me?"

"Well," I said. "I guess it's because you're not my son!"

I thought this might be the end of the conversation but then he adds the comment, "Next time that you go, take me."

I kinda shrugged that off and went on with my day however—

Alex was not done.

Every day thereafter he would ask me the same question as I walked past his work area, "When are you going to take me to Tahoe?"

This happened-- *every day.*

One day I said, "Can you ever let this go?"

His reply was, "Well, if you won't take me to Tahoe for real, at least you could write about it and I would know that I had a good time!"

Well, that was the genesis of *'Take Me to Tahoe.'* It started with a short story published in my book *'Random Samples'* and from there it just took on a life of its own.

We still talk every day and he has always has a comment to make.

The phrases, 'Well, well, well' and 'Glad you could finally make it' are spoken by Alex with some amount of frequency yet always with a tone of admonishment. He keeps everyone in line at the office.

One more thing! Alex assigns everyone a nickname which is how 'Part-Time' became included in the story. For now, he shall remain anonymous. 😊

www.ingramcontent.com/pod-product-compliance
Lightning Source LLC
LaVergne TN
LVHW020709110826
845149LV00012B/2173

* 9 7 9 8 9 9 1 7 1 6 3 1 4 *